Trusting Truth

Faith, Family, Friends & Horses in Appleridge
Book 2

Linda Amick Algire

Town Song Books

York, South Carolina

Cover Artwork & Design Kayleen MacDonald
Book Layout © 2017 Book Design Templates
Copyediting by Espoir Editing

Trusting Truth/ Linda Amick Algire—1st ed.

ISBN 978-1-7337884-5-8 (Hard Cover Edition)
ISBN 978-1-7337884-3-4 (Paperback Edition)
ISBN 978-1-7337884-4-1 (Kindle eBook)

Library of Congress Control Number: 2019949247

Printed in the United States of America

For *Jesse R. Peters*—my horsemanship mentor. Jesse finds happiness in all the right places—God, family, and helping horses with their humans.

Dear children, let us not love with words or speech but with actions and in truth.

1 John 3:18

Also by Linda Amick Algire

Gathering Goodness
Faith, Family, Friends & Horses in Appleridge, Book 1

Thank You God for Everything—Especially Horses

Short Story, My Horse Flicka
Horse Tales for the Soul, Vol. 1

Welcome to Appleridge!
Find a comfy chair, kick off your shoes, and get cozy!

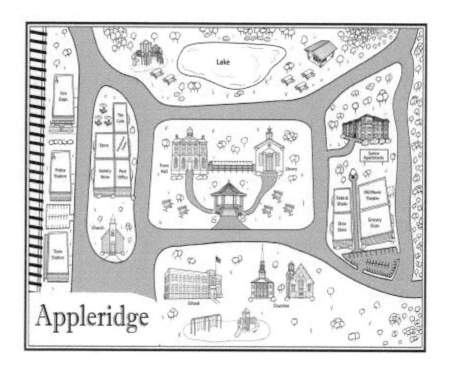

Chapter One

"here are you off to this time?" Hank rolled over to follow Elaine, aka Lainie, with his eyes as she moved around the trailer choosing clothes and throwing them into her bag.

"I told you, Hank, I'm teaching a clinic in Appleridge, Ohio this weekend." Lainie Anderson was getting pretty tired of Hank. "I need to get ready to go on the road, so you may want to get up and gather your things."

Lainie wasn't too sure how Hank ended up in her trailer last night, but she was ready to have him gone. The living quarters of her horse trailer were nice but extremely small. Too small for annoying cowboy one-night stands.

What in the world is wrong with me? I love what I'm doing— teaching people about horses. But I'm not happy. Maybe I'm looking for happiness in all the wrong places. Maybe I should start looking for happiness in the right places, but I don't know any right places.

Lainie moved around the small space like a dust devil—her thoughts spinning.

Teaching people about horses used to make me happy. Maybe I've lost my passion for teaching.

Ok, finding her passion would be a good place to start looking for happiness.

Hank got up slowly and stretched. "Sure, Lainie, I've got things to do. I'm heading out on the road, too."

Hank dressed slowly, keeping his eyes on Lainie. It was funny watching Lainie flutter from one side of the small space to the other, like a moth caught in a jar. "Any chance you'll be back in these parts?"

"Probably; I like the idea of having a place to stay in my trailer with my horse nearby."

"Yeah; me, too." Hank looked solemn.

Lainie stopped her flight to look at Hank. He didn't seem mad at being booted out of her trailer. He wasn't a bad guy, and he was pretty good with horses.

"See you around, Lainie. Are you going to be at the big ranch next month for the instructor gathering?"

"I've blocked out that bit of time. I've clinics scheduled for the next three weekends, so I'll be ready for some down time at the ranch."

"Down time? You know we never get down time at the instructor gatherings. It's more like free labor time with the big guy working us to death and then calling it education. Do you ever think about going off and teaching on your own?" With his hand on the door handle, Hank waited for Lainie's answer.

"I'll admit some days I just want to teach what I want to teach without thinking about making enough money to stay in the organization. I'm not seeing all those promised benefits of being a branded instructor."

Hank nodded. "I sure don't get as much of a kick out of following the big guy around—not at all."

Hank leaned over to kiss Lainie lightly on the cheek. He took his cowboy hat from the hook by the door and left the trailer. Lainie watched him walk over to his own trailer before closing her door. He was a good friend. Well, at least that was what she always thought. Last night probably complicated the friend idea.

Lainie sighed. She mentally listed the million errands she needed to run today. First on the list was a trip to the local feed store to stock up on supplies for her Quarter Horse mare, Shadow. Shadow Me, her registered name, was Lainie's pride and joy. They traveled many miles together.

What would I do without my Shadow? The miles are easy with my sweet girl. But what else would make her happy? What did she really want?

Lainie sat down on the bench she used as a step to climb into her bed tucked in the neck of the gooseneck trailer. What did she want? Good question. She wanted to teach without worrying about meeting a quota. She wanted to get off the road, find a little farm, learn from horses, and teach humans.

At first, she loved being part of the branded horsemanship organization called *Follow the Leader*, and the clout it seemed to carry with the students. Students followed her around like she was a celebrity.

What she didn't love was performing at the shows. Lainie avoided the spotlight as much as possible, but the founder of the organization traveled around the country putting on shows, and Lainie performed on command. It was her job to win converts to the program and build the business.

Lainie shook her head, remembering how she hero wor-shipped Brock Rodgers when she first started the *Follow the Leader* program. It was her dream to study at his ranch and learn from the master himself. Then her dream came true. She won what was labeled a scholarship. The dream quickly turned into her nightmare when the small print required all the so-called scholarship money repaid from future earnings.

She was stuck. The price Brock placed on her education ensured her loyalty for many more years. Well, unless she could find a way out of the contract.

Lainie thought about the division in the instructor ranks—some felt the same as Lainie and others still saw Brock as their hero. She had trouble figuring out who was who. Negativity wasn't tolerated, and suggestions of any kind were considered negative. Lainie kept her comments to herself. A simple comment would cause her loyalty to be suspect, and if that happened, well, she wasn't sure what would happen. Some instructors, who were deemed disloyal, were stripped of their instructor status and mysteriously left the program.

I need to find out what happens after they leave. Does Brock have the power to blackball them from teaching horsemanship in some way?

She was finding it difficult to hide her true feelings. She felt a little twinge of deceit every time she brought a new student into the *Follow the Leader* program. She was spreading a message she no longer believed, and that felt pretty bad. Well, maybe that wasn't totally true.

I know the message is good because the horsemanship being taught is really good. It's Brock and the way he does business that feels bad.

And that was the problem. She was the messenger for someone she didn't trust—someone who was selfish, lacked integrity, and didn't always practice what he preached.

Lainie pulled herself off the bench. Appleridge, Ohio was a good day's drive and she wanted to get started early in the morning, and that meant she better get busy today.

Maybe on the drive I can give this whole situation some more thought. I need a plan and a prayer.

Lainie chuckled—now where did that thought come from? A prayer? She wasn't a praying girl, but she did need a plan.

Chapter Two

Jennie McKenzie turned over and reached for her phone, knocking it off the night stand. She leaned over the side of the bed and used her hand to follow the cord until she found the phone and shut off the alarm.

It was still dark. A nice wake-up tune on her phone wasn't enough to fight the strong urge to pull the quilt up to her neck and snuggle in its warmth for a few more minutes—or maybe another hour. Only the thought of five hungry horses roused her from her toasty bed—actually, three hungry horses and two hungry ponies.

Thinking about the horses motivated her to throw off the quilt and smile. After four years of college in Chicago, she was happy to be home in Appleridge, Ohio. Not quite six months ago she was planning a career as a big city journalist, and now she was buying her grandpa's farm and boarding horses. Only a few months ago she mourned the loss of her childhood horse, Julep, and now Julep was out in the pasture waiting for her breakfast. And today she was starting her new job.

"Today!"

Jennie jumped out of bed and grabbed her jeans, sweatshirt, and socks. She had just enough time to take care of the horses and barn, shower, and drive to her new job. The day just became very exciting.

The *Farm & Family Country Chronicle*, affectionately called the CC, a monthly publication covering agriculture news happening in a tri-county area, was the perfect opportunity for Jennie. She would do just about anything needed—write articles, maintain an event calendar, help build an online presence, and all those other miscellaneous duties that were covered under the *miscellaneous duties as required* caveat found in most job descriptions. It was a small office with three other employees—the owner, Mr. Wilson Mark, who was also the editor, Sherilynn Adams, the office manager/accountant, and Charles Troyer who handled the advertising/marketing position. Charles was retired from his first career in banking and worked part-time at the CC.

It was a gorgeous September morning in Ohio—nice sweatshirt weather—and the horses were waiting at the pasture gate for their breakfast. Jennie opened the gate and they found their own stalls. Horses are very smart and are also creatures of habit. After being fed in the same stall for a while, they could find it easily on their own. Of course, Riley, the only gelding and one of the ponies, would often stir things up a bit by going into the wrong stall to steal the treat Jennie placed in each bucket. Then the horse who belonged in the stall Riley robbed would try to enter another stall, and, well, things became a lot more interesting.

Today Riley behaved and the five stalls each contained the correct equine. Jennie closed the half-doors and walked to the feed room to prepare their breakfast. Great weather was predicted so the three horses, Treasure, Starlight, and Julep, would go back out to their pasture, and the two ponies, Riley and Stuffin, would go to their diet paddock and eat hay. The paddock was a small section near the barn with very little grass. It was perfect for two weight-challenged ponies.

Jennie placed a few flakes of hay into her small utility wagon and pulled it to the paddock. Back in the barn, the horses finished their buckets, and Jennie opened the stall doors for the three mares—Julep, Starlight, and Treasure. Julep would follow Jennie anywhere and the other two mares would follow Julep to their pasture. Then she opened the stall doors for Riley and Stuffin, and they followed her to their paddock, eager to start eating their pile of hay.

With all five equines happy, the feed tubs rinsed, wagon returned to its place, and the barn aisle swept, Jennie cleaned and filled the water tubs. She checked the white board hanging in the tack room for notes. Marcy Streeter who owned Riley and Stuffin left a note asking when the farrier would be at the barn to trim her ponies' feet. Cassy Morton, who owned Treasure, left a note for her friend, Megan Peterson, who owned Starlight.

Jennie smiled. She loved all the horses and their humans who called her barn home, and she especially loved watching the friendship between Cassy and Megan bloom. Making memories, Jennie thought. At her barn they were friends making memories.

Jennie took a moment to look at her calendar. Sam, her friend and farrier, would be at the farm on Saturday.

And I don't have to work. Yay!

The CC didn't require Saturday hours unless she covered a special event—certainly a great benefit for this small horse farm owner.

Seven-thirty! I need to grab my shower and get to work by nine. Easy-peasy! Oh my, did I really just think that? I must be spending too much time with Cassy.

The CC office had a casual dress code, and Jennie chose new jeans, a nice shirt, and light sweater.

I really need to improve my wardrobe for those times I travel for interviews, and now my carefully managed budget has a little bit of wiggle room. Jeremy says I look nice. That thought made her smile. But I'm not a fashionista—that's for sure!

Jeremy James was a friend Jennie teased in high school by calling him Jeremy James, the boy with two first names. When Jennie moved home to Appleridge after college, she and Jeremy reconnected, decided they were *in like*, and wanted to see what happened next. And so far, Jennie thought next had been pretty good.

Jennie was eager to start her new job. She climbed into her truck, affectionately named Blue Boy, for the fifteen-mile trip to Richburg, a small city. A very small city. She didn't think fifteen miles was a terrible commute, and, anyway, she would work from home several days a week. That was definitely a nice perk. Since she was being paid salary instead of an hourly wage, it was understood when occasions occurred requiring extra hours, Jennie could take the equivalent time off when needed. According to Mr. Mark, it would all come out in the wash. Jennie wasn't sure if *come out in the wash* was an acceptable employment law term, but she trusted Mr. Mark would treat her fairly, and he trusted that she would give her best to the job. She was sure it would truly *come out in the wash*.

She arrived at the CC office on the second floor over a small women's clothing shop. How convenient! She needed to visit the shop as soon as possible.

Sherilynn greeted Jennie with a smile and led her to a small desk with a two-drawer file cabinet beside a bookcase, creating a work area in the corner of the large main room. The large room had an office located on each side—one for Mr. Mark and one for Charles. Seniority did have its advantages. Sherilynn had a large work area in front near the door. The U-shaped desk looked like a command station. Jennie would soon discover that sweet, quiet, Sherilynn, was definitely in command at the CC.

"Jennie, I made this little place for you. I thought maybe being in the corner would be a little bit more private, and look, you have a window." Sherilynn seemed very pleased that Jennie was near a window.

"Wow, thanks! I like it." Jennie did like it. The desk held a new computer and came with a nice rolling office chair. It was her first job with her very own desk.

"I have some paperwork for you to fill out. You know, the usual." Sherilynn walked over to central command, picked up a packet, and returned to Jennie's desk. "Mr. Mark will be here at eleven, and he has asked Charles to be in the office today, so we can all meet. He really is a nice boss, but I've seen him mad, too. Oh, Jennie, we don't want to make Mr. Mark mad." Sherilynn looked serious but not afraid. "Anyway, he told me to order lunch so it's a lunch meeting just like in those big offices."

"That sounds great—my first official office lunch meeting." Jennie smiled.

"I'll just let you start on those papers and set up your desk. If you need anything, we have a supply closet right over there. She pointed to a closed door on the opposite wall, across from Jennie's new desk. Just make yourself at home." Sherilynn rushed to central command to answer the phone. "The *Farm & Family Country Chronicle*. This is Sherilynn speaking."

Seated in her new chair, Jennie put her tote bag in the large empty bottom desk drawer. What fun! She had a desk to set up, and with that thought, she sat down and got to work.

As Jennie organized her desk, she noticed that Sherilynn was a very busy employee but a happy employee. She didn't know much about her co-worker, but she would guess her to be in her late thirties. She wore a ring, so married. A picture of a little girl was on her desk. Perhaps her daughter. Jennie thought maybe she should put a picture of Julep on her desk, or maybe a picture of Julep with Jeremy. Jennie often amused herself with silly thoughts.

"Jennie, I'm leaving for a few minutes to pick up lunch. If the phone rings, just let it go to voicemail."

"Ok, but Sherilynn, I could pick up lunch. I'm not very busy and I've noticed you're really busy." Jennie wanted to be helpful and she didn't have much to do. At least not yet.

"Oh my, that would be very nice. It's at the restaurant down the block. We have an account, so it's all taken care of and just needs to be picked up."

Jennie grabbed her purse and Sherilyn's lunch order. She hoped she hadn't set a bad precedent. She didn't want to become the office errand girl, but she really wasn't busy and didn't mind getting outside for a few minutes.

Charles and Mr. Mark arrived around 11:30, and after quick introductions, Jennie helped Sherilynn set out the lunch of club sandwiches and chips on the small conference table in Mr. Mark's office. They sat down and Mr. Mark said a short prayer. Nice, thought Jennie.

"Jennie, I have several assignments for you and I'm very glad to have you, our first full-time writer, on board." Mr. Mark picked up his sandwich and took a bite. He chewed thoughtfully.

After he chewed his bite he continued, "Do you know anything about websites?"

"Yes, a little bit. I don't think I know enough to create a site from scratch but I could maintain a site. I have one for my farm and I do the updates myself. I like to add and switch a few things around to keep it fresh, but I needed help setting it up originally."

"Great! We have a website and it needs to be updated. I'm interested in your ideas and I know Charles here has a few of his own." Mr. Mark looked over at Charles. "There's your cue, Charles; fill Jennie in on a few of your ideas."

"I would like our website to be really active. I want to make it the go-to place for people to find events, news, and information about the area, and maybe sell ad space on the site, too." Charles waited for Jennie's reaction.

"Ok, that's good. I'll be out there finding ideas for interesting articles, so I'll stay alert for what's happening." It would be almost a full-time job to keep up a website of that type but she was willing. "Do you have a tech resource, if I need help?"

"We have the firm that created the website. They provide service for a small fee so we try not to use them too often." Mr.

Mark hesitated and then continued, "We are solvent, the CC is doing well, but print media is not the big game in town anymore. We need to be on budget as much as possible."

"I will certainly give you my best, but web design is not my expertise." Jennie wanted to be very honest and not promise anything she couldn't deliver.

"That's all we can ask," Mr. Mark smiled and then continued, "I have a few things to get you started. We have an issue being printed in two weeks and I need two more articles. Charles, how are you with the ads?"

"Ads are good, most are repeats. I would like to get a few new clients and also start promoting the ad opportunities on the website." Charles leaned back in his chair.

Mr. Mark looked at Jennie. "I know this is your first day, but do you have anything to discuss or suggest?"

"I spent the morning looking at past editions, the website, and making a list of ideas but I'm not ready to make suggestions. I couldn't find the Chronicle on Facebook or another presence on social media. Is that something you've considered?"

Mr. Mark sat up. "We really haven't considered it much. Most of our readers enjoy reading the Chronicle in print because they aren't interested in getting their information online. We have the website and we're getting a decent number of hits, but right now I think we should concentrate on making the website more attractive with great information. We could start a Facebook page if you're willing, I suppose. At some point we will need to step into the online world a little bit more, but I have mixed feelings about that idea, especially if we want to attract the population who prefers printed media."

Jennie smiled. "I could start a very simple Facebook page with information directing readers to our website. It would be a page with good tidbits to make them want to click a link to our website. An up-to-date and active website, with a detailed events calendar, should be exactly what is needed to direct online readers to the Chronicle. We could also include a few current articles on the website each month—just enough to whet a reader's appetite and also get enough hits to make the website attractive to advertisers."

Jennie paused and then continued, "You said you want to attract the readers who prefer printed media. That means I need to become very savvy about that market and write for those readers."

"Yes, exactly. I don't want to be like everyone else, because if we are, we'll lose. We need to court the type of readers who prefer printed media—and then give them an outstanding product. And if it's really good, we'll get those online readers, too. And remember, Jennie, the Chronicle is the *Farm & Family Country Chronicle.* Our readers like agriculture, nature, and the great animal-filled outdoors." Mr. Mark paused. "We'll talk more about it later today."

"Sherilynn, do you have anything to add?"

"No, I'm fine for now." Sherilynn didn't look fine, but Jennie didn't know her well-enough to know for sure.

"Well, then, thank you everyone. Jennie, let's plan to meet in an hour to discuss your assignments." Jennie nodded in agreement and gathered up her things.

Later that afternoon, when Jennie and Mr. Mark met, she was surprised to learn that Mr. Mark currently did most of the writing and layout for the CC and he wanted to turn his duties over to Jennie.

"Jennie, we use QuarkXPress for our layout. I think we discussed it during your interview and you're familiar with the software."

"Yes, I'm probably more familiar with Adobe InDesign, but I'm sure I can learn quickly." Jennie hoped so, anyway.

"I hope you don't feel overwhelmed after our meeting. I know your real love is writing but we are a small operation and we each wear many hats. I promise we work great as a team." Mr. Mark waited for Jennie's response.

"I understand and it's exciting." Jennie didn't add that she thought it was exactly the kind of place to build a great resume. "Mr. Mark, Sherilynn looks really busy; is she feeling overwhelmed?"

"Good catch. I just came from discussing a few things with her and I promised to hire a part-time receptionist to answer phones and do a few other duties several days a week. Sherilynn needs more time to concentrate on the numbers and office administration. She also said she wanted to learn how to work on the website or do the page layout. She's interested in doing more of those things and less receptionist duties."

"That's good." Jennie really did think it was good. "Should we work on it together?"

"Yes, I'll let you two iron-out the details of who does what and when. We need to work together to build our readership, but remember, you were hired primarily to write. I believe well-written, fun, informative articles are the ticket to more readers."

Mr. Mark turned to leave Jennie's corner of the world.

"Ah, Mr. Mark." Jennie waited for him to turn around.

"Yes."

"Do I help with answering the phone?" Jennie hated taking phone messages.

"No, not on a regular basis. Some calls can go to voicemail, and hopefully, hiring a receptionist for the busy times will help, too." Mr. Mark laughed. "I don't want to lose my star reporter because of a few phone calls. Your articles are very important." And with that he left, chuckling.

Jennie's cheeks burned. She wanted to be a team player. *Why did I ask about the phones?*

JENNIE AND SHERILYNN met later in the afternoon for a planning session and assignment of duties. Sherilynn seemed comfortable sending all the calls to voicemail while they met. She wanted to be in charge of either the website or the page layout.

"Jennie, I'll just say it—I don't like team projects. Let's decide what we each should do. We can help each other when needed, but we should have specific duties."

Jennie nodded. "I agree, I don't like team projects, either." She grabbed a notebook. "I think whoever is doing the website should also handle the calendar."

"I agree, and I would like to tackle the website. I'm pretty sure I can learn, especially if you help when I get in trouble."

"Ok. You take the website and I'll help if needed. Will you also take the calendar?"

"Yes, that's a big part of the website." Sherilynn paused. "But, like you said in the meeting, keep your ears open while you're out and about."

"I sure will. I'll be scouting out ideas for articles, and I'm pretty sure that will lead me to events for the calendar—or the other way around. And I'll handle the magazine layout. I think that makes sense since I'm writing the articles. I'll be able to plan the layout based on the types of articles I write, the number of photos, and, of course, the ads Charles sells."

"I think we have a good plan, Jennie."

Jennie took a deep breath. "Sherilynn, I know you've been here for a long time and I feel like I've stepped on your toes without trying."

"It wasn't you, but I did feel a little stepped on during the office meeting, and that's why I talked to Mr. Mark privately. I don't have a college degree or anything, but I learn quickly. I was feeling a little underappreciated."

"I'm glad you spoke up, and for the record, I don't think anyone who handles the entire office should ever feel underappreciated."

"Thanks. I think I'm going to like having you around. I guess I better answer all those messages stacking up, and prepare the ad for our new receptionist. I plan on getting out of here on time today."

Jennie asked, "What are the set work times, anyway?"

"The office is open nine to five, Monday through Friday, so I'm here at those times. I usually pack my lunch and stick close to my desk. If I need to run an errand, I send the calls to voicemail. For the record, yes, we should have set lunch hours and breaks, but we come and go whenever we need. It's never been an issue. Mr. Mark said you were working from home some days. Maybe we can work on a schedule so I know when you'll be here?"

"I'll do that, and when I'm here, I'm fine with staying casual about lunch and breaks. I worked at a family-owned deli in Chicago during college and that's what we did, too."

"It's really nice to have you here, Jennie; don't work from home too often." Sherilynn smiled. "And if you happen to know anyone looking for a part-time job in a very friendly work environment, let me know."

"I have a friend who attends Richburg College. She may know of a student who needs a job and could make her school schedule fit."

"Mr. Mark said to plan for about nine hours a week. I'm going to think about it, but it will probably be three hours on Wednesday, Thursday, and Friday. I think maybe two to five. It'll definitely be nice to have a solid block of time to concentrate on a project without being interrupted."

Driving home, Jennie replayed the day. She was going to like this job. It had a lot of positives. She would certainly be busy, and she liked Mr. Mark, Charles, and Sherilynn. The office was very friendly and casual. Her brief peek into the dress shop downstairs looked promising, too.

She couldn't wait to tell Jeremy all about her day.

AS JENNIE CHANGED from writer extraordinaire clothes into barn hand clothes, she heard a ping from her phone. It was a text from Jeremy.

May I take you out for dinner to celebrate your new job?

Yes, must feed horses first but promise not to get too dirty LOL.

Don't worry, I like horse smell. Are you wearing your silly apron?

Very funny! Jeremy's text teased her about the time she wore her grandma's frilly apron with white rick rack trim to keep her clothes clean during a quick trip out to the barn.

You are a silly boy, Jeremy James, the boy with two first names.

Jeremy sent a quick return text. *LOL touché*

Jennie fed the five hungry equines and finished her barn chores quickly. She gave Julep a few extra minutes of attention and apologized for nothing more. Returning to the house, Jennie changed out of her barn clothes and walked downstairs just as Jeremy pulled his small SUV into the drive.

"Hey, star reporter, how was your first day?" Jeremy gave Jennie a quick kiss on her cheek and then stepped back to look into her face.

"I liked it a lot. It was a nice day, with nice co-workers, and my very first office lunch meeting. Does that make me official?" Jennie teased.

"I believe it does. But lunch was a long time ago, I'm starved. I know I promised dinner but would a hotdog at the soccer field be acceptable, at least to start? I forgot my nephew's playing tonight and I promised I would watch his game."

"That sounds perfect but only if I can get onions on my dog," Jennie teased.

"Oh, alright, I guess I'll have to suffer through onion breath."

"Jeremy James, you better be careful or you won't get close enough to smell my onion breath."

"Ok, I'll be a good sport since I sort of promised dinner and now all you're getting is soccer field food. But I think they have ice cream."

"It just keeps getting better. Let me grab a sweatshirt. Do you have chairs or should I grab a couple from the basement?"

"Nope, I have two that live in the car."

At the game, Jennie and Jeremy enjoyed their hotdogs complete with onions, and since it started to get chilly after the sun left the horizon, Jennie opted for hot chocolate instead of ice cream. Daniel's team won, and chilly or not, they wanted ice cream as their victory treat.

"Hi, Jennie, hi, Uncle Jeremy; thanks for watching my game. Sorry I didn't play much."

"Hey, buddy, when you were out there you looked great." Jeremy gave his nephew a man hug, slapping his back lightly a few times.

Jennie added, "You are one fast little dude."

Daniel laughed and ran to join his team in line for ice cream.

"Jennie, Jeremy said you started a new job today. How was it?" Sarah, Jeremy's sister, joined them on the bleachers.

I really like it. I'm starting to feel like a real journalist, although I didn't write anything today. Today was a get-acquainted day, but I do have two writing assignments."

"I read the Chronicle. It has good information, but I think the writing could be better. It was a smart move to hire a real writer."

"Thanks, but I won't tell my boss, Mr. Mark. He has been doing most of the writing." Jennie smiled to let Sarah know she was teasing.

"I better get this munchkin home. These games sure play havoc with school bedtimes." Sarah waved and walked over to the team busy licking their ice cream cones.

Jeremy and Jennie gathered their chairs to begin the walk to the parking lot.

"How was your first day on the job—really?" Jeremy stopped and looked at Jennie.

"I guess it's too early to really know."

"You're pretty good at sizing up a situation so trust your gut. I'm happy for you."

"Thanks, how was your day? You had class today, right?"

"It was good. I'm getting used to the commute to Columbus, but I'm glad it's only a couple of days a week. I'm getting most of Mom's estate settled, and we're going to have an estate auction in two weeks. What doesn't sell we'll donate to the resale shop. Money raised from donations go to the women's shelter. We haven't decided what we'll do with the house yet."

Jeremy and Sarah's mom passed away several months ago, and Jeremy decided to delay his full-time studies at seminary in Columbus until the estate was settled. He followed his advisor's suggestion to commute for a couple of classes this semester, however.

"I guess you won't need to keep the house if you don't stay in Appleridge." Her comment caused Jennie to feel sad. She hated the thought of Jeremy moving away.

"Why don't you think I'll stay in Appleridge?"

Jennie looked up at Jeremy for a few seconds before she answered, "I guess because you're going to seminary, and pastors don't usually get to choose where they live."

"I see. I'm not sure if I want to pastor a church. I may want to do some other sort of ministry. But you're right—I really don't know where I'll be after seminary. I have a couple of years before I'm faced with that decision. All I know for sure is that I want to make a difference in this world—a positive difference."

Jennie sighed, and told herself not to worry about something that wasn't going to happen for a while, and besides, who knew how long they would be a couple.

Jeremy and Jennie finished their walk to the car in silence, and Jeremy was relieved to see Jennie smile as she opened the car door.

"Should I take you back to the farm, or do you want to go someplace else?"

"Home is good. It's a work night, after all." She started to laugh but stopped quickly. "Jeremy, look!" Jennie pointed to the highway where a truck was in the ditch and an ambulance and a police car were blocking the road with lights flashing.

"Is that Megan's truck?" Jennie grabbed Jeremy's arm.

Jeremy nodded as she quickly closed the car door, and together they ran to the accident. It was Megan, and she was already on a gurney and being loaded into the ambulance.

"Megan, Megan," Jennie called. The attendants blocked Jennie as she approached the gurney.

"Are you a relative?"

"I'm a very close friend of the family. I'll call her parents." Then she heard a quivering voice.

"Jennie-I'm ok-please call mom."

Jennie managed to say, "I will, Megan," before the ambulance doors were shut.

Jennie found Susan Peterson's number on her phone and called.

"Mrs. Peterson, it's Jennie, we spotted Megan's truck in the ditch down the road from the soccer fields. She was able to talk to me and asked me to call. They have her in the ambulance with lights and siren turned on."

"I'm on my way, Jennie."

Jennie turned to look for Jeremy. He was by her side and took her arm for the walk back to the soccer field parking lot.

"Do we go back to the farm or to the hospital?" Jeremy asked, but he was already putting the SUV in gear for the trip to the hospital.

Jennie's friend, Marcy, the owner of the ponies, Riley and Stuffin, was on duty in the emergency department and motioned for them to sit down as soon as they walked up to the reception-ist window. They obeyed and waited for Marcy to fill them in on the details.

"Megan's mom is with her, and it doesn't seem too serious, but she isn't my patient. I'll have her mom fill you in when she gets more details. Even though I know you both, and know how close you are to Megan, I can't release details without permission."

"We understand—thanks." Jeremy looked at Jennie.

She nodded. "Please let Susan and Megan know we're here and praying."

"I will." Marcy rushed back behind the double doors.

"The place is busy tonight, and Marcy seems a little frazzled." Jennie looked at Jeremy, then continued, "She's going to need some serious pony time later. She always stops at the farm to visit her ponies for a few minutes whenever she's had a hectic shift. Judging by the frequency of her late-night visits, I would say it's been crazy." Jennie sighed and pushed back into the hard-plastic chair.

When Jennie returned to Appleridge after college and made the deal with her grandpa to buy his small farm, she also decided to board a few horses for extra income. Marcy was the first to arrive with Stuffin and Riley, and in a few short months, Marcy had become a good friend and mentor to Jennie, Cassy, and Megan. Cassy attended Richburg College and brought her horse, Treasure, with her. Megan was a senior at Appleridge High School, and although she actually lived on a farm, she boarded her horse, Starlight, at Jennie's farm. Jennie's barn was now full, and she enjoyed her good friends—both human and equine.

Jennie heard the emergency doors swish open and turned to look as Dr. Adrian Peterson, Megan's dad, walked in quickly. Jennie waved and he nodded before approaching the information window. The attendant pointed to her left and buzzed him into the inner hallway.

Jeremy and Jennie relaxed a little.

"Dr. Peterson didn't look too worried. I think that's a good sign." Jeremy wanted to reassure Jennie and that was the best he could do for now.

"Yeah, he was in a hurry, but not frantic. Of course, as a veterinarian, I'm sure he has experience in appearing calm under pressure." Jennie shifted in her seat.

"What a date this has turned out to be. I need to plan a little better next time."

Jennie laughed. "You sure know how to romance a girl."

Jeremy loved the way Jennie always found humor in almost every situation, and if the situation wasn't suitable for humor, she always found something positive for her focus. That was something he remembered about her from their high school years together. That and how she loved to tease.

"Hey, didn't you say your boss's name is Wilson Mark?"

"Yes, and I know where you're going with this. And no, I don't tease him about having two first names." Jennie paused, trying to hide a grin. "That's special, just for you."

"I'm so honored." Jeremy loved teasing Jennie about Jennie teasing him. Quite a turn-around, he thought.

As they talked and teased, they didn't notice Susan Peterson until she touched Jennie's arm and Jennie jumped.

"So sorry, I didn't mean to scare you. Megan's going to be fine. She has some serious bruising from the air bags and also a broken wrist. She thinks she braced herself on the steering wheel. She says a large dog or something ran into the road, and she braked quickly and lost control."

"Well, that certainly sounds like Megan. She wouldn't want to hit an animal." Jennie knew she would feel the same way.

"I suppose," sighed her mom. "But she's very lucky she didn't hit another car or tree or anything else. I'm so thankful."

Always interested in details, Jennie wanted more information. "Did she describe the animal?"

"She just said it was large with lots of black fur."

Jeremy noticed that Susan looked anxious to return to Megan.

"Thanks, Mrs. Peterson, for coming out to tell us. If Jennie agrees, I think we will go on home now."

Jennie nodded. "Tell Megan we'll take good care of Starlight and give her lots of attention until she's feeling better. Will Megan go home tonight?"

"They're going to keep her overnight for observation, but she'll be home tomorrow." Susan nodded to the double doors leading to the treatment rooms. "I better get back. They're working on her wrist now. Whatever they do will be temporary until the orthopedic specialist looks at it tomorrow. They'll probably move her to a room soon."

Susan hugged both Jennie and Jeremy before walking back to Megan.

"Wow! I wonder what Megan saw on the road? A black bear would be large and have lots of black fur, but I've never heard of any around here, especially in town." Jennie hoped not because she was always thinking of the horses.

"No, I don't think so. There are bear near some of the state parks and wildlife areas but not here. It was probably a large dog or even a coyote. I know we have coyote in these parts."

"Yeah, I've heard them. I'm glad my little farm is close to town." Jennie's five acres were surrounded by other small farms. The large acreage farms were further out in the country.

In less than twenty minutes they pulled into the farm drive. Jennie got out of the SUV to open the gate for Jeremy. The front fence and gate were new additions to the farm. Someday Jennie wanted to install an automatic gate opener, but for now, it was man or girl power.

Jeremy pulled through and Jennie motioned for him to continue up the drive. It was a short walk to the house from the gate. They met on the back porch.

"I'll walk out to the barn with you for your night check, and then I'm going home. Remember it's a work night," Jeremy teased.

"Ok. Thanks."

They walked to the barn in silence. Once inside, Jennie noticed that the aisle was swept clean, and she hadn't done that in her rush to go with Jeremy. That meant either Megan stopped at the barn before she had her accident or Cassy came to visit her horse, Treasure.

Jennie decided to check the tack room. All the tack and grooming supplies were put away, and all tack closets were closed and locked. She checked the white board hanging in the tack room for any new notes and found one. *Jennie, call me. I'm worried about Megan.* Mystery solved. Cassy was at the farm tonight.

It was dark, but they could see five shapes peacefully grazing in the small pasture directly behind the barn.

"All looks good on the farm," Jeremy said.

"Yes, all is good."

Before they turned to leave, Riley walked out of the shadows to inquire about a treat.

"Sorry, Riley, no treats tonight, but I'll give you a good scratch behind the ears; you always like that." Jennie lightly scratched Riley behind the ears and then stroked his beautiful mahogany pony-sized neck.

Riley soon lost interest and returned to grazing. He was the only gelding in the herd and seemed to like his group of mares. Julep was the alpha mare but Riley helped her lead the herd.

Julep nickered softly when she heard Jennie's voice, but she didn't walk over to the gate. She could usually read Jennie's mind, and she knew this was only a quick visit with no treats promised.

With night check complete, Jennie walked with Jeremy back to his car.

Jeremy wrapped Jennie in his arms.

"See you later, my Jennie girl. I'll close and lock the gate."

Jennie waited for a kiss and wasn't disappointed. Jeremy always knew the exact type of kiss for Jennie—sweet, gentle, and not too demanding.

Chapter Three

t was late but Jennie knew Cassy would be up studying and decided to call.

"Cassy, I saw your note."

"How's Megan? I can't get her to answer her phone."

"She's going to be fine. Jeremy and I went to the hospital, and she's bruised from the air bags and has a broken wrist. How did you find out about Megan? Did you see the truck when you came out tonight?"

"Um—well—yeah, I saw the truck."

"Did you ride Treasure tonight?"

"No, I was so upset about Megan I didn't think it would be a good idea to ride. I groomed Treasure and didn't stay long."

They chatted for a few more minutes. Jennie thought Cassy sounded a little strange—a little guarded. She decided it was probably because she was tired and Cassy was worried. She was sure those two things caused their conversation to be a little strained.

CASSY CLICKED OFF her phone and sighed. Megan really did have an accident. They were texting and then Megan stopped in mid-text. Cassy tried to call but couldn't get Megan to answer. They were supposed to meet at the barn for a quick ride, but Megan never arrived. She hated to be less than honest with Jennie, but she didn't think Megan would want anyone to know they were texting while driving. She needed to know more and decided to call Megan's mom and pretend she heard the news from Jennie.

"Hello, Cassy." Susan didn't seem surprised to hear from Cassy.

"How is Megan, Mrs. Peterson? Jennie told me she was bruised and has a broken wrist. What happened?"

"She says a large animal ran out in front of her, and she lost control when she tried to avoid hitting it. She doesn't know what it was, exactly, just something big and with black fur. Fortunately, she didn't hit another car." Mrs. Peterson sounded tired but also a little skeptical.

"Please tell Megan to call me when she can. Does she have her phone?"

"No, her dad is meeting the tow truck in a few minutes. He said he would look for her phone and other belongings. I'll tell her you called, Cassy. I'm getting in the car now to drive home. They're keeping Megan overnight for observation, but they don't expect any problems. They gave her something for pain and to help her sleep."

"Ok, thanks, Mrs. Peterson."

Cassy hung up. Did Megan really swerve to miss a large black furry animal or was she hiding the truth about their texts? Even if Megan did swerve to miss an animal, they were texting and would need to hide that piece of the story. It was not legal to text while driving in Ohio. Cassy knew she would back up Megan's story. It made her feel a little dishonest, but since no other car was involved, she could justify the little lie. She couldn't wait to talk to Megan.

THE NEXT MORNING the buzz at the Bake & Shake, the local favorite shop for coffee and a donut, was all about Megan Peterson's accident. Appleridge was a small town and news traveled quickly. It usually hit the Bake & Shake first, wandered down the street to a few stores, then ended up being further dissected at The Café during lunch. Jennie's grandpa, Charlie Gantzler, was a regular at the Bake & Shake. He and his group of older retired gentlemen, often called the B & S club, or sometimes affectionately, but less flattering, known as the BS club, were already sharing their opinions about the accident by seven-thirty in the morning.

"Megan said it was a large animal with black fur. I don't know what that would be. It was just about dusk. I suppose it could be just about anything." Mr. Joe Moore, the retired police chief, shared his thoughts, and then the others chimed in.

"You're right about that, it could be just about anything."

"Maybe since it was getting dark, Megan just thinks it had black fur. Maybe it was just a large dog or something with brown fur."

"That could be. I heard Mrs. Williams's big mutt got loose and didn't return home until almost eleven. She lives just down the street. It could have been Moose but he's more brown than black."

"A moose? Are you crazy? We don't have moose in Appleridge."

"I didn't say a moose! I said Mrs. Williams's dog named Moose. You need to get your hearing checked, old man."

The banter continued back and forth like a fast game of tennis, although none of the characters having the conversation actually knew much about the game of tennis. Regardless, they sure did know how to enjoy a good cup of coffee while lobbing their comments back and forth.

The B & S club broke up by nine and a group of older ladies were back in the seats for lunch by eleven. They met for their favorite tuna salad sandwiches on fresh baked croissants. Their conversation was a little more subdued but entertaining all the same.

"Did you hear? Poor Lizzie Williams's dog, Moose, got loose and caused Megan Peterson to crash her truck into a ditch."

"I heard it was a moose, and I didn't know we had moose in Ohio."

"It wasn't a moose! Lizzie's dog is named Moose. It was her dog named Moose."

"I heard Megan broke both her wrists. How in the world will that child go to school with two broken wrists?"

"She'll probably need a tutor."

"Her mom, Susan, is a teacher and she substitutes at the school from time to time. I bet Susan will tutor Megan."

"That could be hard to bear—tutoring a teenage daughter."

"Bear, do they think the animal was a bear?"

"Maybe, I know we have black bear in Ohio but I'm not sure about Appleridge."

By three in the afternoon the seats in the Bake & Shake were filled with the afterschool crowd enjoying milkshakes and ice cream sundaes. The children had a few thoughts of their own.

"Did you hear that Megan Peterson crashed her truck into a big black bear?"

"Did she kill it?"

"I bet there are bear guts all over the road." The boys liked that idea.

"Maybe we should go look?"

"Ewww," the girls said in unison.

"Let's go!" Most of the boys picked up their cones and sundaes and ran down the street.

"Those boys are silly. It wasn't a bear; it was a moose."

"We don't have moose in Ohio. It was a dog named Moose."

"You mean that big brown dog that lives with Mrs. Williams?"

"I think so. I heard my mom say Mrs. Williams was planning a big surprise for Megan to thank her for crashing her truck instead of killing Moose."

"Those silly boys! They aren't going to find any bear guts."

"And not moose guts, either."

The girls finished their ice cream, picked up their back packs, and then the Bake & Shake stopped being news central for Appleridge—at least until another day of newer news.

JENNIE LEFT her second day on the job feeling pleased. She made lists of ideas and stories to write, as well as ideas for monthly columns. Along with a monthly calendar, Jennie thought the columns would entice readers to buy the CC each month. She also considered an idea of having a monthly serial—a continuing story. That was a bit old-fashioned, but Jennie thought their approach should be more nostalgic. The CC should be a very intentional and enjoyable piece of something the world was losing. Jennie wanted to create the right image—to make the CC something very special in an industry that was dying—and not a dinosaur magazine that didn't have the resources to step into a more technological world.

Jennie spent a lot of time researching what would make the CC special, what would attract readers, and how to be intentionally retro but relevant. Jennie also explored new layouts to create a new image—one that had the comfort of something familiar, but yet new and sharp. Perhaps *Retro but Relevant* would be a neat line under the main banner. Better yet, maybe *Retro & Relevant*. Jennie walked down the office stairs to Blue Boy with thoughts swirling like a crazy storm inside her head. She also needed to come up with ideas for the two articles Mr. Mark suggested. He wanted a local flavor piece and also some sort of do-it-yourself article. He said the readers loved do-it-yourself pieces.

On the way home Jennie decided to stop and check on her grandpa. He missed church on Sunday because of a nagging cough and that was highly unusual. Grandpa loved Sundays and spending time with family and friends after church.

She found a parking spot right in front of Grandpa's senior apartment building. Parking was never a problem as most of the seniors no longer owned vehicles. That is what made these senior apartments so attractive—they were within walking distance of almost everything in Appleridge. And they had their own social events to keep the days interesting.

Jennie spotted Grandpa and a few others sitting under a tree. Telling stories, no doubt, thought Jennie.

"Hello, Jennie girl, pull up a chair." Grandpa motioned to an empty chair in their circle.

"Are you feeling a bit better, Gramps?" Jennie smiled as she pulled the chair closer.

"Yup, I went to Doc Phillips yesterday. He thought my cough was due to all the beauty of Fall." Grandpa chuckled. "Those leaves are beautiful, but beauty can be moldy. I guess you're never too old to acquire allergies."

"Were you rolling in the leaves, Grandpa?" Jennie laughed.

"Maybe not rolling but I was playing with those two nephews of yours—my great-grandsons."

"Grandpa, I think you need to start behaving yourself." Jennie pretended to scold.

"I don't know, Jennie girl. When you stop playing, you start dying."

"Ok then, keep playing." Jennie reached over and patted Grandpa's arm. "I just wanted to check on you. Do you need anything from the store while I'm here?"

"No, I'm all set. I was really sorry to hear about Megan, but I'm glad she didn't hit Mrs. Williams's dog. She really loves that old mutt."

"Oh, is that what happened?" Jennie felt like she was out-of-the-loop being over in Richburg most of the day instead of in Appleridge.

"That's what I heard at the Bake & Shake. Mrs. Williams's dog, Moose, ran out in front of Megan, and she swerved and lost control of her truck."

Mrs. Swain sitting to Grandpa's left spoke up, "I heard that she swerved to miss a bear."

"A bear? Really? In Appleridge?" Jennie turned to look at Mrs. Swain.

"That's what I heard at my ladies' lunch today."

"I'll be a star reporter and go to the source. I'll check with Megan." Jennie smiled and stood up. "Gramps, I need to go. Farm chores and hungry equines are waiting."

"You go on. I heard Sam is trimming the horses on Saturday. Maybe you could come and get me, and I could spend some time out there then." It was more of a statement than a question so Jennie knew she would be driving to town Saturday morning to pick up Grandpa.

"Ok, Gramps, he's coming around ten. How about I pick you up at nine?"

"Sounds good. We'll stop and get some donuts for the barn gang, my treat."

"I'll hold you to that promise." Jennie waved as she walked across the lawn to her truck. It was good to see Grandpa feeling better.

Jennie wanted to check on Megan but decided to go home and feed the horses first. Megan could actually be at the farm. She probably couldn't drive but Cassy may have picked her up. Those two were getting as *thick as thieves*—as her grandpa would say.

Small towns sure were funny, especially when it came to gossip. It wasn't malicious gossip, but it was seldom accurate. Maybe it should be called something like mythical or imagined gossip. Just like that old game of telephone—you never knew what the story would be when you reached the end of the line. She definitely needed to start at the front of the line and talk to Megan.

BOTH CASSY AND MEGAN were in the barn grooming their horses.

"Hello, you two! I've missed you both." Jennie walked down the barn aisle.

"Hi, Jennie; we've missed being here. School is crazy right now." Cassy stopped brushing Treasure.

"Cassy picked me up so I could have some time with Starlight." Megan was awkwardly holding a brush in her left hand. Her right wrist was in a cast.

"Are you feeling ok? Did you need surgery?" Jennie motioned to Megan's wrist.

"I promised Mom I would be careful and I didn't need surgery, it's just a hairline fracture. Everything looks good and not much swelling, so they put the cast on this morning. I'll wear this for about six weeks. I guess I'll be pretty useless around here."

"Don't worry about being useless, I'm just glad you're going to be fine. Jeremy and I sure were scared when we saw your truck. It looked like you slammed into the ditch pretty hard."

Cassy and Megan glanced at each other, then looked away quickly. Jennie suspected they were having a silent conversation. Jennie suddenly felt like a parent and she didn't like that feeling. She didn't consider herself that much older than Cassy and Megan. Still, there was something definitely odd about them right now.

"I'm glad to see you and know you're going to be ok. The Appleridge grapevine has been pretty active lately. By last report you hit a moose and have two broken wrists instead of one." Jennie laughed but Cassy and Megan looked stunned.

"What?" Megan put her head down.

"Oh, don't worry. Apparently, Mrs. Williams's dog, Moose, was running loose about the time you put the truck in the ditch, and she thinks the black furry animal that caused you to swerve may have been her Moose. Then, somehow, that turned into a real moose until the fine citizens of Appleridge decided we didn't have moose roaming the streets of Ohio." Jennie could tell both Megan and Cassy didn't find the humor in her report but continued. "I guess they've watched too many Northern Exposure reruns."

Both girls gave her a questioning look and Jennie realized she just threw a time machine moment at them both.

"I'm not sure if it really was a dog or anything. I saw something black out of the corner of my eye. That's all." Megan walked over and sat down on the bench in front of Starlight's stall.

"Your accident will be old news as soon as something else happens in Appleridge. It'll be fine." Jennie paused. "Hey, if you're almost finished, let's get these beauties fed."

Cassy led Treasure to her stall and Megan carefully took Starlight to her stall. Jennie went outside to get Riley, Stuffin, and Julep. All they needed to do was open the pasture gate and all three trotted to the barn and found their stalls. Cassy and Jennie gave each horse a feed bucket, then carried the hay out to the paddock. Megan sat and waited. Her first outing since the accident was tiring her out a bit.

"It's going to get a bit chilly tonight but I think they'll be fine with hay under the overhang. I need to check the white board to see if Marcy left a note about blankets for Riley and Stuffin since they're both clipped and ready for the competition in a few weeks."

After Jennie walked to the tack room, Cassy turned to Megan. "Why do you look so worried? I'm not from a small town but even I know how a little bit of gossip is pretty normal. It doesn't sound malicious—it's just small-town news."

"I'm worried because my dad wants to talk to me tonight when he gets home from the clinic. He said we needed to discuss my cell phone. I think he found it in the truck."

"Oh—ok, I'm sure it lost its charge or something else happened during the accident. Do you think our texts are still on the screen?"

"I don't know but they don't have to be for him to be angry."

"Why? I'm sure he's relieved that you weren't more seriously hurt. I'm sure he's angry about the damage to the truck, but why are you so worried about the phone?"

"Because it wasn't in my purse, and when I got my license, I signed a contract of responsibility for driving. I promised to always keep my cell phone in my purse while I was driving so I wouldn't be tempted to look it. Even if Dad doesn't know we were texting, it wasn't in my purse and that makes me at fault."

"Really? Your parents made you sign a contract?" Cassy found that strange.

"Yes, and I also have a contract for being financially responsible for the truck and Starlight, and then there's also the contract for when I'm home alone for a weekend, and there will be another when I go off to college."

"My dad's an attorney and he never thought that up." Cassy frowned. "Well, maybe he did, but ours are verbal agreements. I have to keep my grades at a certain level to keep Treasure here while I'm in school, and I do have a budget."

"My dad likes the details and I'm the second daughter. I suppose raising my sister, Belinda, gave him some ideas, plus my failed internship last summer probably didn't help."

"I know your dad loves you, Megan—it will be ok. Let's get you home or I'll be in trouble for keeping you out too long tonight." Cassy was trying to lighten the mood a bit as she picked up both her and Megan's grooming bags and walked to the tack room just as Jennie was leaving.

Jennie caught bits and pieces of the conversation while she was in the tack room but pretended she didn't hear. She waited for Cassy, and they walked down the barn aisle together.

"Marcy left a note. The ponies don't need their blankets. It's going to be in the upper forties tonight. If you're finished, let's go ahead and let them out."

Cassy and Jennie opened the stall doors and motioned for the five equines to find their hay in the paddock. The pasture gate was open so they could also graze tonight, although the grass wasn't growing much this time of year.

"I need to get up to the house and do some work. My new job already has homework." Jennie paused. "You're welcome to come on up for a few minutes."

"I think I need to get Megan home. She looks really tired." Megan didn't argue.

Cassy and Jennie waited for Megan to get up from her seat on the bench and walk with them to the door. Cassy's car was parked near the barn, and they both climbed in and waved.

Jennie took one final look around the barn, shut the door, and started her short walk to the house.

Interesting, thought Jennie. Megan was obviously feeling a little guilt. She found that refreshing considering her age and the offense. Some teenagers would sneer and not feel a bit guilty. They would say something like, "What's the big deal, everyone does it, and, anyway, I didn't kill anything." Jennie knew Megan was better than most. She had good parents, good friends, and her experience last summer taught her plenty about integrity, or the lack of integrity. Megan spent most of the summer learning from a horsemanship trainer who fell into the lack of integrity category.

Jennie pulled her hoodie sweatshirt over her head and decided to make a light supper. She checked her phone and smiled at the text from Jeremy.

You were in my thoughts as I drove home tonight.

Jennie replied. *Thinking of you and smiling.*

Jennie thought about inviting Jeremy for supper, but she knew he was usually a bit fried after his classes and commute, and she really needed to get some ideas down on paper for her articles. As she ate, she wondered how she could turn Megan's experience into an article. She would talk to Megan first, and wouldn't use her name. How could she write about small town gossip and keep the story positive?

Some people would say that all gossip is bad, but Jennie didn't feel any malice in the stories people shared today. That's it, she thought, she heard stories. People loved stories and local events and accidents fueled the stories. Maybe if it wasn't malicious it wasn't truly gossip.

Jennie finished eating and sat down at her computer to write. Her fingers flew. She didn't worry about content when writing a first draft. She simply put all her thoughts down on paper and edited later.

Three hours later, Jennie stood up and stretched. Oh my, it was almost midnight and she had a meeting with Mr. Mark first thing tomorrow morning. Jennie saved her work, made several print copies, and shut down her computer for the night. Her thoughts were still in draft form, but she needed to be up in six hours, and she hated getting up.

Tell Us a Story

People love stories. Fact or fiction, it doesn't matter, a good story is a good story. In towns across our state, interesting, funny, creative stories are being told at every post office, local restaurant, grocery store, and, yes, even church.

Some may call it gossip, but it isn't always malicious. Malice is usually missing from local accounts, because in a really small town, a place where everyone knows everyone or at least a friend or family member of everyone, truth can be stretched but malicious gossip will eventually lead to a personal reprimand—from someone. There's accountability on a personal level in a small community. It's not a post on social media, sharing opinions that would never be spoken in person. In spite of the name, social sites are never face-to-face.

That's why I like small-town stories. They're face-to-face-to-face, and some of the information gets more interesting as the story is told. Like the old game of telephone, stories get more creative as they are shared.

Let's put our creative storytelling to work, or better yet, to play. Beginning next month, you'll find a new column called *Tell Us a Story*. We will print one line and readers are encouraged to send what they think should be the next few lines. The Chronicle staff will pick the next line, or several, for print in the next issue. Readers are then encouraged to continue adding to the story each month. Be creative, but also appropriate with thoughts and language. Send your creative sentence by the fifteenth of each month to: Jennie @ Farm & Family Country Chronicle .com (take out spaces) or call the office and leave a message for extension 4. Please speak slowly and clearly or the story really will become the old game of telephone!

Here's our first line: It was a windy day and the front door flew out of her hands and slammed shut.

Have fun!

AS JENNIE WORKED on her ideas for the CC, Megan Peterson sat at the Peterson kitchen table, sharing chocolate chip cookies with her father. Megan sat quietly but her mind wasn't quiet.

Funny, this is quite a Hallmark moment, too bad it's going to be spoiled with whatever Dad is going to say. Why doesn't he just start talking and get it over with?

Adrian Peterson cleared his throat and looked at Megan. "I'm glad you're feeling better. I need to talk to you about the truck. Don down at the garage thinks the cost of replacing air bags and seat belts may be very expensive and more than the truck is worth. He doesn't think the frame was bent or damaged, but he wants another day to make sure. I guess that will determine our direction. We won't mess with a bent frame. You'll get some insurance money but not much since the truck is old. I'm sure your premiums will increase regardless."

Megan looked at her dad. "I trust Don's decision, but I really hate to lose my truck. It's been such a good truck, and I don't think I have enough saved to pay for another right now."

"We also have to talk about your cell phone." Megan's dad pulled the phone from his pocket. "Don found it on the floor of the truck. It may be fine and only need to be charged."

Adrian handed Megan the phone. She reached out tentatively. "Thanks, Dad."

"You have your purse. You somehow were able to grab it when the paramedics arrived. The phone wasn't in your purse, so I have to ask, were you talking on the phone when you lost control of the truck? I'm asking as your father, but I'm surprised the officer filing the accident report didn't ask that question."

Megan hesitated. Technically she wasn't talking on the phone. Maybe she could say no and wait for the next question. No, her dad was no dummy. There would definitely be other questions, and Megan knew she needed to be honest.

"I wasn't talking, it was worse. I was texting." Megan waited for the explosion, but it didn't happen.

"Thank you for being honest, Megan. I suspected it was something like that, especially when Cassy didn't want to share these cookies tonight. You were texting Cassy, right?"

"Yeah—to see if she was going to the barn. It was quick and something I don't usually do, but I was on a familiar road, and there wasn't any traffic, and…"

"And it was wrong, and I'm just glad you didn't hit someone, and all we're looking at is a broken wrist and a wrecked truck."

"I know you're disappointed in me, but you don't seem quite as mad as I thought you would be. I mean you aren't screaming."

"I'm disappointed, but I'm also relieved you didn't lie to me. Did you lie about the black furry animal?"

"No, not really, I did see something out of the corner of my eye that caused me to panic and swerve. I suppose if I wasn't looking at my phone I wouldn't have swerved and crashed the truck so I can't blame whatever it was."

"Losing your truck and a broken wrist are considerable punishment. You won't be able to ride Starlight in the parade. You won't be able to paint signs to earn money. You're going to feel the effects of one poor decision for a long time. I'm very thankful you didn't hit a car, someone's pet, or, too terrible to think, a person—adult or child. I think that would haunt you forever."

"I've thought about those things and I'm thankful. I guess that's why I'm not trying to justify my actions. Something I'm pretty sure I would have done a year ago. I've grown a bit this year, Dad."

Adrian smiled. "Yes, you have. Your experience last summer was well worth the pain, wasn't it?"

"I didn't think so at the time, but yeah, I guess. I learned to be honest, to take responsibility, and to treasure my integrity, because someone I admired and trusted did none of those things, and I don't want to be like him. At one time I wanted to be like

JJ. I wanted to train with him, follow him across the country, and be in the spotlight with amazing horsemanship. I worked hard for that opportunity, and when I was chosen for the internship, I fought with you and Mom until you agreed to let me to leave home and follow my dream."

"But it wasn't what you thought and you learned a valuable lesson about yourself."

"I sure did. I learned I'm stronger and smarter."

"Stronger and smarter, I agree, but tell me more." Megan's dad smiled as he grabbed one more cookie and, when Megan gave him a look, said, "Ok, ok, only one more. Your mom sure can bake a mean chocolate chip cookie."

"JJ did amazing things with horses, but then I discovered that JJ didn't have much integrity. He never took responsibility for his actions, and he definitely wasn't honest. I didn't want to be like him, didn't want to travel or study with him, and no longer trusted anything he said or did. It was a pretty big breakup, wasn't it?"

"It was, and you handled yourself with integrity, with honesty, and took responsibility for your decisions. I'm very proud of you, and that's why I can sit here and calmly discuss this recent mistake without anger. If you had attempted to justify your actions, or not take responsibility for your poor judgment, I would have gotten very angry, very quickly."

"I guess we both grew last summer," Megan teased.

"Don't push your luck, Meggie Moo." Adrian only used that special name on occasion.

"By the way, Mary called to check on you, and you may want to give her a call soon."

Mary Gray was a mentor of sorts for Megan. When Megan was kicked out of the horsemanship internship in South Carolina last summer, she stayed with Bobby and Mary until her mom and dad could pick her up and bring her home to Ohio. Her dad and Dr. Bobby, another vet, had quite an adventure together. During that time, Mary, who painted barn signs and other things, inspired Megan to also paint. Art was something Megan always enjoyed and she learned quickly. She enjoyed the work and formed a bond with Mary. Trailering the horses to the state park for long rides also helped them develop a good friendship.

"Dad, are Dr. Bobby and Mary still coming up for Quarter Horse Congress?"

"Yes, and I'm sure your mom would love some help getting ready for our guests. Even one-arm help is better than no help."

"Dad! That probably isn't a politically correct thing to say."

"You're right. Someone who actually lost an arm wouldn't think it was very funny. But couldn't they laugh and say, "I'll show you" and then I would learn? It seems that everything is potentially offensive. What ever happened to people demonstrating their worth, instead of demonstrating because they didn't like the words? My comment wasn't intended for malice."

"I know, but even if comments aren't intended to hurt, sometimes they do hurt." Megan knew how comments often hurt.

"Then isn't it good to have a conversation so that an opinion can be changed, or at the very least, more understood? Opinions are often wrong but actions speak the truth. If a one-armed person was offended, instead of throwing a temper tantrum and calling me a—not sure what—wouldn't it be better to explain or show what they were actually able to accomplish with one arm? Then I would think, that's impressive."

"Dad, when did you get so philosophical?"

"I don't know. I'm trying to understand why people get offended so easily but aren't interested in teaching or sharing. Nonetheless, young lady, your mom would appreciate some help from her currently one-working arm daughter."

"I'll help but now I need to go to bed. I'm pooped and tomorrow's my first day back in school."

"Goodnight, sweetie, and I'm proud of you." Adrian didn't rise. Strangely, he sat in his chair with a goofy grin.

"Just so you know, I saw that cookie you just took and are hiding under the table. You're a real cookie monster."

"Are you calling me blue? Because I don't know if that's offensive or not."

"Good night, FATHER." Megan couldn't stop smiling as she left the kitchen.

It had been a very long but interesting day in the town of Appleridge. Funny how some people think small towns are boring.

Chapter Four

ainie climbed out of her bed and stretched, still stiff from yesterday's long drive. She was pleasantly surprised at the accommodations for her and Shadow at the host farm. The farm owner, Trina Shaw, had a special place for Lainie to park her trailer, one with an electric and water hook up, and a nice pen waiting for Shadow under the roof of a run-in barn. This morning she would take a short ride on Shadow, and then meet with the clinic organizer to go over a few details. She didn't see much of Appleridge as she drove through the town last night, but maybe later she would drive to town for lunch and a quick look around. It seemed nice enough for a small town.

JENNIE AND MR. MARK sat at the conference table sharing ideas. When Jennie explained her idea for the Tell Us a Story column, Mr. Mark sat back and said nothing for a minute or two. Jennie nervously waited for a comment.

No comment. He must think my idea is stupid, and he's trying to decide how to tell me without calling me stupid.

"Jennie, I think your idea will be fun for our readers, but we need to think this through a bit more. Let's talk about it at next week's staff meeting and we'll get Sherilynn's and Charles's input. I have a few thoughts. Should we set a time limit for running the column? What will we do if we don't get submissions? Or, too many? If we try the idea, let's create an email address for the submissions. It could be something like tellusastory @ country-chronicle. I don't like the idea of using your email for this purpose, and besides, we get quite a few email addresses with our website."

"I'll give it some more thought and a separate email address is something I didn't consider. This week I realized how much people like to share stories and thought I could create a positive outlet. I only came up with this last night, so it was probably a little premature to present the idea." Jennie felt a little foolish because she knew the idea needed more thought.

"I like new and different ideas—keep them coming. Did you consider writing about the accident and the stories that followed as your human-interest piece?" Mr. Mark relaxed into his chair and waited for Jennie's answer.

"Yes, I did, and that's how I came up with the Tell Us a Story idea. I'm still thinking about how to write about the stories that circulated after the accident. I want my article to be positive." Jennie continued, "I have also written a piece on local fall festivals. It should be ready for your review today or tomorrow. I wrote a little about the history and what makes each festival special, how they unite the local community, and also attract visitors. My how-to piece is on how to stack firewood. It includes places to purchase firewood, how large is a cord, what will fill a pick-up truck, and a few fun facts. I want my pieces to be both informative and fun to read." Jennie was proud of her firewood piece, but she was also very aware that this was her first month writing for the Chronicle and she was still learning what their readers and her boss expected.

"I look forward to reading this month's edition." Mr. Mark smiled.

"Don't you want to read them before then?" Jennie was surprised.

"No, I've read your work, I hired you as a professional, and I trust they'll be good. I realize it may take you a while to learn what our readers expect and enjoy, but you'll need to learn that for yourself."

Jennie was amazed but tried to appear mature and confident. She needed to remember she was a professional and not a student waiting for a grade from her professor.

"Thank you for your confidence. I promise to learn quickly." Jennie was sincere.

Mr. Mark gathered his papers and added, "I know you will, Jennie."

Jennie returned to her desk. She decided to work on the Tell Me a Story idea later. This afternoon she would polish her articles for her debut into the CC. She wanted her first efforts to really shine.

The day passed quickly as Jennie worked. She took a break for lunch with Sherilynn and then went right back to work, hardly leaving her desk. Jennie thought of a few more story ideas and wrote them down on her growing list. She never wanted to be caught without an idea of what she should write next. So far, that didn't seem to be a problem.

When Sherilynn motioned that she was leaving for the day, Jennie realized it was already five-thirty. She waved and promised to lock the door and turn out all the lights except the one on Sherilynn's desk. Jennie shut down her computer, cleared up her desk, and grabbed her purse. She didn't like being in the office alone, and besides, she had five hungry equine mouths to feed, and one feline named Beauty.

She stopped by Sherilynn's desk and scribbled a note. Jennie wouldn't be in the office tomorrow. Instead, she was exploring new story ideas. She scheduled interviews on Friday because it was a nice way to end the week. Tomorrow's interviews were with a visiting horse trainer conducting a clinic at a local farm, and with Dr. Peterson for a possible article on the benefits of micro-chipping cats, dogs, and horses. Both interviews were close to home.

JENNIE QUICKLY FED the barn gang and then showered and dressed in jeans, new boots, and an equestrian shirt and vest for her interviews. She wanted to look nice for her meeting with Dr. Peterson, but also have a great equestrian look for her horsemanship interview.

Dr. Peterson scheduled a bit of time after his early morning surgeries and the start of routine visits with furry patients. He was waiting for her when she arrived at the clinic and stopped to grab a coffee as he led Jennie to his office. Jennie declined his offer to get one for her.

As Jennie's vet for years, father of Jennie's best friend, and her hero last summer, Dr. Peterson was no stranger to Jennie. They skipped the formalities and greetings and got right to work. Jennie had a few questions and Dr. Peterson had several websites and pamphlets for Jennie to use for her article. He explained the benefits, the costs, and then he inserted a chip into a dog while Jennie watched.

"I'll scan several of my patients to see which ones have micro-chips."

He then scanned several cats and dogs in the clinic to show her the identifying number on the scanner display, and how the owner's information could be retrieved from a database using the number. This was not new information for Jennie, but she found the details fascinating.

"Do you think any of your clients would be willing to be interviewed? I'm interested in stories about people who found their lost pets because of the micro-chip." Jennie always loved to give her stories a personal touch.

"I'll ask several that I know have good stories and give them your contact information if they're interested in sharing. Some have really good stories. Of course, your personal story is the perfect story. Just remember that we never pressed charges because we couldn't prove who was actually guilty, so don't use real names." The smile leaving Dr. Peterson's face told the whole story. Jennie knew Dr. Peterson was thrilled to get Julep back but still regretted not being able to press charges.

When Dr. Peterson's daughter, Megan, took Julep to South Carolina last summer for the horsemanship internship, several ranch hands reported that Julep had died while Megan was away at a competition. Dr. Peterson's friend and fellow vet in South Carolina, Bobby Gray, found Julep at a sale while scanning horses for micro-chips. She hadn't really died; she was stolen. It was quite the rescue story. Fortunately, this story also had a happy ending because Megan gave Julep to Jennie and then rescued another horse from the ranch. Their story had a good ending, but with horses being stolen every day, Jennie was driven to share information to make it more difficult for a horse to simply disappear. She understood the heartbreak of losing a beloved horse. She also knew that many stolen horses ended up on a slaughter truck to Mexico or Canada where the price per pound drove the crime.

Jennie didn't linger. Dr. Peterson was busy. She knew she had a great personal interest angle with Julep's story, and if she could get a few more stories featuring cats and dogs, her article would be not only informative but compelling.

The drive to the farm hosting the horsemanship clinic was next on Jennie's agenda. What a great day to be out and about! She rolled down her window and enjoyed the fresh air on the short drive.

At the farm she noticed cars parked in a pasture with an open gate and maneuvered her truck into the pasture. She picked up her folded camping chair from the back of the truck, grabbed her bag holding a water bottle and notebooks, and started the short walk to the barn. There were about twelve horses in the arena with their humans and maybe fifteen more students with notebooks sitting in chairs along the arena fence. Everyone seemed busy taking notes as the instructor led the class. It appeared to be what Jennie called a ground session. The class was learning horsemanship skills working from the ground and not riding. Jennie was learning more about ground work from Marcy, and she was very interested. The class looked fun.

Trina Shaw, the farm owner, came over to welcome Jennie. "Welcome." She whispered so as not to disturb the lesson. "Are you Jennie?"

Jennie nodded. "Hey, I know you." Jennie laughed, probably a little too loud, as several of the auditors turned in their chairs to see who was talking. Trina was a hugger and embraced Jennie but then quickly motioned for Jennie to follow her a short distance away from the arena. "And I know you. Funny, we never talked about horses at church."

Trina was fairly new to the area and recently started to attend Our Savior Lutheran where Jennie also attended. They didn't realize they knew each other when Jennie called to get permission to visit the clinic.

Jennie laughed again, but this time no one was disturbed. "I bet we'll talk horses at church from now on."

"We sure will. Go ahead and sit with the auditors. I need to run to the house, but I'll see you at lunch."

Jennie opened her chair and placed it behind the group, a perfect position to observe both the class in the arena and the students sitting along the fence. The instructor, Lainie Anderson, was entertaining and knowledgeable. The class seemed to be having fun, and the horses were relaxed. So far, it seemed good. The exercises seemed fairly simple so she made a note to ask about the level of this particular class.

While doing her pre-interview research, Jennie learned that you could choose to be a student with your horse or you could pay to audit the class without a horse. There were apparently different student levels, but Jennie didn't fully understand the descriptions. She was very surprised at the cost of the class as it seemed very expensive.

Trina introduced Jennie to Lainie during the lunch break.

"It's nice to meet you, Jennie. If you have any questions, just ask."

They didn't talk long. The students were lining up to talk with their instructor. The class was a bit star-struck by Lainie—gathering around and hanging on every word.

The students saddled their horses following lunch, and the afternoon was filled with riding exercises. The clinic looked fun, but Jennie was sure that the average 4-H child could do most of the exercises presented in this particular session.

Maybe I'm missing something, but I don't see the "bang for the buck." She realized she was a bit more obsessed with what you get for a dollar than most people. *The information is good, but I would expect more, or maybe I'm missing something.*

Just before the class ended, Jennie thanked Trina, and picked up her chair for the walk back to her truck—thinking about her notebook full of her observations. She could take this story several different ways. Should she highlight the farm and what it offered, or talk about the horsemanship program Lainie taught? She wanted to tell a good story, give good information, and be very objective—not an easy task. Especially since she knew Trina personally.

She introduced herself to two middle-aged women, also walking back to their truck, and explained she was writing an article for the Chronicle. Jennie liked to give her articles a personal slant. She wasn't too surprised when they seemed willing to stop and chat. Everyone had been friendly and welcoming at the clinic. She was surprised, however, that they weren't as positive as Jennie expected.

"Hi, I'm Jane, and if you don't use my name, I'll share my opinion." Jane's friend smiled, but didn't share her name.

"Hi, Jane, I'm Jennie McKenzie and I write for the *Farm & Family Country Chronicle*. I'm not familiar with this horsemanship program, but I already figured out that it has faithful followers. Are you a Follow the Leader student?" Jennie noticed that Jane's friend still didn't offer her name but she looked friendly.

"Yes, we love the program. It has good principles, but I have trouble with the faithful follower description."

Jennie quickly replied, "Oh, I'm so sorry, I didn't mean to be derogatory about dedicated followers."

"No, you weren't, but I am. I would love to learn more, and the clinics seem fun, but I can't afford to spend that much money for fun. I like Lainie, the instructor. She's my favorite of all the Follow the Leader instructors."

"I'm going to read and learn, but I'm not paying to audit anymore—at least not as much," Jane's friend added, but still no name was offered. "Even the auditing fees are getting beyond my budget."

"It's funny, but I thought the same thing about the fees, but since the class was full, I guessed the fee must be typical." Jennie glanced at the remaining students and auditors still gathered around Lainie.

"I'm not sure; maybe they have a lot more money than me. I have to stick to a strict budget just to have my horse, so I try to do all the free things in the area, and there seem to be plenty to do. I wish we had a good local instructor who could teach the

Follow the Leader program. I sure would like to take a class like this sometime." Jane seemed to flip from anger to wistful.

"I can certainly understand a budget. I find it necessary as well. I also noticed the students seem very attached to the instructor. If I promised not to use your name in my article, would you be willing to give me your contact information? I'm also interested in doing an article on the free horsemanship activities in this area."

"How about you give me your contact information? I'll email some ideas, and we can email back and forth if you have more questions." Jane smiled, pleased to be asked for her opinion.

"Thank you, that's a good plan." Jennie opened her portfolio and pulled business cards from the front pocket for Jane. She also gave Jane's still nameless friend her business cards—her farm card and her *Farm & Family Country Chronicle* card.

"Thank you for your help and any info you can send my way. I'm from Appleridge but I've been away for a while and it seems the horse community has changed quite a bit in my absence."

"We live south of Richburg. There's a lot going on in our area." My name's Sonja and I could send you some things, too." Now that Jennie seemed safe, Sonja didn't want to be left out of the conversation.

"Thank you, Sonja. I look forward to hearing from you both, and maybe we'll meet again at another event."

Interesting, thought Jennie as she put her chair and bag into the truck. She had no idea where she would take this story, but she had a feeling it wasn't going to go the direction she originally planned. She loved this job and couldn't wait to get home and hit the internet, hunting more information.

As it turned out, Jennie didn't spend much time on research. It was Friday night and that meant a pizza with Jeremy. He called while she was in the barn finishing the evening chores.

"Hey, do you feel like a pizza and a movie if I bring both?"

Jennie laughed because a pizza and a movie had been their regular Friday night routine for a while now.

"Sounds good—I'm just finishing barn chores."

"Are your dear friends and boarders at the barn tonight? Do I need to bring extra pizza?"

"No, I'm not expecting anyone tonight. Marcy may stop on her way home to love on the ponies, but she enjoys a bit of private time after a long day."

"Ok, I'll place the pizza order. Is pepperoni and cheese ok?" Jeremy laughed because he knew the answer before he heard the reply.

"Make it pepperoni, mushrooms, and onions, please, and not one word about the onions."

"It will be my pleasure." Jeremy loved Jennie's obsession with onions. Well, at least he loved teasing her, but smelling onion, maybe not so much.

JENNIE AND JEREMY devoured their pizza as neither had eaten much for lunch. Jeremy also brought a bag of the locally made potato chips to munch on during the movie.

"You are a very bad influence, Jeremy James, but thanks for bringing the chips as a movie snack."

"It's my pleasure." Jeremy smiled as Jennie grabbed a large handful of chips. "But, hey, save some for me, onion breath."

"I knew that was coming sooner than later." Jennie smiled and continued eating chips. BBQ chips, actually. It couldn't get much better.

The movie was funny and had a great ending. Jeremy got up and stretched as he reached for their plates, cups, napkins, and one totally empty chip bag. He took his load to the kitchen as Jennie also stretched and carried the pizza box with two slices remaining.

"Do you want to take these last two slices home?" Jennie secretly hoped he would decline and he did.

"No, I know how much you love cold pizza." Jeremy didn't like cold pizza.

"I do, but not for breakfast tomorrow. I'm picking up Gramps and I think we may go out for breakfast. He wants to visit with Sam while he trims the horses' feet in the morning. Why don't you stop out if you aren't doing anything? It'll be a leisurely horse day here at the farm.

"Ok, maybe. I'm running a few errands in the morning and Daniel has a soccer game. Maybe I'll bring Daniel after soccer, if that's ok?"

"You bet! Daniel loves the ponies, and we may put him to work."

"I'm sure he'd be fine doing anything that involves being with Riley and Stuffin. Hey, come here." Jeremy reached for Jennie and pulled her close. "Not bad for onion breath." He teased, as he lowered his head for a nice long kiss before leaving.

Jennie watched Jeremy stop outside the gate, then get out of his SUV to shut and lock it, before driving down the road. Jennie knew it made him feel good knowing she was inside and safe for the night. She loved her time spent with Jeremy. He was fun and thoughtful. Of course, their relationship was still very new. Maybe he would change over time, and wouldn't always be so fun and considerate. Somehow, Jennie didn't think so—she thought he was exactly who she thought he was.

LAINIE DISMOUNTED from Shadow and walked the mare to her pen under the roof of the barn. She usually treated herself to a relaxing ride after a long day of teaching. Tomorrow she would tack up Shadow during the afternoon riding portion of the clinic and teach from horseback. She often used Shadow to demonstrate a particular exercise or technique. It was a good class, although several of the students were trying to force their horses into obedience instead of waiting for what their horses offered. She needed to find a way to work on that tomorrow. Some didn't understand a correction is for their benefit and not criticism. When did a correction become negative, especially when it was offered as positively as possible? Lainie shook her head. She no longer believed in herself as an instructor, but she couldn't let it show. She didn't want to be outed as a fake. It was getting hard, though.

Lainie pulled a business card from the back pocket of her jeans—Jennie McKenzie, *The Farm & Family Country Chronicle*. Jennie seemed nice enough, but she wore a puzzled expression on her face most of the day. She was very interested in Lainie's background and the Follow the Leader program. Lainie wondered if Jennie McKenzie would return tomorrow.

Chapter Five

In the morning, Jennie picked up Grandpa, talked him out of his offer to buy donuts, and instead they drove to the Café. Gramps didn't mind getting something different than his usual Bake & Shake breakfast of donuts or muffins, and coffee. The Café was usually busy on Saturday, but since Gramps liked to sit at the counter, they quickly slid onto two vacant stools.

"Order something good, Jennie, my treat." Grandpa wasn't looking at a menu so he must have his mind already set.

"Thanks, Grandpa, but I was going to treat you today," Jennie said truthfully.

"I think I better treat so you have plenty of money to pay your landlord." Grandpa chuckled, as he was her landlord.

"Ok, then; thanks, Grandpa." Jennie was hungry and wanted an omelet but thought maybe she should find something cheaper.

"I know you want an omelet, Jennie girl, go ahead, I won a bet yesterday at the Bake & Shake so I have some extra dough." Grandpa thought that was funny—getting more dough at the bakery.

"What kind of bet, Grandpa?" Jennie closed the menu. Yup, she would let Grandpa's dough pay for a veggie omelet, hash browns, and toast.

"Oh, I won the bet for guessing how many people would order chocolate-blueberry-pumpkin muffins between seven-thirty and nine at the Bake & Shake yesterday. We each put in a dollar and then come up with something to guess."

"Grandpa, really? That makes you a gambling man."

"You do realize, Jennie, the real gamble is eating a chocolate-blueberry-pumpkin muffin, but actually, it was pretty tasty." Grandpa smacked his lips just as the waitress, an older woman named Bernice, walked up to pour coffee and take their order.

"Well, Charlie Gantzler, so we pulled you from the dark side this morning, and away from the Bake & Shake. By the way, I heard you relieved my husband of a whole dollar yesterday."

"I did, Bernice, and now I'm spending it and a few others right here treating my granddaughter."

"Well then, let me take your order quick before you change your mind." Bernice cackled as she took their orders, and still had a grin on her face as she walked away.

"Grandpa, have you ever heard of something called natural horsemanship? I interviewed an instructor teaching a natural horsemanship clinic yesterday. She reminded me a little of what I've heard about JJ, who ran the internship program that Megan attended last year, and you know that wasn't a good experience."

"I think I've heard that term before, but I always think good horsemanship is good horsemanship and bad is bad. I'm not sure what they mean because nothing we humans do with horses is truly natural."

"I think it helps people understand how to think like a horse."

"Did the teacher show the students how to think like a horse?" Grandpa seemed to be enjoying the conversation.

"She tried and I liked the exercises. The participants, for the most part, were having fun. Some of the horses didn't seem too thrilled. The instructor cautioned the students to partner with their horses and not use force of any kind. Some didn't seem to understand, because they were just making their horses do what they wanted."

"Ah, so that's the bad horsemanship. We know that good horsemanship teaches and waits for the result." Grandpa took a sip of his coffee. "What reminded you of JJ and Megan's experience?"

Jennie thought for a moment. "I guess it's because I remember how infatuated Megan was with JJ, and the students at the clinic seemed to be like that around Lainie. Lainie's the instructor for a program called Follow the Leader. I interviewed several students, who paid to watch today, and they said they would love to bring their horses and participate but didn't have the money."

"You didn't see the old bang for the buck?" Grandpa knew how closely Jennie monitored her budget.

"Yeah, I guess. I haven't sorted it all out yet. I know I've been away from horses for a while. Maybe things have changed. The instructor talked about it being her mission to help horses by helping people. I found that interesting but didn't get a chance to ask her more. I'm sure going to dig further. I have Lainie's email address. I'm going to ask her a few questions, and I also need to find out more about this Follow the Leader program."

"Sounds like you have a good article in the making, Jennie girl, and I bet Megan has some good information after her experience last summer. It does sound like the same type of program.

Megan was willing to give up an awful lot to follow that trainer to South Carolina."

"I'll talk to Megan, but so far, she doesn't seem too eager to offer any details. I think she's still recovering from her terrible experience, and now she also needs to heal from her accident."

"That Megan is a good girl; she may need to talk, and it may help to talk to a good friend."

"I suppose. I'll start the conversation and see where it leads."

Bernice brought their orders and there wasn't much conversation as they both dug into their huge breakfasts.

"I THINK I'LL have to roll myself to the truck, Grandpa. I'm stuffed." Jennie couldn't believe she ate a three-egg omelet, a large serving of hash browns, and two pieces of toast.

Grandpa laughed. "It was good. We won't need much lunch."

"I won't need any lunch or supper, but I'll probably have some, anyway."

"Oh, I bet you'll burn through breakfast if you have many chores to do today. Let's go. All this talk about horses has gotten me itchy to touch a few. Do you think Marcy will be out today?"

Jennie grinned and stopped to look at Grandpa before climbing into the truck. "Why? Are you thinking this is a good day for a carriage ride?"

"Yup, and maybe Marcy will hand me the reins again." Grandpa opened his door and climbed into the truck with more agility than most people half his age. All the horse talk had certainly put a spring in his step this morning.

AFTER PULLING INTO the farm drive, Jennie climbed out to open the gate. She decided to leave it open for Sam and the others. Back behind the wheel, she followed the gravel drive to the barn and parked.

"Gramps, I have chairs in the barn. Sam should be here any minute so I'm going to put hay in the stalls and call the horses."

"I'll wait in the aisle and make sure they all get where they need to get. Does that Riley still try a few tricks?"

"Not very often, but when he does, he certainly causes a ruckus." Jennie walked to the back of the barn and opened the gate. None of the horses seemed very interested in returning to the barn. It was a beautiful day, and they were enjoying their pasture time. Jennie waited, and Julep finally caught sight of her and quickly trotted to the barn.

"I can always count on you, Julep. Jennie pulled a peppermint out of her pocket, and Julep gently took it from her hand. "Come on, girl, let's get you in your stall and the rest will follow."

Riley was second. He never wanted to miss anything. Once he was in his stall, the other three calmly walked into the barn and found their stalls.

With all five in their correct places munching hay, and Grandpa settled in a comfortable folding chair at the end of the aisle, Jennie checked her phone for messages.

"Sam will be here in a few minutes. Good thing we didn't have to wait long for breakfast since he's a little early. Cassy is on her way and will pick up Megan. Marcy is working the afternoon shift today and wants to know if the ponies can be trimmed first so she can take the carriage out for a short session. I think you're in luck, Grandpa."

Sam arrived pulling a small trailer containing his farrier equipment—horseshoes, nails, rasps, hoof knives, a grinder for sharpening knives, and a stand called a Hoof Jack—everything and anything he would need while trimming and shoeing horses.

"Hey, young man, good to see you on this fine day." Grandpa didn't get up from his chair, but Sam walked over quickly to shake his hand.

"Hello, Mr. Gantzler, good to see you. Are you going to hold a few horses today?"

"Only if I can hold a few horses while sitting down since I'm pretty comfortable in this here chair." Grandpa did look relaxed and comfortable.

Jennie knew Sam was teasing. "I promised Marcy we would do her ponies first. She has to work later and would like to drive this morning, if possible." Jennie went into Riley's stall with his halter then led him down the aisle to Sam. "I'll hold him."

Sam greeted Riley, offered his hand for a sniff, rubbed his hand down Riley's neck, then along his back, and on down a back leg. Riley picked up his foot and Sam went to work.

Riley was a good boy, and it didn't take too long to trim four pony feet in spite of the banter between Grandpa, Sam, and Jennie. Marcy arrived just as Jennie was leading Stuffin into the aisle for her turn with Sam.

"Hey, gang, may I join this party?" Marcy seemed in good spirits.

"You sure can, but so far it's been pretty tame," Grandpa teased. He liked Marcy. "Jennie says you're getting the carriage out today. Any chance I could hitch a ride?"

"Sure—it's always fun to have you on board, Mr. Gantzler. Jennie, do you mind holding Stuffin for Sam so I can groom Mr. Riley? I really hate to rush when I'm with the ponies, but I promised to start my shift at the hospital a littler earlier than planned."

"I'll hold her, no problem. Actually, I should make Grandpa hold her since he wants a carriage ride," Jennie teased.

"Are you riding Julep today?" Marcy tied Riley in the aisle near enough to stay in the conversation.

"Not sure. It depends on how much time is left after all the horses are trimmed. I may play at liberty instead of riding." Jennie loved liberty—playing with a horse from the ground with nothing attached. No halter or lead line. The horse was at liberty to stay with her or leave. It was fun, and when Jennie and Julep played, it often looked like a dance as they mirrored each other—a dance choreographed by trust.

As soon as Sam finished trimming Stuffin, Marcy tied her in the aisle for grooming. She was usually the easier of the two. Riley loved to roll in dirt or mud but Stuffin usually rolled in grass. Once groomed, both ponies were ready to harness. They both understood the command to stand and not move while being harnessed and hitched to the carriage, but to be safe, Grandpa stood at their heads as Marcy brought the carriage forward and attached the traces. She was a pro and so were Riley and Stuffin. They completed the process in only a few minutes.

Marcy put on her helmet and climbed into the carriage. She then handed Grandpa a helmet and motioned for him to climb up and sit beside her on the left. He didn't argue about the helmet. He knew Marcy made wearing a helmet mandatory for a seat on her carriage.

"Walk on." Marcy encouraged the ponies, and they pulled the carriage with its passengers out of the paddock and into the pasture following a mowed path.

"Jennie, is Treasure being shod today? I know Cassy was considering pulling the shoes and trying to keep her barefoot for a while." It was getting warmer and Sam pulled a bandana out of his back pocket and wiped his face as Jennie held Starlight for her turn.

"I think so; I'll send a text to confirm." Jennie searched her pocket for her phone. She was notorious for losing her phone, not hearing her phone, and pretty much ignoring her phone most of the time. This time it was in her back pocket fully charged.

"Cassy must have heard you, Sam." She motioned to the front of the property where Cassy was pulling in the drive with Megan in the passenger seat.

"Hey, Sam, have you heard from Belinda lately?"

"Yeah, I heard from her yesterday."

"Are things going well at school? I know she's pretty busy." Jennie missed her best friend and Megan's older sister, Belinda. They reconnected briefly during the summer but now Belinda was at the University of Florida for vet school, and Jennie hadn't heard from her for a while.

"I think so. She seems happy. She called to share something about a hoof case her class saw at the clinic." Jennie noticed Sam seemed a little flustered when he talked about Belinda. Neither Sam nor Belinda wanted to admit they were a couple, but in Jennie's opinion, they made a really nice couple.

Megan and Cassy were now in the barn and bursting with news. Jennie noticed that Megan seemed happier and not so guarded today—like the old Megan before her accident.

"Well, what are you two so happy about?" Sam noticed, too.

"Megan has decided to attend Richburg College next year, and we're going to share a dorm room."

Megan joined the conversation. "Actually, we want to share an apartment but Mom and Dad said I need to experience dorm life for my freshman year."

"I'll stay one more year in the dorm and share a room with Megan." Cassy grinned. "I would only do that for a really good friend."

Jennie followed the volley of conversation from Cassy to Megan to Cassy again. She wasn't surprised to hear the news. Megan and Cassy were becoming very good friends. What did surprise Jennie was Megan being excited about going to college.

"Wow, Megan, what a change for you. I guess your experience this summer convinced you that college was a good idea?" Jennie couldn't resist sharing her thoughts.

"A lot has happened in the last few months. Enough to convince me that taking a bit more time to decide my future is a good idea. I'm pretty sure I want to do something with art, and horses, but I don't have to declare a major, yet."

"I'm happy for you both." Jennie was happy, also, that she would have her two boarders around a little while longer. Jennie enjoyed having both Starlight and Treasure, and their owners at her barn, and the extra income didn't hurt.

"Hey, are we shoeing Treasure today?" Sam wasn't going to let all the talk stop him from his work. He had a full Saturday schedule.

"Yes, shoes today, but I'll have them pulled next time and keep her barefoot for winter." Cassy walked over to Treasure, greeted her, and then took her halter off the hook.

"Hold on, Cassy, let me finish Starlight, then I'll trim Julep. I'll finish with Treasure, since she's the only one being shod—if that's ok."

"Ok, that's good. Megan and I are here hanging out with the horses all day."

Megan reached for Starlight. "I can take over now, Jennie."

"Hey, sweetie," Megan talked to her mare as she stroked Starlight's neck with her good arm and then reached in her pocket for a peppermint—Starlight's favorite treat.

In less than an hour Sam finished Starlight and Julep, then waited for Cassy to bring him Treasure.

"Good timing, Marcy." Jennie called out when she saw Marcy approach the barn. But it wasn't Marcy driving; it was Grandpa.

Grandpa directed the pair of ponies into the barn paddock with a huge grin on his face. Marcy reached for the reins. He handed them over and waited for Jennie to help him climb down from the carriage. He was still grinning as he walked back to his chair in the barn aisle.

Cassy handed Treasure's lead rope to Jennie so she could help Marcy unhitch and unharness the ponies and then took Riley out to the wash rack. Marcy followed with Stuffin. Both ponies were a little sweaty from their workout and needed baths before spending the afternoon in the pasture. Cassy, Megan, and Marcy stood at the gate and watched both ponies drop to the ground for a good roll.

This time, Riley rolled in the grass instead of the dirt. Marcy laughed. "Yay! Good boy, Riley."

Jennie decided to turn Julep out with the rest of her herd since she was finished with her trim. There was so much activity at the barn, Jennie didn't know if or when she would ride, and it wasn't fair to ask Julep to stand in her stall on a gorgeous fall day waiting for Jennie to decide.

Cassy tied Starlight in the aisle for Megan to start awkwardly grooming her horse with her left hand.

It was a very busy day at Fawn Song Farm and Jennie loved it.

"Gramps, may I make you a sandwich? It's almost 1:00." Jennie always worried about her Grandpa even though he was very self-sufficient.

"No, I think I'll take a walk on up to the house to use the facilities. I would like to bring a sandwich back with me and maybe a cold drink. Do you have any root beer?"

"Of course, Gramps, I keep it on hand just for you." Jennie walked over to help Grandpa out of the folding chair—and he gladly accepted her help.

"Thanks, Jennie girl." Grandpa was self-sufficient but not too proud to accept help when help was needed. Jennie thought more senior citizens would be wise to learn that lesson.

"Sam, how about you, would you like something?"

"No thanks, I have my lunch in the truck and I'll eat it on my way to the next barn."

"Cassy and Megan, I know you usually bring lunch and drinks. Do you need anything today?"

Megan turned away from Starlight. "No, we're all set. Mom packed us a great lunch."

"Mrs. Peterson is a great lunch packer," Cassy added.

"Oh, I remember her picnics well." Jennie laughed. "I've had my share."

Jennie and Belinda spent many horse days together as youngsters, and Mrs. Peterson usually brought a small cooler to the barn or packed lunches that would fit in their saddle bags when they spent the day riding along country roads. Jennie remembered those lunches fondly, and she wondered if that was why she was always checking to see if her friends had plenty to eat and drink while they were at her barn.

"Marcy do you want something before you leave?"

"No thanks, I'm heading out now." She paused at the barn door.

"Thanks for being a great *gator* today, Mr. Gantzler."

"Anytime, Miss Marcy, I welcome a ride anytime."

Marcy competed with her pair of ponies in the sport of combined driving, and during the marathon phase of the competition, a passenger called the navigator or *gator* is responsible for helping with direction and timing the pace as they travel through the course. While traveling, the navigator stands on the back step and moves his or her weight when and where needed to help the carriage stay balanced around tight and fast turns.

Marcy's thoughts continued as she climbed into her truck and drove off the farm. At his age, Marcy knew Jennie's grandpa couldn't stand on the back step and balance the carriage. Too bad, thought Marcy, he sure was good at everything else required from an excellent gator. Both she and the ponies loved his quiet but very clear demeanor.

Grandpa and Jennie returned to the barn with their lunch and root beer just as Sam was closing the door of his farrier's trailer. Megan was still grooming Starlight, and Cassy groomed a now perfectly shod Treasure.

Jennie was content. She really enjoyed this life with horses and friends. It was so different from the life she thought she wanted while living in Chicago. Then, she dreamed of racing around the city capturing exciting events in beautiful written essays and articles. Now, she loved traveling the country roads in search of personal interest stories for the Chronicle and hanging out in her barn.

"I've heard you sigh twice. Is something the matter?" Grandpa was finished with his sandwich.

"No, Gramps, everything is perfect. Those are sighs of contentment. I'm feeling as contented as you look while holding that bottle of root beer on this glorious fall day."

"Ah, I know just what you mean, Jennie girl, I know exactly what you mean." And Grandpa sighed as he took a long swig from his bottle.

With lunch finished and the barn quiet, Grandpa looked at his watch and then at Jennie.

"You can run me home now, Jennie girl. I have enough time for a short nap before the music starts."

"Music? What music?" Jennie was already up and folding her chair.

"We're going to have entertainment at the senior center tonight—a group from the high school playing music and a dessert social."

"What are you bringing to the social, Gramps? Do we need to stop at the Bake & Shake to pick up something on our way to your apartment?"

"No, I'm covered. We had the option of making a small monetary contribution to buy a few things in lieu of providing a dessert." Grandpa waited as Jennie carried the two chairs to the tack room. She didn't like anything cluttering up her barn aisle.

Walking down the aisle from the tack room, Jennie stopped to tell Cassy and Megan she was leaving for a while to take Grandpa home, but would be back before feeding time.

"Ok, thanks." Megan was sitting on her tack trunk waiting for Cassy to finish grooming Treasure.

"Oh yeah, if Jeremy stops by, please let him know I'll be back fairly soon."

Cassy straightened up and looked over Treasure's back at Jennie. "Would you mind if Jeremy rode Julep while we ride?"

"No, I don't mind. Wait! We? Are you riding, too, Megan?" Jennie stopped and looked at Megan.

"Yeah, Cassy will saddle Starlight for me and help me get up. I won't do much, and probably no wild gallops," Megan teased.

"Funny. You know, I just want you to heal quickly. Sorry if it feels like I'm trying to tell you what to do."

"No worries; Mom wasn't thrilled, but I promised that if Starlight was too full of herself, I wouldn't ride."

"Ok, be careful, guys. I'll leave the house unlocked in case you need anything."

Jennie and Grandpa walked out of the barn in silence.

"She'll be fine, and if she falls and causes more damage or breaks another bone, I call that a valuable but hard lesson learned."

"I guess. Do I get pretty bossy, Gramps?"

"I wouldn't call it bossy, exactly, but you do like to put all the pieces in the correct place. The problem is your correct place may not be someone else's correct place. Your place may be the wisest, and may be the best, but people have to learn what's best for them. You know what I mean?" Grandpa opened the truck door but waited before he climbed into the truck.

"I know what you mean. I've learned quite a bit while making my own decisions lately." Jennie waited until Grandpa was in the seat with the door shut before she walked around to the other side and climbed in.

"Have I made a few decisions you didn't think put the pieces in the correct place?"

"Ah, yes. Not many, but a few." Grandpa laughed. "And I'm sure there will be a few more times we both make choices that are questioned by others."

Jennie thought her grandpa was perhaps the wisest grandpa in the world.

Chapter Six

Sam pulled over on the side of the road under a few trees to eat his lunch. He wasn't feeling very hungry, but he needed to eat. Being a farrier was hard physical work.

Sam wished the physical work would drive away all the worry stealing his usually healthy appetite. He wished he was happy like everyone seemed to be at Jennie's barn. Those folks sure did seem worry-free. But then, they weren't worried about having enough money to pay their bills.

Sam was good with money. He learned a long time ago how to squeeze a dollar. His dad died young and his mom was terrible with money. Even as a young boy, he learned to budget the money he earned mowing lawns and doing odd jobs. Many times, his meager income kept their electrical power on and a few groceries in the house. He vowed at a young age he would never worry about money, and now here he was, worried about money.

He hated debt. He put himself through farrier school without a loan, and he bought his start-up supplies with cash. He borrowed money to buy a truck. He didn't feel any shame since a truck was a necessary business expense. Sam was careful with his money and scrimped when possible. He wasn't stupid. That's why he filed his own taxes. He didn't think he needed to pay an accountant for something he could do himself. But now, he knew that was a very bad decision. The recent letter from the IRS proved him wrong and was the cause of his worry. They wanted money—lots of money—more money than Sam had in the bank at the moment, and they didn't want to wait.

Sam wasn't sure what happened. He wasn't trying to cheat. He paid what he honestly thought he owed. Something was obviously wrong. Maybe he took the wrong deductions. Sam worked all day—every day but Sunday. He had a full list of clients. He didn't think he could add more business, and he definitely didn't want to raise his fees. His prices were fair for both him and his clients. He didn't want to borrow money from the bank to pay taxes. His mom certainly couldn't help. Sam knew he needed to find a way to pay for an accountant or maybe legal help.

Sam sure didn't want people, especially his clients, to find out he had been stupid with money. He had no one to ask for advice. He thought about asking Jennie's grandpa. He seemed wise and like he could be trusted. He definitely couldn't talk to Belinda right now. She would be able to sense something was wrong as soon as she heard his voice.

He and Belinda told people they weren't an official couple, but they wanted to be married someday. They were waiting for Belinda to finish school and for Sam's business to be successful. Belinda told Sam she was proud of what he was accomplishing with his life and his skill as a farrier, but Sam always felt like he wasn't good enough. All through school he struggled with his family's lack of money. His clothes were from the thrift store, and he never owned his own horse. A kind family allowed Sam to ride, and he joined 4-H with their horse in exchange for help on the farm. Sam always wanted his own horse, and now he had a Quarter Horse mare named Sadie. He didn't want to think about losing Sadie. No, he would find a way to always care for her. He kept Sadie at a nice boarding barn and it wasn't cheap. Sam wondered if Jennie would consider letting Sadie live at her farm. He thought Jennie would help him out, if possible, but Sam hated the thought of sharing his situation with Belinda's best friend. No, he would figure out something else.

Sam put his unfinished sandwich back in the cooler, started the truck, and headed to his next stop. He needed to keep going, keep working, and keep making money.

JENNIE DROPPED Grandpa off at his apartment and decided to make a quick stop at the grocery store. She needed a few items and she also wanted to find something special for dinner—just in case Jeremy was able to get to the farm. As she pulled a small grocery cart from the rack of connected carts, Jennie heard her phone sing a song. She pushed the cart to the side, out of the way of fellow shoppers, and pulled the phone from her purse. She missed the call but saw it was from Belinda. Her ears must have been burning. Reception was poor in the store so she walked outside before trying to catch up with her friend. She didn't bother to listen to the voicemail before she called.

"Hey, that was quick." Belinda sounded good.

"I couldn't get my phone out of my purse fast enough. I didn't listen to your message."

"That's ok. Nothing important, I just wanted to catch up and also ask if you've seen Sam lately."

Jennie hesitated. "Yes, I just saw him. He was at the farm this morning. Funny, I asked about you and he said—well, he mentioned he heard from you. Something about a hoof case you saw at the clinic."

"Oh, really?" Belinda now didn't sound so good. "He said he talked to me?"

Jennie searched her memory. "No, I think he said he heard from you, but I assumed that meant he talked to you."

"I called and left a message about the hoof case several days ago, but I didn't actually talk to Sam, and he hasn't returned my call."

"You know, he did seem a little strange today, and more quiet than usual." Jennie was starting to feel uncomfortable.

Sensing that Jennie felt bad, Belinda added, "I know he's busy. I was just worried. It's not like him to ignore a message, and the case really is interesting." Belinda made an attempt to steer the conversation back to their normal banter.

"I guess you must feel out of the loop all the way down in Florida. After all, Appleridge is the center of the known universe." Jennie also wanted their usual fun conversation.

"That's for sure. First Megan wrecks her truck and Dad lets her off the hook—that was pretty amazing. We both know that whole story about the black dog was to cover the fact she was texting."

"That's what I thought, and I wondered how she explained it to your dad and lived to tell the story. Of course, the entire town of Appleridge told their own stories, and it was pretty entertaining. She's at the barn with Cassy and they both act like all is well in their world."

"Mom said Dad considered Megan's broken wrist and the loss of her truck enough punishment. Apparently, she fessed up and didn't try to lie. I guess they don't consider the little story about a black dog a lie. Those little stories some people call white lies will always get you into trouble."

Jennie laughed. "Yeah, we told our share and always paid the price."

"And, so will Sam. He wasn't being truthful when he implied he talked to me—when he said he heard from me. Something is up and I intend to find out the whole truth and nothing but the truth."

"Uh-oh, and here we were doing so well." Jennie really thought they had moved on and forgotten Sam for a moment.

"Don't worry. I'm more worried than angry. Sam's not a liar or a cheat. If anything, he holds himself to an unrealistically high standard and that's not good."

"I'll keep Sam in my prayers. I know he doesn't rely on faith, but prayer can reach everyone."

"Yeah, it doesn't matter if someone thinks he needs it or not. Thanks. Got to go—knowledge awaits. Love you, girlfriend."

"Love you; bye." Jennie ended the call with regret. Her attempt to help her friend feel better about Sam failed. She closed her eyes right there in front of the grocery store, ignoring the cars and customers pushing shopping carts and prayed.

Father, please be with my friends Belinda and Sam. I know something is wrong but not what is wrong, but you do, and you love them both. Please send your peace to sooth their troubled hearts. Please show them your love. Thank you and I love you.

Jennie knew if she didn't pray immediately, sometimes she would forget, and when you promised to pray, you needed to pray. A broken promise was the same as a lie of omission, wasn't it?

AS BELINDA WALKED to class, she also prayed. Something didn't feel right. She was worried about Sam.

She knew Jennie wouldn't just brush off the call. She would dig until she found an answer. Belinda could trust God and she could trust Jennie. Now she felt better. She would call Sam again after class. If he didn't answer, she would leave another message. A message telling him she missed him and just wanted to hear his voice. As much as Belinda loved to claim she and Sam were not a couple, and she was not looking for a serous relationship until after she graduated, she also knew with certainty—she did not want to lose Sam.

SAM WAS EXHAUSTED. It was unusually warm for September and he squeezed in extra horses at his last stop. Fifteen horses today to be exact—six barefoot trims, five horses trimmed with front shoes only, and four horses trimmed with shoes all the way around—it was a very long day. The shower felt good, and he was finally hungry. Sam's phone, recently thrown on the kitchen counter, rang. He glanced and saw it was Belinda. He hesitated. He didn't answer but could hardly wait to listen to her message.

"Hey Sam, it's me, but I guess you already know. Please call because I miss talking to you. You always make me feel good. I hope you're ok. I'm sure you can't call because you're busy. After all, you are absolutely the best farrier in the area. Love you. Bye."

Sam's stomach clenched at hearing Belinda's voice. He wanted to talk to her. Why was he being so stupid? She said, *love you*. Oh sure, it was probably just a casual sort of *love you* one said friend to friend. But still, she said it. He would call her back tomorrow. He wasn't sure what he would say if he called tonight. The only thing he knew for sure—he didn't want to lose Belinda.

JENNIE PULLED INTO her drive, disappointed she didn't see Jeremy's SUV parked near the house. Hopeful, she glanced at the barn, and nope, not there. Her phone played music as she carried her bag of groceries into the house. Jeremy.

"Hey, did Daniel play?"

"Yeah, a little. You know Daniel sits the bench quite a bit."

"I know, but he seems to have fun." Jennie smiled because Daniel didn't seem to mind.

"That he does, and his team won. I didn't realize this was a tournament, and since they won this morning, they need to play again later this afternoon. That means I won't be back in Appleridge to spend time with my favorite girl."

"I'm happy for Daniel, but sad for your favorite girl. I guess that means she'll spend the evening doing what she does best."

"Are any juicy stories in the works?" Jeremy teased.

"You know the *Farm & Family Country Chronicle* only prints the juiciest stories, but I'll never tell." Jennie realized that was exactly what she was doing—not telling about Belinda and Sam.

"Is it ok if I pick you up for church tomorrow?" Jeremy wished he could talk Jennie into going to the later service, but she would go to her usual early service because it was less traditional. Jeremy loved the music and worship band at the early service. What he didn't love was getting up early.

"Yes, you may—bright and early."

"I do this only for you, Jennie, only for you." Jeremy was serious.

"Jeremy James, 9:30 in the morning isn't that early."

"Maybe not, unless a good uncle spends the entire day at his nephew's soccer tournament and doesn't get back to Appleridge until the wee hours of the morning."

"You exaggerate, Mr. James. Surely you do." Jennie smiled.

"Perhaps I just want you to feel sorry for me."

"I do feel for you." Jennie knew that wasn't a lie. She had very strong feelings for Jeremy.

JENNIE CARRIED her plate of cheese and crackers into her office. She only needed a snack for dinner tonight, and besides, she didn't feel like cooking anything. It would be a great evening to put the finishing touches on her *Farm & Family Country Chronicle* pieces. She wanted them to be well written, informative, and easily read. If someone took the time to read anything Jennie wrote, she wanted the reader to feel like it was time well spent. It wasn't just about her; she wanted to help make the CC the best publication in their area—or the entire state. Hey, why stop there? Maybe it would become the best in the country.

Jennie laughed. Maybe she should stop dreaming and get busy. Dreams didn't come true without a lot of passion and hard work. Maybe she should add that to her list of future articles—interview people who were living their dreams and share their stories—stories about passion and hard work.

Sam suddenly came to mind. He was a great example of some-one willing to work hard from a very young age to overcome huge obstacles that were not his fault. Jennie sat holding her face in her hands. Sam—what was happening with Sam? He deserved success and happiness. She remembered how Sam always re-mained positive even though his friends—Jennie, Belinda, and Jeremy—complained about silly things. Not Sam, though any complaints he had to share were certainly valid.

Why was she so worried about Sam? Not answering his phone and letting her make the wrong assumption really weren't shat-tering issues. He's probably working too hard and is a little stressed. For the second time that day, Jennie said a little prayer for Sam. Sam would be fine, but maybe God was nudging her to do something. She believed sometimes prayer led to action, and Jennie wouldn't mind being an answer to someone's prayer.

CASSY AND MEGAN showered and primed, were ready for something fun. They didn't know what, exactly, but they didn't want to stay home on a Saturday night. Cassy was staying with the Petersons for the entire weekend.

"Hey, how about watching a movie tonight?" Megan picked up the control to scan Netflix offerings.

"That sounds good, but right now, in spite of your mom's awesome lunch, I'm starved." Cassy opened the refrigerator to see if Mrs. Peterson had anything stashed for a snack.

"I'm hungry but I'm sure Mom didn't cook anything. I heard Dad say he was taking her out for supper. She's been working pretty hard lately—helping at the clinic when she isn't substitute teaching. She said it feels like she has a full-time job without the benefits."

Cassy walked over to the cookie jar and lifted the lid. "Yum, I see chocolate chip cookies!"

"I'm surprised there are any left. Dad has been hitting the cookies pretty hard lately." Megan laughed at the memory of her dad trying to hide cookies under the table.

"Did I hear the cookie jar being opened?" Adrian Peterson walked into the kitchen freshly showered, wearing casual but nicely pressed clothes.

"Busted!" Cassy stuffed the first cookie into her mouth.

"Cassy, as soon as you chew, how's school?" Adrian Peterson moved closer to the jar to steal a cookie for himself. "It could be a while until we get to the restaurant so I better have a cookie or two to hold me over."

"School is good. Weekends are better."

"Were you at the barn the night Megan wrecked her truck?"

Now where did that come from? thought Megan. She gave her dad a puzzled look.

"Now Dr. Peterson you aren't going to catch me. Megan already told me she fessed up and you know we were texting." Cassy smiled sweetly.

"Cassy, Cassy, you ruined all my fun. I wanted to see if you were going to make up a good story."

"I'm not a good storyteller so I usually stay quiet. You know, share nothing unless forced and reduce the risk."

"Yes, that's a common strategy, and usually quite successful. Megan has used that a few times."

"Dad, I'm really trying!" Megan seemed very disappointed.

Adrian added quickly, "I'm teasing. I know you're trying and I'm proud of you. However, I reserve the right to tease you once in a while." Adrian hoped he sounded sincere because he was sincere, and he hoped Megan accepted his words in the spirit they were intended. He was relieved when Megan smiled.

"Ok ladies, I've caused enough trouble for one evening." Adrian left the kitchen, still thinking he wasn't very good at being funny.

"I like your dad. Why did you get so upset?" Cassy took another cookie and sat down on a stool.

"I don't know. I guess because I want him to be proud of me. I haven't always been easy to love."

"No worries, girlfriend. He's very proud of you. I can tell because he was upset that he made you upset. I don't think my dad would even notice. But I can't do family counseling on an empty stomach. What if we picked up supper at the Dairy Queen and then watched a movie?"

"Sounds like a plan!"

LAINIE THOUGHT today's session went well. This was a nice group of students. They seemed to want corrections and suggestions. She hoped the farm owner, Trina, would invite her back again. It was a lovely facility. Now she needed to find a place to camp with Shadow for a few days. She didn't need to be at her next clinic until Thursday and it wasn't a long drive.

Trina walked by the grooming stall just as Lainie started to hose the sweat from her mare. It was an unusually warm day for Ohio in September, and the class ended the day with a fun but long group trail ride. Lainie wanted to get Shadow in her pen with a flake of hay, just in case any students needed a bit of help trailer loading their horses. It always happened, and it was never a quick fix. Although in a hurry, Lainie knew she should thank Trina for her hospitality.

"Trina, do you have a second?"

"Sure." Trina stopped and looked at Lainie.

"I just want to thank you for your hospitality. I really enjoyed the students and the farm. It's such a nice place."

"Thank you, Lainie. I love it here. It's always been my dream to run a nice boarding barn and clinic facility." Trina's smile shared the passion in her voice.

"Are you a Follow the Leader student?" Lainie had wondered why Trina wasn't in the clinic, although she did ride with the group at the end of the day.

"Oh, not really, I don't consider myself a groupie of any program. No offense." Trina looked like she wished that comment hadn't left her mouth. "But I do love to offer all sorts of clinics. I'm open to anything that helps people enjoy their horses a little more, and be safer. Not everyone at the barn can afford a Follow the Leader clinic, but I like to have one or two a year for several of my boarders who are crazy about the program—and Brock Rodgers."

"No offense taken; I understand." Boy, do I understand, thought Lainie.

"Some of the girls are going into Appleridge for an end-of-clinic group dinner at Joyce's house. Are you going?"

"Yes, but I'll need directions." Lainie hesitated and looked at her shirt. "And I need to clean up a bit."

"You're welcome to ride with me," Trina offered. "I'm just going to wash up a bit and change my shirt."

"That sounds good. I need to talk to you about places to stay with Shadow. I don't need to be at my next stop until Thursday and it isn't too far."

"Lainie, you can stay right here, and if you're interested, I'm pretty sure some of my boarders who couldn't afford the clinic would be able to afford a short lesson."

"Thank you, but I expect you to charge for my extended stay. After all, I'm using your facility, water, and electricity." Trina's offer to stay at the farm thrilled Lainie.

"I won't charge you to stay, but I would truly appreciate it if you could help a few of my boarders. A few really need help."

"Sounds like a plan." Lainie was eager to help. "We'll have to keep the arrangement private. I'm required to charge a set amount per my contract. Perhaps, we could keep it all informal. I'll be here and help without actually calling it a lesson."

Trina smiled. "Sounds like a plan. Let's get ready; I'm hungry."

Chapter Seven

ainie got up from her chair to throw her paper plate in the trash. She needed a break from the conversation. All the women were really nice and very interested in hearing more about her adventures as a Follow the Leader instructor, but Lainie just wanted to be herself. Boy, she sure would love to tell some of the secrets she kept tucked away. Wouldn't they be shocked if she shared a few things about the big guy, Brock Rodgers? Lainie pasted on her smile and returned to the back porch to join the group.

"Hey, Lainie, I really enjoyed the clinic. When will you be back in this area?"

Lainie looked over at Sharon and smiled. "Soon, I hope. This is a great group."

Teresa, the clinic organizer, spoke up. "We'll talk about a spring clinic before you leave, ok?"

"Sure, I'm interested." Lainie wouldn't mind coming back because she loved the farm and students. And, it would be good to have the date on her calendar. It was important to show Follow the Leader a full schedule.

One by one the group said their goodbyes, thanked Joyce for her hospitality, and headed home.

Trina waited by the door as Lainie talked to Joyce. They were the last to leave.

Strange, thought Lainie, it's only nine on a Saturday night; why is everyone leaving so early?

Trina must have read Lainie's mind, because as they walked to the truck, she asked Lainie about going to church with her in the morning.

"Um, well, I'm not really the church type of girl. Is that why everyone left so early?"

"Probably. Most in our group attend church. What type of girl is a church girl?"

"Oh, you know, good, really good." Lainie didn't want to insult Trina because she really liked her.

"Good? Maybe most try to be good but none achieve the goal." Trina laughed at the puzzled expression on Lainie's face.

"I go to church because I like being around people who aren't perfect and know it but are trying to be a little better. And I love worship—the prayers, the music, and my church family."

"Don't you get tired of the judgement and the holier-than-thou attitude of some church goers?" Lainie knew she didn't measure up to what most church people would think acceptable.

"Hmmm, that wouldn't be a good church experience. Don't get me wrong, no church is perfect, it's possible to have a bad experience, but judgement is God's domain and I believe he would rather love us instead. I'm not sure why some people think they need to judge on God's behalf, but it certainly doesn't seem very Christ-like to me." Trina had had a bit of experience with people judging her unfairly.

They were almost back to Trina's farm. Lainie wasn't as uncomfortable as she usually became when someone tried to preach about church. She was actually intrigued. Trina seemed different—more caring, more accepting. She wanted to get to know Trina better. If she went to church with Trina, maybe they would also go out for lunch. It seemed she was either always eating alone or eating with a group who expected her to be someone they could admire. It would be nice to be loved for just being who she wanted to be.

"I don't really have anything to wear to church. I only have jeans and boots."

"You can wear jeans and boots. I often wear jeans. Some will wear dresses, and some will wear shorts and flip flops in the summer." Trina smiled and continued. "I go to the 9:30 service at the Lutheran church because of the praise band. We really celebrate when we worship, but don't worry, you won't be asked to do anything that makes you uncomfortable."

"Ok, Trina, you win. I'll find a clean pair of jeans and shine my boots. What time will we leave?"

"Great! It's not far—in Appleridge. We don't need to leave until 9:10 or so." Trina smiled. I'm going to do one last night check of the horses and then grab a glass of ice tea and sit on the porch to enjoy this beautiful fall evening. You're welcome to join me."

"That sounds good; thanks. I'll check on Shadow and meet you on the porch." Lainie was happy for the invitation. She wasn't eager to go to bed, and there wasn't much to do in her trailer.

Lainie grabbed a Diet Coke from her little fridge and walked to Shadow's pen. Shadow raised her head from the hay she was eating and nickered a greeting.

Lainie stood by Shadow's side and stroked her neck for a few minutes. Then she checked her water and gave her another flake of hay. She would need to ask Trina about the nearest feed store. Maybe Trina could point it out tomorrow. Lainie couldn't travel with much hay and feed so she always tried to buy a little bit when possible.

What would she do without her Shadow? Lainie couldn't imagine life without her mare. Sometimes it seemed like Shadow was her only friend. At least the only friend who loved her just as she was.

A VERY NERVOUS LAINIE drove with Trina to church the next morning. Church! Lainie couldn't believe she'd actually agreed to go to church. Darn that Trina. Why did she have to be so nice? Since she appreciated Trina's friendship and hospitality, she couldn't say no. Maybe it would be ok.

Trina noticed Lainie rubbing her hands together. She seemed very nervous.

Father, please be with Lainie today. I know she's nervous. Help her feel your love and the love of my friends.

"Thanks for coming with me today. How about lunch following the service? Do you have anything scheduled?" Trina decided lunch was a safe topic.

"Nothing officially scheduled. It depends on who shows up at the barn today. I'll watch for anyone who would like a little help."

"Thank you so much. There are several I certainly hope show up. They couldn't take the clinic, but help will certainly be appreciated." Trina turned into the church parking lot.

Lainie noticed quite a few younger adults going in the building, and Trina was right: most were wearing jeans. Lainie relaxed a little. Then she saw the reporter, Jennie, walking toward the door with a cute guy. They were talking, smiling, and seemed to be in their own little world.

"There's Jennie. It's funny, but even though we greeted each other every Sunday, horses never came up in our conversation. Jennie is usually with Jeremy. I'm fairly new so don't ask me the scoop about those two." Trina laughed.

Trina led the way into the church. Stopping at the door, she took a program from an usher. Or whatever you call them, thought Lainie, as she reached for one. They found seats toward the back, on an end, two rows behind Jennie and Jeremy. This is good. Yesterday Jennie sat in back observing her class; now the tables were turned, and Lainie could sit and observe. Lainie was surprised to see a keyboard player, a man and woman with guitars, a violinist, and a drummer waiting in front of the church. This was obviously going to be a new experience. Lainie thought only pianos and organs were allowed in church.

The pastor walked in, also wearing jeans, and without the usual pastor robe. He greeted everyone and then made a few announcements. A group of people walked to the front to lead the singing as the musicians started to play. The words to the song were up on a large screen over the worship team's heads.

Lainie was totally intrigued. She loved to sing, so why not go for it? She wasn't familiar with the song, but it seemed easy enough to follow. Trina also sang along and then lifted her arms in the air. Lainie noticed several others lifting their arms. This church was nothing like she expected.

After singing three songs and a prayer, they were invited to sit and listen to today's message. Lainie listened carefully. She was able to follow along fairly well. It was a message about living a passionate life for Christ, and how each person is called to use their passions and gifts to share Christ's message of love and grace.

Maybe teaching people to be safe and enjoy their horses is a good way to share my passion, but does it share love and grace? What is Christ's message, anyway?

Lainie remembered being told she better behave or she would go straight to hell. She never liked that message. She would never be good enough to avoid hell, so why try? She planned to enjoy herself while she was here since there was nothing better later. This pastor was saying something different. Lainie would ask Trina a few questions during lunch.

Lainie looked around, surprised when the service ended after another song.

Wow, that was a quick hour, and it was actually fun.

Jennie and Jeremy turned to leave, and Jennie smiled as she spotted Trina and Lainie.

"Jeremy, I want you to meet Lainie and you already know Trina, but what you don't know is she's a horse girl, too. They're both serious horse girls."

"Hi, Trina, and nice to meet you, Lainie, and I'm sure there's more to this story." Jeremy laughed as he glanced at Jennie, waiting for more information.

"This would make a great story over lunch. Would you like to join us for lunch? Jeremy and I aren't too sure what we're doing yet, but we plan on going somewhere." Jennie mentally

95

reviewed her pantry and decided she needed to make a quick stop at the grocery if they wanted to come out to her place.

Trina looked at Lainie. "We're going to grab lunch but haven't picked a place. What do you think, Lainie?"

"That would be fun. You guys will have to pick, I don't know my way around Appleridge."

"The Café started offering Sunday brunch. If we hurry, we could beat the Baptists to the buffet, as Jennie's grandpa likes to say." Jeremy hesitated, looked at Lainie, and then added, "I sure hope that didn't offend you."

Lainie laughed. "No, it's funny. Can I surmise that the Baptists also like to go out for Sunday brunch?"

"Yup, and they get out of church later so we always beat them to most restaurants, unless we talk too much." Jeremy was relieved his attempt at humor was well received.

"Well, ok then, let's go. Lainie and I will meet you there." Trina was already searching her purse for her truck keys.

"Ok, save us a seat."

As Lainie and Trina walked to the truck, Jeremy and Jennie stopped to say hello to a few more people, and then walked out to Jeremy's SUV. On the way, Jennie filled Jeremy in on how she met Lainie and connected with Trina.

"They seem really nice. I was surprised to see Lainie in church." Jennie rolled down her window.

"Why?" Jeremy looked both ways as he pulled out of the church parking lot.

"Not sure, but I noticed she seemed very uncomfortable when we said a prayer at lunch during the clinic."

"A lot of people are uncomfortable praying in public."

"That's me, sometimes." Jennie confessed. "I wish a prayer could just roll off my tongue like your beautiful prayers."

"Thanks. God hears all prayers. It takes a little practice to get comfortable. You start small, share what's in your heart, and don't worry how it sounds, God knows your intent."

Jennie nodded that she understood.

The Café wasn't far and since it was still early, all four were sitting in a booth by 11:15. Lainie looked around the half-empty restaurant, smiled, and remarked. "We beat the Baptists."

They all laughed as they looked at the menu board for specials.

"I can't believe I'm eating here two days in a row. I'm feeling quite spoiled." Jennie usually didn't eat in restaurants very much.

"Enjoy." Jeremy added, "My treat, everyone."

Lainie and Trina started to object but Jeremy was firm. His mother was a stickler for manners, and it didn't feel right to pay for Jennie's meal but ignore the other two women in their party. He treated women as equals, but he was also taught that manners were manners.

"I am thankful to have a nice lunch with three beautiful ladies."

After they ordered, conversation flowed easily. Horses, of course, were the main topic.

"What did you think of the clinic this weekend, Jennie? I know you're writing a story, so I'm pretty interested in what you thought." Lainie never beat around the bush when she wanted to know something.

Jennie put down her fork and finished chewing her last bite. "I thought the sessions were really good, and they looked fun." She hesitated. "But they also seemed easy and some of the students didn't seem challenged enough."

"Yes, that's the problem with a large clinic. I usually have to teach for the group, and some weren't ready to do much more. My main goal is to teach them to communicate with their horses and the tasks lead to that goal."

"Why are the clinics so expensive? No offense; I'm not saying you aren't worth the money. Well, strike that, maybe that's what I'm asking. Are you worth the money?"

Both Jeremy and Trina looked at Jennie, surprised that her question was so blunt, and then quickly looked at Lainie, waiting for her reaction. All four forks were suspended in mid-air.

"You know, I'm not sure how you asked that without offending me, but you did, and I'm not offended. That's a skill. Ok, do I think I'm worth the money? Yes and no. I think I'm really good. I give my best to the class. I also have to stick to the fee guidelines for Follow the Leader. Do I think the cost keeps a lot of good people out of the clinic? Yes. Could I get in trouble for saying this? Yes. I really hope this is a friendly lunch and my comments are off the record."

Trina and Jeremy continued to eat in silence but were very alert to the conversation. It was friendly because both Lainie and Jennie were keeping it friendly, but it was also like being in the eye of a possible storm.

"My goal is to always write the truth. With that said, my personal integrity is very important. Writing for the Chronicle doesn't require the latest scoop or scandal. I want to write a good article and one that helps both you and Trina, but is also truthful. While I don't need to report anything you don't wish to reveal, I also won't write anything that may not be true just to promote the Follow the Leader program. Something tells me this article doesn't need to be about Follow the Leader. I'm more interested in what you bring to Appleridge, what you believe about horsemanship, and what your passion is."

Relieved, Jeremy laughed, then teased, "You did listen in church today."

"I've never been a fan of church, but I also listened today. I have a lot to think about, and it may not be what you would guess." Lainie looked at Trina and continued. "Trina, you share your love for Jesus very well, and your farm is the passion you share."

Trina looked like she was going to cry. "Thanks, Lainie, that's sweet."

"Lainie, I'll let you read my article before it's submitted. It's my desire to touch readers with a very personal story, but that story needs to be true."

"I can't ask for more than that; thanks."

"Will you still be around tomorrow? Why don't you come out to my farm tomorrow evening? We can talk more then." Jennie was sincere. She wanted to talk more.

Lainie looked at Trina. "What do you think?"

"I think you and Jennie should talk in private, but I would like to visit your farm later, Jennie."

Jeremy paid the check, and since they noticed a line at the door of The Café, the group decided to hurry out.

Trina stopped just outside the door. "Thanks for lunch, Jeremy."

"It was my pleasure, ladies, and I hope to see you again."

On the way back to Trina's farm, Lainie was quiet—thinking.

"Did you enjoy the service and lunch?" Trina couldn't quite read Lainie.

"Yes, I actually did. Thanks, Trina."

"Good; you seem quiet, so I wasn't sure."

"Oh, sorry; my mind is busy thinking. Do you think there's a market here in Appleridge for horsemanship clinics and lessons? I really like this area."

Trina hesitated. "Yes, but not at Follow the Leader fees. Could someone like you teach privately and make a living? Yes, I think so. Could you make a killing and become wealthy? Probably not so much."

"That's what I was thinking. I've heard that expression before—make a living, not a killing."

"It was something my dad always said. He owned a small-town grocery store, and when large companies tried to buy him out, promising him enough to retire wealthy, he always refused to sell. He cared about the town and all his employees. He cared about making an honest living and wasn't looking to sell out to make a killing. He felt those large stores would kill a small town. Big isn't always better." Trina was proud of her dad and missed him.

"Your dad sounds like a very caring and wise man." Lainie could see that his daughter had the same attributes.

"Yes, he was. I had a great childhood. My brother now runs the store and it still provides a nice living, and the town still has a locally owned grocery."

Lainie wanted to ask Trina what took her away from the small town and brought her to Appleridge, but as they arrived back at the farm, she noticed several people with horses in the arena.

Trina nodded toward the arena. "Oh, good, those young ladies are who I wanted you to meet. Do you feel like helping, or do you need some time to digest your lunch?"

"No, I'm good. I'll start out slow and see where it goes." With that, Lainie was out of the truck and walking to the arena. She seemed to have a spring in her step.

"I CAN ALMOST hear the wheels turning in your head. You're thinking about what you want to ask Lainie." Jeremy glanced over at Jennie.

"You know, I don't think I'll need to ask anything. Something is troubling her, and I think she needs to simply talk."

"I think so. I suppose you already did a bit of research?"

Jennie smiled. "Yes, a bit. She hasn't been a Follow the Leader instructor for long. Before going in that direction, she already had a nice reputation as a rider and trainer on the eventing circuit. Cassy will certainly love the opportunity to talk with Lainie since jumping and dressage are her interests. And I found a connection between JJ and Brock Rodgers. That was interesting."

"You know, I'm just a cowboy, Jennie. What's eventing?" Jeremy was doing his best cowpoke imitation, tipping back an imaginary hat.

"Well, cowboy, eventing is sometimes called combined training and it's a three-part competition that includes dressage, stadium jumping, and cross-country jumping. It's the riding version of combined driving. That's what Marcy does with the ponies."

"Oh, and was Lainie good?" Jeremy wondered what caused Lainie to switch to Follow the Leader.

"From what I can tell, she was very good. It makes me wonder why she became an instructor with Follow the Leader. She certainly doesn't need to ride on Brock Rodgers's coat tails."

"That was my thought, exactly. I think something happened, maybe something big. That's probably your story, Jennie."

"Yeah, it probably is the story, and one I need to handle carefully, because it's probably a very precious story to tell."

When they pulled into the drive at the farm, Jennie noticed Marcy's car down by the barn. "I'm glad Marcy has today off. She's been working long shifts at the hospital. She'll enjoy a nice afternoon with her ponies."

"I'm going to go on home and change my new jeans into old jeans and grab my boots. Do you think Marcy will let me drive the ponies?"

"Maybe; if not, do you want to ride Julep?" Jennie didn't share Julep with just anyone, but Jeremy wasn't just anyone.

"Thanks, but I enjoy just hanging out with the horses—and driving Marcy's ponies."

"Jeremy, what ever happened to Bert?"

Bert was the bay Quarter Horse gelding Jeremy owned while he was in high school but needed to sell when he left for college. Jennie wanted to ask the question before but could never seem to find the right time. She knew Jeremy loved Bert as much as she loved Julep.

"He was with a family of kids. I bet he loved being a babysitter. He was a good old boy."

"Maybe we could find him. Sam gets around, and maybe he knows if Bert's still in the area."

"Oh, I can't keep a horse right now, anyway."

Jeremy said nothing more, so Jennie let the conversation drop—for now. She would definitely ask Sam when she got a chance.

Chapter Eight

ennie felt good as she drove to the Chronicle on Monday morning. She'd had a great weekend, and had a bunch of writing ideas and notes stuffed in her bag. She would spend the morning putting the finishing touches on two of her pieces. The micro-chip article was ready for the next edition, and it would hit the stores at the end of the week. She would spend the morning finishing the layout. Charles did an awesome job of selling new ads, and Sherilynn was turning the Chronicle website into an eye- catching and informative place for all the latest events around three counties. Jennie needed to deliver on the articles and layout—no pressure!

She loved working at the Chronicle. It was challenging but not overwhelming. Her co-workers were good at their jobs and eager to help her when needed. Returning to the farm each night was a special blessing, and tonight Lainie was coming to meet the gang. Life is good. She had friends, horses, and Jeremy. Jeremy was becoming a huge part of her life. She made a mental note to check in with her mom, dad, and sisters. Her good but busy life hadn't included her family lately, and that wasn't good. Jennie shook off the feelings of guilt that tried to creep into her day. *Go away, I'm busy.*

JEREMY PICKED UP his book bag and keys, locked the house, and walked to his SUV. He enjoyed his classes but hated the commute to Columbus. This semester he was in seminary part-time while he handled the details of his mom's estate. Her passing was sudden and left a hole in his life, just when they found a deeper connection. Jeremy was thankful for his sister, Sarah, and her family—especially his nephew, Daniel. He also had Jennie. Yes, he was thankful for Jennie, and prayed that somehow God would guide them in a life together. Jeremy was fully aware that God may call him to a ministry that wasn't in Appleridge, and he knew how much Jennie loved her family and the farm. When Jennie mentioned finding Bert again, she must have been thinking they could bring him to her farm. Jeremy didn't know what to say so he didn't say much. For now, he would just enjoy their time together.

JENNIE LISTENED to the radio during her drive to Appleridge. She was excited about the latest issue of the *Farm & Family Country Chronicle* and hoped Mr. Wilson would be pleased. The layout took a bit of time. She didn't have much experience in that department, but she was learning quickly.

Entering Appleridge, Jennie decided to swing by the grocery store before going home. She needed a few basic things and would find a few snacks for this evening—just in case. She hoped all her boarders would be at the farm tonight. She wanted them to meet Lainie. She had a feeling Lainie needed a few friendly faces in her life. Trina seemed to care about Lainie and that was good. Trina seemed like someone who would make a very good friend, and Jennie wanted to get to know her better.

As she parked Blue Boy, her trusty but older Silverado truck, at the store, Jennie saw Sam climb out of his truck. She quickly grabbed her purse, got out of her truck, and ran to catch up with him.

"Hey, Sam!"

Sam stopped and looked around. "Oh, hey, Jennie. How are things at the farm?"

Sam seemed a little uneasy. "Great, all the horses are great. No issues. Have you heard from Belinda lately?"

Sam hesitated, then answered, "I heard from her, yes. Between her classes and my work, we seem to leave a lot of messages."

Interesting, thought Jennie, he's trying to be honest. "I know how that is; Jeremy and I seem to text more than we talk."

Sam seemed eager to change the subject. "Is Jeremy in town most days?"

"He commutes to Columbus three days a week, but you can usually catch him at his mom's house on Tuesday and Thursday. Call him on his cell—or shoot him a text." Jennie laughed. "Why?"

"Oh, no reason, really. He seems like he knows a lot, and I wanted to ask him a few questions, is all." Sam was looking everywhere but at Jennie.

"He's a smart guy, and he's also your friend, Sam." Jennie wondered why she added the part about being Sam's friend. It just popped out.

"Yeah, I know."

"Sam, do you remember Jeremy's gelding, Bert?"

"I sure do, nice horse. Too bad about what happened to him."

"What happened to him?" Jennie didn't think this was going to be good news.

"The family that owned him didn't have a lot of horse knowledge and they used black walnut shavings for bedding."

"Oh, no! Where did they get the shavings?"

"They had a few trees cut down on their property, and it left a pile of shavings. They had no clue standing on black walnut shavings could kill a horse. It was a pretty serious case of laminitis, and they didn't recognize the early symptoms. The kids were devastated, as you can imagine, and the parents vowed never to have another horse."

"I'm so sorry to hear this—for many reasons. People don't realize keeping a horse isn't quite as simple as a dog or cat. Too bad every new horse owner couldn't have a mentor of sorts."

"That would be a great program, matching up experienced horse people with new horse people. You wouldn't believe the people I attempt to educate about hoof care. Some welcome the information, some think they already know everything and ignore my advice, and I usually end up dropping some clients because they don't want to do the best things for their horses." Jennie heard Sam's passion for his work and his love for horses in his voice.

"Your clients would be wise to listen. You have a lot of knowledge and are really skilled."

"Thanks, Jennie."

"Hey, do you think I should tell Jeremy about Bert, or just let it go?" Jennie always had a hard time just letting things go, but she was willing to try if it was the best for Jeremy.

"Jeremy knows what happened to Bert. The family called and asked him to come out when Bert was suffering. Jeremy helped them make the decision to euthanize Bert when it became obvious that he was suffering with no hope of recovery. Jeremy even prayed with the family and thanked them for the years they cared for Bert. I still can't figure out why he wasn't mad."

"It doesn't surprise me that Jeremy prayed and tried to help the family. He's that kind of guy." Jennie was also thinking how surprised she was that Jeremy didn't share what happened when she asked him about Bert. "I guess I better let you go."

"Yeah, I need to get going. I'm beat but I want to stop and spend some time with Sadie tonight."

"I bet you never get enough time to ride." Jennie knew Sam worked long hours.

"It's hard because I'm usually tired from a long day." Sam paused. "Hey, if I ever needed a place to keep Sadie, would you be able to make room?"

Jennie thought for a moment. "I'm pretty full but I would make room for you and Sadie." Jennie wondered what was going on at the farm where Sam kept Sadie. She also knew it probably took a lot for Sam to ask. She should have extended the invitation before he asked. He would be a perfect boarder.

"Thanks, I don't have a reason to move just now, but it's nice to know she would have a place to go if needed. I know you don't have another stall, but Sadie doesn't need a stall. I could probably build a run-in shed if you were open to that idea."

"Since I like to keep the horses out as much as possible, I've been thinking about building a nice run-in shed, but first I need to fit it into my budget somehow."

"Oh, I know about budgets. Money never seems to go as far as you think it should." Money, thought Sam, it always came down to money.

Just as Sam was turning to walk into the store, Jennie reached out her hand to stop him. "Before you go, do you know if Belinda is coming home for the Apple Festival?"

"I'm not sure. I didn't ask but I don't think so. She doesn't have a break, and I don't think she likes to miss her classes."

"I didn't think so, either. It's a long trip for a short weekend. See ya later."

They parted ways at the entrance to the store. Jennie grabbed a shopping cart but Sam didn't stop for a cart. Jennie didn't think Belinda would travel home for the festival, but she wanted to check Sam's expression when she asked about Belinda. Just as she thought, Sam didn't want to talk about Belinda. Strange.

Sam's truck was already gone when Jennie exited the store with her groceries. She decided to worry about Sam and Belinda later. Right now, she was trying to understand why Jeremy didn't tell her about Bert, especially when she mentioned Bert and asked about him. Jennie wondered when the tragedy happened. She didn't think to ask Sam because it really didn't matter. What mattered to Jennie was that Jeremy didn't feel comfortable sharing the story with her.

It was still early, and Jennie decided to swing by her parents' house. She hadn't talked to her mom in a while, and since they attended the later, more traditional church service, she always missed them at church. Come to think of it, her mom hadn't hosted their famous Sunday night suppers lately. Jennie realized she missed gathering with her family for supper on Sunday evenings.

It only took a few minutes to drive to her parents' house on the edge of town. Although the front door was open, with the

Victorian-style screen door allowing the cool breeze to float through the house, she walked around to the back deck off the kitchen.

"Hello, hello," Jennie called as she reached for the door.

"Well, hello stranger."

Her mom, Ellen McKenzie, turned away from the stove to greet Jennie. Jennie caught the slight reference to her being AWOL for the past few weeks. Moms were clever that way, and Ellen McKenzie was a particularly clever mom.

"I thought I would stop by since I was in town picking up a few groceries."

"How's your new job?"

"Good—I really like it."

"Long hours?" Her mom's questions were quick and a little snappy. Whoa, thought Jennie, Mom isn't happy.

"Not too bad. I get to work from home some days, and I've been doing a few interviews around the area. Hey, what are you cooking?"

"Oh, just a pot of chili since I had quite a bit of ground beef in the freezer that I need to use up. Do you want to stay for supper?"

"When will it be ready? I have a friend coming out to the farm later."

"I just started it, so not for a while." Her mom gave the pot a good stir and turned to face Jennie again.

"Mom, I was thinking about our Sunday night suppers. We haven't had one for a while."

"No, we haven't. Why? Do you miss them?"

"Yes, I like them."

"I wondered." Another short and slightly snappy comment, thought Jennie. Oh boy, Mom isn't going to make this easy.

"Did you also miss our usual picnic on Labor Day?"

"What picnic? Did I forget?" Jennie didn't think she would forget a picnic.

"I didn't plan one just to see if anyone noticed. And guess what: no one noticed."

Ellen poured herself a class of ice tea and sat down at the kitchen bar. Jennie grabbed a stool and sat down beside her.

"I'm sorry, Mom. I feel like I've disappointed you somehow."

"Yes, you all have. No one seems to care if we get together or not, and I'm certainly not going to be the type of mom who demands your presence."

Jennie didn't know how to respond or if she should even try to respond.

"I've always tried to make holidays special for my girls, but you all seemed to have plans for the Labor Day weekend, and didn't ask about our usual picnic. I waited but no one noticed that I didn't plan a picnic. And guess what: no one asked. Not you, not Sallie, not Connie. So now I have all this ground beef, bought to make delicious hamburgers on the grill, but now I need to use it up and here we are with chili again tonight."

A few tears escaped down Ellen's cheeks, but she caught her breath. "I stopped planning Sunday nights. And guess what: no one noticed."

Jennie didn't know what to say, but she reached over to give her mom a hug. Ellen stiffened at first, but then relaxed and hugged Jennie back.

"Mom, I'm sorry. I noticed. Sorry it took me so long to ask. Sorry about Labor Day. I guess I got so wrapped up in my new job and I forgot it was Labor Day."

Jennie was busy, but she wasn't going to make any more excuses. It wouldn't help her mom feel better to hear all the reasons why Jennie was too busy to notice.

"What about Dad? Did he notice?"

Ellen sniffed and searched for a tissue in her pocket before answering. "No, he didn't notice. He doesn't notice much anymore. I talk and if I stop talking in mid-sentence he doesn't seem to notice, so I know he isn't listening. I've been feeling pretty ignored lately. Maybe it's always been like that, but I never noticed before. Ha ha, never noticed. Well—I'm serving notice right now." Ellen thought what she just said was funny, but she was too emotional to share the humor at the moment.

Jennie had never heard her mom say anything even slightly negative about her dad. Maybe her mom was having some sort of emotional issue right now—maybe something hormonal.

Ellen sensed she was upsetting Jennie, so she brushed away the tears, got up to stir the chili, and said, "Tell me more about your job."

Jennie was torn between talking about her job to diffuse the emotion or dealing with her mom's comments. She took her cue from her mom who didn't look too eager to share anything more and seemed to regret what she already shared.

"Well, it's good. The first issue of the Chronicle with my work comes out this week. I did the layout and several articles. I like my co-workers, and they're really good at their jobs. I like the small office and being able to write from home some days. The pay is better than my part-time job at the library, basically because it's a full-time job." Jennie was making an attempt to be humorous.

"It sounds really good. By the way, how's Megan?"

"She comes out to the barn with Cassy. She has a cast on her wrist, but she didn't need surgery."

"And Jeremy? Is he getting his mom's estate settled?"

"I think so. He doesn't talk about it too much." With that thought, Jennie realized she never asked Jeremy those things. She needed to do a better job of noticing Jeremy, too.

Jennie heard her dad, Edward McKenzie, open the back door. "Hi, Jennie, are you staying for supper? That smells good!"

"No, I haven't been home from work, I have groceries in the truck, and five equine mouths to feed."

"Don't forget Beauty."

"You're right—change that to five equines and one feline."

After repeating what she told her mom about her job when her dad asked the same questions, Jennie gave them both a hug and left.

Wow, just this morning I was thinking life is good, and it is, but it's also very complicated. Life is complicated and relationships are complicated. Jennie vowed to pay better attention to her family and friends. She needed do whatever she could to help the people she loved. She thought about Sam and Belinda, wondered why Jeremy didn't tell her about Bert, and didn't understand why her mom was so distraught today. She knew her mom felt ignored, but Jennie sensed there was something more. She would talk to Connie and Sallie, because she needed to do a better job of staying in touch with her older sisters as well as her mom. She would have to pray and ponder her concerns about Sam, Belinda, and Jeremy.

Driving home, she worried Lainie would arrive early and leave if she wasn't at the barn. She ran into the house to put groceries away and change her clothes.

Marcy pulled into the drive just as Jennie started her walk out to the barn, waved, then parked near the barn.

"Hi, Marcy, I was just getting ready to feed. Are you driving the ponies tonight?"

"No, not tonight; I just want to love on them a bit. I'm off work tomorrow and will be out in the afternoon."

Jennie and Marcy brought the equine crew into the barn and gave each a flake of hay to munch as they filled their feed buckets. They chatted as they worked. Marcy seemed tired but in good spirits. Jennie was relieved. She didn't know if she could handle another relationship issue tonight, and she still needed to talk with Lainie.

"I met a Follow the Leader instructor at a local clinic and asked her to come out to the farm tonight. I want to write an article, not really on the Follow the Leader program, but on her personal journey. Apparently, she was well known in the combined training world before joining the Follow the Leader ranks as an instructor, and I'm intrigued.

"What's her name?"

"Lainie Anderson."

"I've heard of an Elaine Anderson."

"Yeah, I think that's her. I'm going to ask tonight. I think maybe that's my story."

"I'll groom my ponies and give you some privacy. But I would like to meet her. Is she going to stay in the area?"

"I don't think so. She travels around teaching clinics and lives in her horse trailer. I hope to introduce her to Cassy, especially since Cassy has done a bit of the same type of competition with Treasure. I don't think Cassy will be here tonight, though. She said something about a school event."

"What about Megan?" Marcy walked to her tack closet to remove her grooming bag.

"Not sure. She mentioned having a lot of make-up work, although she didn't miss too much school after her accident. She's a senior, though, and taking some hard subjects. She's trying to catch up after not caring about school for most of her life. I'm sure she has a lot of homework."

"Has either one mentioned the Apple Festival parade? I want us to enter the parade. Riley and Stuffin will handle the parade excitement fairly well, but I still want someone with me on the carriage just in case. It's always nice to have someone ready to hop off and stand by the ponies' heads if needed. You never know what you'll encounter in a parade."

"I'm sure Jeremy would love to ride with you. It'll be fun. I don't think Cassy is too eager to try Treasure in a parade. She may have been willing to try if Megan was able to ride, but Megan's broken wrist changes everything. I could ride Julep and Jeremy could ride on the carriage, or we could take turns riding on the carriage. I bet Cassy and Megan would love to hand out candy. They may even want to dress up. We need to come up with a plan for our entry."

"Both you and Jeremy could ride on the carriage. The ponies could pull all three of us—it's on pavement and fairly level. Maybe we could all meet and plan this week. I'll bring the snacks. How about getting together Friday or Saturday night?"

"I could do either night, but let's try Saturday night. We're all usually here on Saturday. What time do you work Saturday?"

"Barring any problems at the hospital, I could be here by 7:30 PM."

Jennie walked over to the white board and picked up the marker:

Fawn Song Farm Gang!

We need to plan our parade entry.

Can you meet Saturday night at 7:30?

Snacks Provided

Then underneath she signed her name followed by a YES, and Marcy signed her name followed by a YES.

"Did you have any ideas, Marcy? I guess I should find out if this year's parade has a theme."

"I heard at the hospital that the theme is—Apple of My Eye."

"Hmmm, that's going to take some creative thinking." Jennie laughed.

"My thoughts exactly, and I hope our two teens have some great ideas. They're both pretty creative."

"That they are." Jennie turned when she heard a truck coming up the drive. Lainie had a diesel, and it was pretty hard not to hear when she arrived.

"There's Lainie. Let me introduce you before you get busy."

"Hi, did you find the place ok?" Jennie called out as she walked to the barn door to welcome Lainie.

"I did; good directions. I didn't even need to use my GPS." Lainie glanced over at Marcy.

"Lainie, this is Marcy Streeter. Marcy, Lainie Anderson. Marcy owns these two cute Welsh ponies, Riley and Stuffin."

They walked down the barn aisle and Jennie introduced each horse and pony, giving a brief history of each. She saved Julep for last.

"And this is my horse, Julep, and boy do we have a long story to tell some night over a small campfire."

"Now I'm really intrigued. She's a nice-looking mare. This barn is full of nice-looking horses and ponies." She grinned as she added the tag—and ponies.

"Marcy, what do you do with your ponies? Drive?" Lainie figured she didn't ride. Marcy wasn't a big woman, but the ponies were too small for an adult to ride, even a fairly small adult.

"I compete in combined driving." Marcy beamed. She loved driving her team.

"Wow, I've always wanted to learn more about that discipline." Lainie hesitated, she usually didn't share her background but something about Marcy and Jennie made it feel right. "I have a background in combined training. I guess we both like the thrill of three disciplines."

Marcy didn't reveal that she knew Lainie previously competed under the name Elaine and not Lainie. She was pretty good at knowing when to share and when to wait for a person to share when they were ready.

Jennie took in the whole conversation. She could learn a lot from Marcy on how to listen, and not always reveal what you know or think. Yup, she decided, listening more would serve her well in the future.

"It's been really nice to meet you, Lainie, and I hope we meet again. I've had a long day at the hospital. If I don't get busy grooming my kids, I'll lose my motivation."

"Nice to meet you, Marcy, and I totally understand."

Jennie pulled out two folding camp chairs and placed them in the aisle near the door.

"I'm going to let the horses munch on their supper hay as we talk. I'll let them all back out after Marcy's finished. It's a nice night."

"Sounds good. You have a lovely farm, Jennie. Have you had it long?"

"In a way, all my life—it's my grandparents' farm, and I'm buying it from my grandpa. He's given me terms I can afford."

"Very cool; is your entire family in Appleridge?"

Jennie was beginning to wonder who was being interviewed, her or Lainie, but she thought maybe Lainie was using small talk to help them both get comfortable.

"Now that I'm home, yes, I was the one who left for school and thought I wanted to live in a large city as a journalist."

"What happened?"

"I couldn't fill up the horse-shaped hole in my heart, and I couldn't afford a horse in the city. Oh, yeah, I missed family, too," she added with a laugh.

"I can totally understand missing horses. They're like air for horse lovers. You can't breathe without them."

"Where are you from?" Jennie wanted to do less talking about herself and more talking about Lainie.

"I actually grew up not too far from here, in Pennsylvania. I grew up riding, but we didn't have a farm. I boarded my horse at a pretty fancy barn. My dad is a doctor and my mom a lawyer. They couldn't understand my crazy addiction to horses but were willing to feed the monster—for which I am very thankful. I'm an only child, and they had intense careers. My horse was my best friend."

"Is Shadow that horse?" Jennie noticed the brightness leave Lainie's face when she asked.

"No, I lost that first horse. His name was Skippy. At least that's what I called him. His registered name was Skip to the Beat and he was an off-the-track Standardbred that could jump the moon." Lainie laughed at the surprise on Jennie's face. "I know what you're thinking; Standardbreds pull sulkies; they don't jump. He wasn't a pacer. He not only had a true trot but also a great canter and gallop. I don't think he liked sulky racing much. He didn't have a very good track record."

"Wow, this is a great story."

"Well, it is, up to a point."

Jennie waited for Lainie to continue and when she didn't, Jennie decided to prompt.

"What happened?" Jennie kept her voice soft. She wanted Lainie to know she cared about what happened.

"Skippy and I did really well in competition, and my parents thought I needed a better trainer to win even more. They counted blue ribbons and championships and became obsessed. The new trainer didn't think Skippy was good enough to take me much further and convinced my parents that a better horse would take me to the national championships or even the Olympics. They didn't really care that I loved Skippy and was having fun. I was told to sell Skippy and look for another horse. When I refused, they sold him behind my back."

Jennie gasped. "That's terrible. What did you do?"

"I refused to go back to the barn or to ride with that trainer again. I worked at several other area barns training horses and giving lessons to new riders. I thought I could earn enough to buy Skippy back. I earned a pretty good reputation for both riding and training and was determined to show everyone I didn't need that stupid trainer. I never earned enough money to buy Skippy before I left for college, so my plan changed. I decided to somehow make peace with my parents so they would pay for college. I was determined to find Skippy after I finished school, and found a good job, so I could afford a horse."

"Jennie, I'm leaving." Marcy didn't try to interrupt but she also didn't want to leave without saying goodbye. "Should I leave the munchkins in their stalls?"

"Yes, let them eat their hay, and I'll turn them out when they're finished."

Jennie waved goodbye to Marcy and then turned back to Lainie, who sat quietly with her head down. Jennie was riveted. What a story. She waited for Lainie to look up, but she seemed in another place. Jennie was sure she was re-living every detail as she told the story, and she was also sure it was a story rarely told.

After a few minutes, Lainie continued just as if she'd never paused.

"I went away to college, earned a teaching degree, basically because I couldn't decide what I really wanted to do, found a job, and moved out of my parents' home. I'm not too sure they missed me or even noticed I was gone, but that's another story for another time. I searched for Skippy and found him, but the family didn't want to sell. They loved him. I guess the next part is a good story because they still have him, and he's a treasured member of their family. The family has two daughters. The oldest is now in her first year of college and the youngest is in high school and rides Skippy in 4-H, but she doesn't jump him much because she thinks he's getting too old."

"Do you ever visit or is it too difficult?"

"I'm welcome to visit anytime. I've been helping them with a few things when I'm in their area. The mom is taking carriage-driving lessons because she's determined to drive Skippy after her daughters leave home. I helped her find a good instructor—one who understands horse behavior. The instructor knows Skippy raced at one time and will introduce the carriage slowly. We don't know if he carries any bad baggage from his racing experiences. Probably not, but she wants to be sure he isn't afraid."

"It sounds like he has a forever home. Not with you, but a good home." Jennie saw that as a positive.

"Yes, and they've promised to give him to me if for any reason he needs to find a new home." Lainie looked relieved. Like a bit of baggage rolled off her shoulders as well.

"Thanks for sharing your story. I have a feeling that's not the end of the story, though."

"It felt good to tell it, although I'm not too sure I want it printed."

"I understand. That's a very private story and it's safe with me. But why did you leave the jumping competition world and become a Follow the Leader instructor? Do you have time to tell that story?"

"It's pretty straightforward. While I competed, I met quite a few trainers and riders who didn't care what they did to win. They used force to get what they wanted and brutal equipment—things like tight flash nosebands so the horses can't open their mouths, tie-downs so they can't lift their heads, severe bits for control, and other really awful stuff. I'm sure you've seen it all."

Lainie waited for Jennie to respond.

"Yes, probably not as much as you because I've never been in high-level competition, but I've seen enough on casual trail rides to make my stomach queasy. I'll never understand why some people pretend to love horses and then treat them like objects to control."

"I know, it's sad, because they'll never know the joy of being truly connected to a horse." Lainie could tell Jennie was on the same page.

"You and I are in total agreement. I guess that's why I was intrigued by your clinic. You were trying to get your students to understand. Some did, but others tried to force a connection."

"Good observation, Jennie. It's sometimes hard to understand why students pay good money to attend a Follow the Leader clinic but then don't understand or accept the concept that you can't force the relationship."

"So—is that why you teach the Follow the Leader program? You know I've never studied the program, but I understand what you're teaching. There are a lot of good horse people who understand."

"I knew there had to be a better way to communicate with horses, but I didn't have a mentor. I worked at big show barns, and they want to win—at all costs. I'm not saying all show barns are bad, but most don't care about anything but winning. That's how they stay in business. When I saw Brock Rodgers demonstrate his Follow the Leader program at the state fair, I was totally intrigued. Here was a person who truly cared about the horse. I remember he said it was his mission to help horses."

"Ok, I'm going to ask a really tough question, and I hope you don't take offense."

"Go ahead." Lainie waited.

"Do you think you can have both a mission and make a million? I mean, why the focus on money? How can you spread your message to the masses if the masses can't afford to come to your clinics?"

"At the time, I never really thought about it. I was so mesmerized by the message that I was willing to pay any price to learn. I guess I expected all Follow the Leader students to feel the same way. I was totally on board with everything about the program. I'm usually very discerning about things, but not this program. I became a faithful follower, and I put Brock Rodgers on a pedestal."

Jennie sat back and debated about where to go next with her questioning. She decided to press a little.

"Lainie, you used the word *was*. Are you still mesmerized by the message?"

"Very astute, Jennie, catching that slip-up." Lainie wasn't offended. "I still believe in the message. It's a great message. I'm not as thrilled about the politics of the program, and I agree with you about the fees. I'm helping to make Brock Rodgers rich, and that was never my goal. Brock has fallen off my pedestal. He expects instructors to follow him without question. He considers any suggestion a criticism. He sets quotas for bringing in new students, and for the number of lessons and clinics we teach. That causes a lot of problems."

"What kind of problems?" Jennie knew Lainie was sharing her heart. She put her pen and notebook down and waited.

"It causes some instructors to forget the horse and focus on winning the most students. It's just like those bad trainers in the large show barns."

"That's not horsemanship," Jennie commented.

"Exactly. When the horse is forgotten, it isn't horsemanship, and it isn't what should be taught if you follow the program I love."

"Some of the instructors aren't walking the walk, so to speak, and for you, personally, that's the dilemma?" Jennie could understand the struggle Lainie faced.

"You got it. I value my integrity, and I feel my integrity is being challenged, and in some ways lost."

"I can tell you're a person of integrity. I can't imagine you losing it." Jennie couldn't imagine such a thing.

"I'll give you an example. Brock totally loses it if a student complains to the corporate office. Many instructors do whatever is necessary to avoid an unhappy student. I'm guilty, and that really tugs at my heart. I would never willingly abuse a horse, but when a student doesn't take correction well, I avoid offending them, and sometimes that isn't best for the horse."

"Oh, you mean like when that girl in the clinic who was kicking the stuffing out of her horse, and when you asked her to stop kicking, she insisted she wasn't kicking, and then she kept on kicking?"

"Yes, exactly; I didn't correct her again because she was very offended, and that poor horse will have to endure her kicks because I didn't make her stop, or worse, I didn't risk offending her in order to teach and stick by my principles. I could tell she was the type to complain."

"Are there any instructors who keep their jobs and their integrity? Is it possible?"

"There are a few. And I totally admire their ability to handle Brock and still keep their integrity intact. They're mostly long-time instructors who have such a large following that kicking them out of the program would come back and slap old Brock in the face. They can somehow ignore Brock without offending him. I don't have that ability."

Lainie was quiet. She seemed to be thinking.

"I want to help horses. I want a mission, not a million. I love teaching horsemanship, but I'm losing my passion to represent Follow the Leader. If Brock doesn't follow his own program, and treat his instructors, students, and horses with the same respect he preaches, his mission is no longer my mission."

There, she said it; now what would Jennie say?

"Do you have a contract? Do you have to stay with the program?"

"Yes, sort of, because I have a non-compete clause. If I leave, I won't be able to teach anything similar to Follow the Leader for two years, and I have to reimburse Follow the Leader for my education. I think I could fight that one because I actually did pay for my education. Boy, did I pay!"

"I don't suppose your mom could look at the contract. You said she was a lawyer, right?"

"No, I can't share this with her. I really can't. We have very little contact. It's not that I don't want to connect. My parents are self-absorbed."

"You couldn't teach the Follow the Leader program, but do they have a patent on good horsemanship? Isn't good horsemanship just good horsemanship? You don't need to use the same terms or patterns. Wait a minute, of course you could use the same patterns. I mean, how in the world can they stop you from using a circle or figure eight, for crying out loud?" Jennie was getting riled. She hated bullies and it sure sounded like Mr. Brock Rodgers was a big bully.

"You're asking good questions. I guess I've been bullied into not asking those questions. Brock always gets rid of instructors who question anything. He considers it disloyal."

"You have been indoctrinated and controlled. They've used common control tactics— cause doubt, discourage individual thinking, and threaten punishment."

"I can't risk this getting out; you understand, right? I've never shared this story and here I am sharing it with someone I just met—and a reporter, to boot."

"I understand, but I would still like to write a story about you, and about your compassion for students and horses. I want to help you find a way back to your passion again. I know you're a great teacher and would do well on your own. There has to be a way. Are you willing to at least think about a different future?"

"I sure am, and it would be a relief not to worry about student quotas set by Follow the Leader, and it would be nice to offend a student once in a while—in a nice way, of course."

Bang, bang, bang. Jennie turned to look at Riley who was kicking the stall door with his front foot.

"I think someone has finished his hay and wants to go out to the pasture. I don't want to reward his kicking, but I do need to let them out. Any suggestions for Mr. Riley?"

"Probably just ignore him. Don't make a big deal or draw attention to the kicking."

"Yeah, thanks. I agree."

After a few minutes, Jennie walked to Julep's stall and opened the door. Julep stopped for a treat and then waited for Jennie to release the rest of the herd. As herd leader, Julep would walk them out to the pasture. As Julep waited by the rear barn door, Jennie opened Treasure's door, followed by Starlight's. Riley didn't kick again, but he was anxious. Jennie didn't want him tearing out of the barn at a run, so she haltered both Riley and Stuffin to lead them to the pasture. Lainie reached for Stuffin's lead line, and they walked the ponies out to the pasture together. Jennie pulled two horse cookies from her pocket and gave one to Lainie for Stuffin. She took off Riley's halter before giving him the cookie. She hated to have a horse pull away from her before she was ready, and with Riley's attention on the cookie, she was able to take the halter off without that happening.

Back in the barn, they hung up the halters, and folded up their chairs.

"Thank you for trusting me with your story, Lainie. I'll respect your privacy. You'll get final approval. I don't think I'll write it, yet; something tells me the story is still developing."

"Thanks; I don't trust easily, and I'm not sure why I trust you, but I do." And she did.

Jennie gave Lainie a quick hug. "When do you leave the area? Do you have time to come to the farm again? I want you to meet Cassy and Megan."

"I'm pulling out sometime Thursday afternoon, but I may be able to come back Wednesday night, and I'll bring pizza."

"Now that's an offer I can't refuse." Jennie never refused pizza if she could help it.

After saying goodbye, Jennie watched Lainie pull out of the drive, heading back to Trina's farm.

Father, please be with Lainie and help her find peace. I know you have a great plan for her life. Help her to seek your plan.

As she finished her prayer, Jennie vowed to never abuse Lainie's trust.

And, Father, please show me how to help Lainie—and, Sam, and Jeremy, and Mom. Thank you.

What an emotion-filled day. Life was good but also very hard. Jennie wanted to help Sam, her mom, and now Lainie. Could that be what Jesus wanted her to do? Could this be how she was called to share love and grace?

Jennie didn't have answers, but she knew where to find peace. Tonight, her prayers were very lengthy and she fell asleep before she finished. That often happened. Her grandma always called it falling asleep in the arms of Jesus.

Sweet dreams, Jennie girl.

As Lainie drove back to Trina's farm, she felt a quiet sense of peace. She didn't know why; all she knew was it felt good. She trusted Jennie, and she couldn't quite figure that out, either. Maybe she could find her passion for teaching horsemanship again, and maybe she could figure out a way to leave the Follow the Leader program and survive financially. For the first time in a long while, Lainie felt content. She would hate to leave Appleridge on Thursday. After less than week, it felt like home. She even liked going to church with Trina.

God, I feel you in my life, and I can't believe I'm talking to you right now. I'm not very good at it, but, God, I said that prayer in church. You know the one about asking you into my life. Sorry it took me so long, but anyway, I just wanted to say thanks.

Oh yeah, thought Lainie, I'm supposed to end a prayer with Amen.

Amen.

Chapter Nine

ennie woke up tired. Not only did she get to bed later than usual after her talk with Lainie, but all night she tossed and turned. Problems, problems, problems; everyone had problems, and now their problems were her problems. As she ate her breakfast, Jennie jotted down a few things.

Sam—ask Jeremy to talk to Sam, what is bothering Sam?

Belinda—call her more often, listen more, I miss my friend

Jeremy—tell him I'm sorry to hear about Bert, DO NOT make him feel bad about not sharing the story

Mom—call her today, listen more, and don't forget Sunday night suppers

Lainie—find someone to review her contract, give encouragement, keep everything confidential, and above all, protect Lainie's trust

This relationship stuff is really hard.

She added *say a prayer* to the bottom of her list, and then she added it again at the top. I need to start with prayer and end with prayer, she thought—everyday.

THE CHRONICLE OFFICE was crazy with last-minute details before this month's issue went to press. Jennie didn't have a lot of time to think about her mom and friends, but she prayed for them every night. She called her mom on Tuesday during lunch and they planned a supper for Sunday night. She called Jeremy Tuesday night and he promised to call Sam. Jennie didn't mention anything about Bert. She would tell him she was sorry about Bert in person.

Jennie made a note to call Dr. Peterson. Even though the Petersons had a lovely barn, Megan paid Jennie to board Starlight at her barn. Horses like company. Starlight wouldn't be happy being the only horse at the Petersons' farm, and Dr. Peterson didn't want to buy another horse to keep Starlight from getting lonely. He didn't want to get back into what he called *the horse business*. Megan would be in college next year, and the Petersons were looking ahead to retirement. Jennie didn't think they would sell the farm, but maybe they would lease the barn? And maybe Lainie would be interested in a lease?

Arriving home on Wednesday night, Jennie was happy to see Cassy's car parked at the barn. Maybe she would get an opportunity to introduce Lainie to both Cassy and Megan.

After changing her clothes, she sat with her cat, Beauty, on her lap for a few minutes of petting. Beauty purred and pressed her head into Jennie's hand. She loved to have the top of her head rubbed gently.

"Beauty girl, did you miss me today?"

Jennie didn't expect Beauty to answer, but she liked talking to her. Sometimes it was lonely at the farm. Jennie kept busy during the day, but evenings were often lonely.

Strange—if I'm lonely why don't I do a better job of staying in touch with friends and family?

That's a good question to ponder later. Right now, she needed to put Beauty down and go to the barn because she wouldn't be lonely tonight.

Jennie loved Wednesday nights. Usually all three horse owners and friends came to the barn, and tonight, Lainie would join their group. She also invited Jeremy, and he said he would try, but it would depend on how late he stayed at school, and then whether the commute was good or bad.

Jennie knew it was just a matter of time before Jeremy announced his move to Columbus. He would attend seminary full-time after Christmas, and he would need to live closer to campus. Jennie was ok with that thought, but she hated to think about Jeremy leaving the area or even the state after graduation. She chastised herself for worrying about something that was still a few years off. And besides, she and Jeremy were still testing the waters of their relationship, and nothing was permanent—yet.

Jennie threw a flake of hay into each stall and then opened the gate to the pasture. Some days she kept the paddock gate open and the horses used the barn overhang for a small shelter. No need for shelter today. Today was beautiful with clear skies. She thought Sam's idea for a run-in shelter would be a great addition to the farm. Maybe she could somehow fit one into her budget. Worth a try, she thought.

As Jennie finished feeding, she heard laughing and looked up to see Cassy and Megan walking into the barn.

"Hey, guys, what's so funny?" Jennie was happy the girls were fast becoming best friends.

"Oh, nothing much. Megan was just telling me about Mrs. Williams trying to give her a reward for not hitting her big dog, Moose."

"She insists Moose was the big black animal that caused me to swerve and put the truck in the ditch, but I'm not so sure—and you know why. Of course, I can't tell Mrs. Williams why I'm not so sure. She is a real sweet lady, but she can be very insistent and she won't take no for an answer."

"What's the reward?" Jennie wasn't too sure why this was funny.

"Oh, she wants me to ride in the parade on her decorated golf cart with Moose. I'd be so embarrassed. I don't want to hurt her feelings, but I'm not going to pretend I'm some sort of hero or anything. It's crazy."

"It really isn't funny, but I was teasing Megan about the whole thing," Cassy confessed, but she didn't look a bit sorry.

"Mrs. Williams doesn't give up easily. We may need to come up with something to make her happy. Maybe she could help us with our parade entry?" Jennie, the problem solver, was on the job again.

"Maybe, but that will be about as hard as coming up with something for this year's theme. That's a tough one." Megan shook her head.

"Hey, Marcy and I are counting on you two. You're the creative ones in our little group." Jennie really was counting on them.

"Oh yeah, well you're the writer, so get those creative ideas flowing." Cassy wasn't going to let Jennie off easy.

Jennie played along. "I guess I better get busy, but I agree, that theme is silly, and I'm still counting on you two."

"Megan, before you start grooming Starlight, could I talk to you for a few minutes? It's about someone I've invited to the barn tonight. Cassy, you can stay?"

"Sure, ok." Cassy looked at Megan and she nodded.

"I'm sure you've heard about the Follow the Leader program. It was new to me, but, Megan, it sounds similar to what you were doing with JJ."

"Brock Rodgers isn't a good topic to mention around JJ. JJ claims Brock stole his ideas to start the Follow the Leader program. But, to answer your question, yes, it's the same type of horsemanship, and great principles if followed. Sadly, all JJ and Brock can see are stars and dollar signs. Somehow, they forgot about the principles they preach."

Jennie almost blurted out, *that's what Lainie said*, but quickly clamped her mouth shut when she remembered that wasn't her news to share.

"Lainie Anderson is in Appleridge. She taught a Follow the Leader clinic at Trina Shaw's barn last weekend, and she's stopping by tonight. I wanted you two to meet."

"Why? You know I'm not too fond of my experience with JJ, and Brock is from the same mold." Megan wasn't happy.

"Trust me on this, Megan. I'm not too sure why I think you should meet, but I think it will be fine." Jennie turned toward Cassy. "And you may know Lainie as Elaine Anderson when she competed in combined training?"

"Sort of, I remember the name, but I've never met her."

"She needs friends." Jennie didn't think this was going well. "I don't mean you have to be her friend; I just think you may want to be her friend. It feels like I'm being nudged to make sure you three meet and then I'll leave the rest up to God."

"You think it's a God thing?" Megan looked a little embarrassed and Cassy looked plain uncomfortable. Neither one was big into faith, but they respected Jennie enough to not run for cover.

Jennie was still new at sharing her faith, so she kept it casual. "Maybe, who knows, but the worst thing that can happen is we have another friend who loves horses."

"Friends are good, and horse-loving friends are the best." Cassy could always find a shiny nugget in every situation.

"Thanks, guys. But, you're still not off the hook for this parade theme thing. I'm coming up dry for ideas." In truth, Jennie hadn't thought about it too much this week.

JEREMY ENDED the call with Sam. They planned to meet at The Café for a cheeseburger in about forty minutes. Sam needed to take a quick shower first. Since Jeremy spent the day in classes, and not under a horse, he was ready to go. Something was up with Sam and he could tell Jennie was worried. That was Jennie, always trying to solve problems. He wouldn't call her a busybody, exactly, but she was usually in everybody's business. Not pushy or in a bad way—she always wanted to help. She had a good heart. Heck, maybe she should be the one going to seminary, not him. He debated about calling Jennie but decided to wait until after he talked to Sam.

"HEY, BUDDY, it's been a long time." Jeremy walked up to Sam who was already sitting at the counter. Sam got up for a man hug—shaking hands with one hand and the other hand slapping each other's back.

"Is the counter ok or do you want to take that booth over there?" Sam gestured to the booth in back of the café.

"It's up to you. Are we talking about anything serious?"

"Well, maybe. Yeah. Let's grab the booth." Sam led the way after he checked with the waitress and Jeremy followed.

The both ordered cheeseburgers, fries, and Pepsi. "That was easy, boys." They laughed when Bernice the waitress called them boys. They had a history. She called them boys back when they both were really little boys.

"What are you doing working nights, Miss Bernice? You've been here long enough to get the day shift." Jeremy knew the answer, but he liked to tease the older woman.

"Now, Jeremy, you know I bowl in the ladies church league on Wednesday mornings so I switch my hours and work the supper shift. You're just lucky it's Wednesday and you get me." She laughed as she slapped shut her order book. "Be right back with your Pepsis, b-o-y-s." She drew out the word boys.

"Miss Bernice sure is a character." Sam chuckled and added, "Almost as much of a character as Mrs. Williams."

"Yeah, I think they're related or something." Jeremy thought they were related but he never knew how exactly.

Sam and Jeremy talked about Sam's work, Jeremy's school, and resurrected a few memories about their time in 4-H together while they waited for their food. Jeremy could tell Sam was dancing around what he really wanted to say.

Bernice brought their meals.

"Ok, if I say a prayer?" Jeremy waited for Sam's response.

"Um-yeah-sure-ok." Sam looked around to see if anyone was looking. There were only a few customers and none were looking in their direction.

"Father, we thank you for this time sharing a meal together. Good friends are a real blessing. Father, please give Sam the peace to share whatever is on his heart and help him to feel the love you have for him. Amen"

The prayer felt good. Sam never prayed, but it felt good to have Jeremy pray for him.

"You guessed correctly. I do have something and I need advice. I'm not sure if there is anything you can do to help me. I know we haven't kept in touch much after high school, but I still consider you one of my closest friends."

"I am, Sam. Good friends don't need to be together all the time to be good friends."

"Thanks. I've gotten myself in a little trouble. I didn't see it coming, and I wasn't trying to do anything wrong. The IRS says I owe them money, a good bit of money, and money I don't have right now. I've been doing my own taxes since I started my business. I don't have a lot of deductions so I thought I could save some money by doing them myself. I keep thinking it's some sort of mistake. I don't mind telling you this could seriously hurt my business."

"Maybe it is a mistake and a good accountant could straighten it all out." Jeremy wanted to help, but he didn't even do his own taxes, and he didn't have a business.

"I know, I guess I just hoped you could send me in the right direction. Send me to someone good and not too expensive. I would be embarrassed to have my clients hear about this. I thought maybe you knew someone."

"Ok, let's think. Did you mention this to Belinda? She's really plugged into the business community in the whole Appleridge area. I think her dad was president of the Chamber of Commerce last year, and she knows quite a few of the clinic's clients."

Sam's face turned red. "I don't want Belinda to know I'm so stupid."

"Oh, man, you're not stupid. Stupid would be if you ignored the whole thing." Jeremy could tell by Sam's reaction that this was a big deal for him.

"Don't you think Belinda would want to help, and maybe her dad, too?" Jeremy kept his voice low. Appleridge was a small town and he didn't want Sam to suffer if they were overheard.

"You know I love Belinda. There, I said it, I love her. But I also know I'm not good enough for her. She's going to be a veterinarian. That takes a lot—she's really smart. I'm just a farrier. I work on horses' feet all day and come home smelling like horses' feet. This whole deal has just been a huge reminder that I need to let Belinda find someone better. I'm not asking Belinda; heck, I've been avoiding her calls."

"And you're not happy, because you miss her."

"Yeah," Sam admitted.

"You know what, Sam, you are stupid." Sam looked shocked. Jeremy hoped this got the reaction he wanted. "If you think Belinda is the kind of girl who loves a person for what he does instead of who he is, well then, that does make you stupid."

Sam said nothing. He looked like he wanted to get up and run for the door, but he sat instead, staring at his half-eaten plate of food. Jeremy hoped Sam's thoughts were going in the direction he wanted.

Finally, Sam looked up. "That was a trick, right?"

Jeremy grinned. "Right, smart fellow. You love Belinda because she's kind, honest, funny, and yes, smart. She loves you, and all I need to do is look at her when she's with you to know that's true. She doesn't care how much money you make, or how much you owe. She's proud of you, Sam. You have skill. Don't sell yourself short. As a future vet, Belinda can truly appreciate the value of a skilled farrier. Heck, you'll probably get all her referrals on the tough cases. A good farrier is worth his weight in gold."

"I knew you would shoot straight with me; maybe that's what I hoped to hear." Sam took a deep breath and asked, "But now what? Your advice is welcome, but don't hurt me."

"Now what? Well, first I would call Belinda. Jennie said she's worried about you and misses you. Just talking will take a bit of the worry away from you both. Ask if she knows a good accountant. Trust her. Sharing this will send the message you trust her and value her opinion. Then get a good accountant and find out how to fix this IRS mess. I know you aren't a cheater, and I'm sure it's all a big mistake. Maybe you'll owe a bit of money, but I'm going to guess it can be fixed quickly."

Sam didn't say anything, but he nodded so Jeremy knew he was listening and receptive.

"This next part is going to be me preaching. It's what I do. Well—not so much preaching but sharing my faith." Jeremy waited for Sam to protest. No protest came. Sam seemed to relax instead.

"You are good enough. God believes you are good enough. You are his son, he loves you, and he thinks you're good enough. I know you aren't a churchgoer, but that doesn't matter. You don't go to church to become good enough. You're already good enough."

"Thanks, friend, but why do people go to church if it's not to get good?"

"They go to meet good friends, to love each other, to worship a great God who thinks they're good enough, and then to learn how they can help others find that same peace. You're my friend and I don't want you to miss this wonderful thing called grace." Jeremy picked up his now sort of cold cheeseburger. "I would love to share more, when you're ready."

Sam nodded and started to eat along with his friend. He would call Belinda tonight. He missed her. He hated to think she was unhappy and worried—and he was the cause.

"Thanks, I'll let you know about the faith stuff. Oh, before I forget, I hope Jennie wasn't too upset about Bert. She looked like she was trying not to cry when we walked into the grocery store."

"What about Bert?" Jeremy already had a feeling—a bad feeling.

"She asked if I knew where Bert was and I told her the whole story. I'm not sure, but I think she wanted to find him for you."

"Oh, boy—now I have a little explaining to do. She asked me about Bert and I didn't share the story. Instead, I brushed it off. In case you're wondering, I'm stupid." Jeremy decided he didn't want to eat a cold cheeseburger after all.

"Sorry, man, if I caused you some trouble." Sam looked worried again.

"No, it'll be fine. I'll bring it up before she does and I'll spill my guts."

They got up for another man hug and slap and walked to the front to pay their bill. Sam pulled out his wallet and said, "My problem, my treat." Jeremy, knowing it was a matter of pride, didn't argue.

Driving home, Jeremy thought about Jennie. He hoped he wasn't in trouble about the whole Bert thing, and also because he wasn't going to drive out to the farm tonight. He was tired. He needed to think. He would call Jennie later and ask her to dinner tomorrow night. They could talk then. He had a lot to talk about—probably even more than Sam.

ON HIS WAY HOME, Sam heard his cell ring and pulled the truck over to answer. His gut told him it was Belinda and he shouldn't ignore the call. He was right.

"Hey."

"Well, Sam, it is Sam, isn't it? I think I remember what your voice sounds like."

Sam didn't hear anger in Belinda's voice so he decided to play along with a preemptive answer.

"It's me; the one and only. I miss talking to you, too."

"I was worried about you and about us." Belinda sounded sad.

"I was being stupid, but I had dinner with Jeremy tonight and he set me straight."

"Good old Jeremy. What happened?"

Sam explained everything to Belinda and she listened without interrupting. When he finished, she hesitated, then said softly, "Thanks for sharing, I know that was hard, and Jeremy is right. You are good enough. You're better than good enough. I was afraid I lost you and I didn't know why, and it hurt."

"I'm sorry. I guess I was just embarrassed. I didn't want you to think I was stupid. You're all the way down in Florida meeting some pretty smart guys, and I was afraid you would think we weren't good together."

"I'm a little angry with you right now." Belinda's voice wasn't soft now. "Ok, maybe not angry but sad. Sad that you thought I was that shallow. That's not me and it's never been me."

Belinda was angry and more than a little bit. Sam knew he needed to do some serious damage control.

"I'm sorry, I'm really sorry, but to be truthful, we've danced around commitment, so I guess I don't know where we are in our relationship. I know you want to wait until you're out of school for anything serious, but it's hard to feel secure without commitment. Don't you think?"

Nothing but silence.

Uh-oh, I pressed too hard.

"You're right. And I probably wouldn't have been so worried if I knew where we stood in our relationship. All I know is I don't want to lose you, Sam. I love you. There I said it first."

"I don't want to lose you, Belinda." Sam hesitated. "I love you."

"Now that wasn't so hard, was it?" Sam could hear the smile in Belinda's voice.

"No, it actually felt pretty darn good."

"It did. So—we have a committed relationship. That means we trust each another, we're best friends, and we're planning a future together. Ok?" Belinda felt light—happy.

"Ok, and it also means you'll end up living with someone who smells like horses' feet most of the time." Sam was serious but was also teasing.

"That may not be as bad as what you'll smell. Vets do some pretty stinky procedures. It's not all fun and glamour," Belinda kidded back.

"Yeah, I can just imagine our future laundry room."

"I can, too, and I can imagine doing laundry with you forever." Belinda wasn't teasing now.

"Does that mean we have to take turns with the laundry?" Before Belinda could respond, Sam quickly said, "Just kidding, I'm pretty good at it and promise to always do my share."

"Right answer, love you. It's late and I know you're tired. I know I'll sleep better tonight and I pray you will, too."

"I will, I definitely will, and even better when I get this IRS mess behind me."

"I'll text you some names, ok?"

"Night, love you." As Sam clicked off his phone, it felt like he could slay the IRS dragon and win. Belinda loved him. And if Jeremy was correct, God loved him, too. It felt good to be loved.

Chapter Ten

ennie greeted her co-worker with a smile. "Morning, Sherilynn."

"Hi, Jennie, we have a staff meeting today bright and early. We're meeting in an hour."

"Ok. Thanks." Jennie glanced across the room at the conference table and added, "It won't be a long commute. I'll be there."

"You're funny, Jennie."

"Laughter is good medicine—that's what my Grandpa always says." And it was.

Sherilynn looked like she was going to respond but just then the phone rang.

"Good morning, the *Farm & Family Country Chronicle*." She waved as Jennie proceeded to her little desk in the corner.

One issue down and now more articles to write for the next. Jennie wondered if the staff took a slight break between issues, but if the staff meeting was any indication, the answer was no.

As Jennie waited for her desktop computer to boot up, she thought about Lainie's visit to the farm last night. It was fun. Lainie was very entertaining and she seemed to enjoy meeting Cassy, Megan, and Marcy. Megan shared her internship story, which surprised Jennie, and although Lainie was sympathetic and nodded her head in agreement a few times, she didn't share her thoughts about the Follow the Leader program. She also didn't defend Brock when Megan mentioned the conflict with JJ.

Lainie mentioned that she knew JJ but didn't elaborate. She did mention her desire to stay in one place and teach her own program someday. Jennie thought that was revealing, but she didn't think Cassy or Megan took notice.

Jennie thought the story about Lainie's name change was interesting. Apparently, Brock didn't think the name Elaine was sassy enough and started calling her Lainie, saying it was a name people would remember. Jennie wondered if Lainie would go back to Elaine if she left Follow the Leader, but she couldn't ask that question in front of the others.

Lainie promised to stay in touch with Jennie and she certainly hoped they would stay in touch. No, thought Jennie, not hoped, she would make an effort to call her once in a while. Besides, she still needed to get the name of a cheap but good lawyer for Lainie. She would ask Jeremy tonight.

Jennie looked forward to tonight—a dinner date with Jeremy. No pizza at her place this time. Jennie wondered if Jeremy needed to tell her something important or if he was just trying to make up for the whole Bert thing. She wondered if Sam mentioned their conversation about Bert when he had dinner with Jeremy. Guys were just as good at that sort of thing as girls. Sometimes better. Maybe not gossips, but definitely curious.

Jennie was deep into research and ideas for her next articles when Sherilynn called her name and motioned for her to come over to the conference table.

"Mr. Mark and Charles both had early appointments, but they'll be here in a few minutes. I wanted to show you a few ideas before the meeting, if you have time."

"Sure." Jennie grabbed a steno pad, her favorite tablet for note taking, and a pen. She sat down at the table beside Sherilynn.

"I had a few ideas for the website. I want to, you know, clean it up a bit. I think it's too busy. If we want our website to be the place for people to check for events and happenings around the area, I think it has to be clean and easy to navigate."

"I totally agree. It looks sort of like a website that has been changed and updated too much. Maybe it needs a total makeover?" Jennie was glad Sherilynn brought up the idea of fixing the website. It looked tired and old.

"That's a thought. I think I would enjoy creating something new instead of trying to fix this one. But I'm not sure I can pull that off." Jennie thought Sherilynn could pull off anything she put her mind to.

Jennie pointed to several screen printouts of ideas. "I really like this style. It looks old but not tired and old. It looks retro but fresh."

"Thanks. I hope Mr. Wilson and Charles like it, too."

They heard sounds coming from the stairway and then both Wilson Mark, owner of the Chronicle, and Charles, the ad manager, walked into the room.

"Hello ladies."

The men grabbed coffee and seated themselves at the table.

"First order of business is how very pleased I am with this month's Chronicle. It looks great." Mr. Mark held up a copy and then distributed copies around the table. I've got more in the car. These are so fresh the ink may still be wet."

Jennie couldn't help but page through, quickly looking for her articles. She did this month's layout, so it wasn't like she didn't know where they were, but it was more exciting to see them in print instead of on a computer screen.

"Other than giving my congratulations on a job well done, I don't have any new business. You all know your jobs and what is expected. We're printing a small supplement for the Appleridge Apple Festival, but we've discussed that already. Are there any questions on the supplement?"

Jennie spoke up, "I'm scheduled to meet with the organizers early next week. We're printing a schedule and a few articles describing the events, right? Should I use photos from our files?"

"Yes, use a few of last year's photos, and I believe they're still using the same logo, but ask at the meeting."

Charlie spoke up, "We get quite a few advertisers to cover the cost. It's a popular ad opportunity. I never have trouble selling ads, and, actually, most businesses are already on board. However, if you know of anyone who wants an ad, we can always squeeze in more."

"Ok, sounds fine. Is there anything else today?"

Sherilynn waited a beat, then spoke, "I was just sharing some ideas to update our website with Jennie. We both think it needs a makeover." She pushed some of her pictures across the table to Mr. Mark.

"I love Sherilynn's ideas. The old-style country look is retro but still new and fresh." Jennie gave Sherilynn her full support.

"I like it." Mr. Mark slid the examples over to Charles who nodded his approval.

"Do you feel confident enough to take on this job?"

"Yes and no. I still want to work more on the design. I would like to have all my ducks in a row before I start. And, I want to be able to finish it before Thanksgiving or I'll wait until after the New Year."

"And that's why I trust you to run this office." Sherilynn beamed at Mr. Marks praise.

"Ok then, with this month's edition printed, I want you all to clean up anything you've started, and take the rest of the day and all day tomorrow off. Come back fresh and ready on Monday to put out another great issue."

Everyone clapped and offered their thanks, but all stayed seated.

"What about the phones?" Sherilynn asked because phone calls were important in their business.

"I'll be here and answer calls the rest of the day, and tomorrow I'll record a message saying we will return all calls on Monday. I'm no fool, I know Sherilynn will check messages from home, I know Jennie will write, and she also has a few interviews scheduled on Friday, and I know you, Charles, will chase a few ad leads. Regardless, please enjoy some time away from the office, if possible.

Mr. Mark beamed at his staff. "We look out for each other and I appreciate your dedication. I want to show my thanks. I'm no dummy. I know the best way to motivate a staff is to throw out a few perks on occasion. Now go—all of you."

Jennie didn't need to be told again. She rose from the table and walked over to her desk to gather her things and log out of her computer. Mr. Mark was right; she did have a couple of interviews, and she would work from home, but, still, it was a nice surprise and treat. Jennie knew there weren't many employers who appreciated their staff like Mr. Mark. And he was right. Employees who feel appreciated are eager to work harder. It was such a simple concept, but one that was rarely endorsed.

She glanced at the time. It was only 10:30. Jennie decided to call her mom and treat her to lunch.

"Hey, Mom, are you on any deadlines today?" Jennie knew her mom was usually busy with her at-home sewing business.

"Hi, honey, nothing major needs to be finished today, why?" Mom sounded more like herself today.

"I've just been given the rest of the day off and would like to treat you to lunch at The Café, if you're free. I could be back in Appleridge by 11:15 or so."

"Well, what a treat. Sure. I can be ready by 11:30. Should I meet you there?"

"No, I'll pick you up if you don't mind riding in Blue Boy." Jennie's truck was an older model Silverado and hand-me-down from her parents, but she kept it clean.

"Oh, that's fine. Blue Boy and I are old friends."

Jennie laughed. "Ok, see you then."

"Bye, sweetie, drive safely."

Jennie noticed her mom seemed to be really pleased at the invitation. She wanted her mom to be happy. She deserved to be happy. She was a great mom.

LAINIE LOADED SHADOW into the horse trailer. The next clinic wasn't too far. She didn't need to rush. Lainie couldn't figure out why she felt like crying.

Straighten up, girl; you love to teach clinics and meet new people.

149

The pep talk she gave herself didn't help. Lainie didn't want to leave. She felt like her life was just getting started in Appleridge. That was strange. Maybe she would like the next place just as well.

Trina walked out to the trailer. "I'm glad I didn't miss you. I wanted to tell you to come back anytime you're in the area and have a few days free." She gave Lainie a hug and Lainie hugged back.

"Thanks, Trina, I will." Lainie continued to check all the doors, checked to make sure the lights worked, and the hitch was secure. She was hauling precious cargo. She climbed into her truck and started the engine, waved one final goodbye before putting the truck in gear, and pulled out of the spot she temporarily called home.

It's that sort of thing. That's why I like it here. Trina's offer to come back was genuine and not just small talk. Jennie's offer to help and her listening ear were genuine. Even Marcy treated Lainie like an old friend. Lainie knew genuinely kind people were rare, and she met quite a few at this stop.

I can always come back. Someday me and my Shadow will come back.

JENNIE'S MOM was ready and waiting when Blue Boy stopped in front of her house. She walked to the curb and hopped in the truck with a smile on her face. She looked pretty— and happy.

Reaching over to give Jennie a quick hug, Ellen smelled like her favorite lotion, Vanilla Bean.

"Thanks for the invite, sweetie, I was a little restless today. I finished several small projects this morning but didn't feel like starting a new project."

"Have you been busy, Mom?"

"I have been busy. I did all the new uniforms for Appleridge High's varsity cheerleaders. They couldn't find what they wanted in the catalogues."

"Wow, that's cool." Jennie's mom was a very talented seamstress. She ran a business from home and it was a good business.

"Now that Dad's retired, are you ready to slow down?" Jennie glanced at her mom before pulling out onto the street.

"No, I love to sew and your dad spends most of his time out in the garage puttering around or at the Bake & Shake with your grandpa."

"What? Dad has joined the old B & S coffee club?" Jennie was shocked.

"He has his own group. I'm not sure what they're called yet."

Jennie thought a few moments. "Let's call them the BS & More club."

"Jennie!" Ellen pretended she was shocked.

They arrived at The Café and found a seat easily; the lunch crowd was a little slim today. Bernice took their orders. They both wanted the spinach quiche special with a side salad. Jennie couldn't wait any longer and pulled out a copy of the *Farm & Family Country Chronicle* to hand across the table to her mom.

"Here it is, Mom, my first edition."

Ellen paged through the small magazine with a grin on her face. "I can't wait to read this; it looks good. A new look. May I keep this copy?"

"Yes, you may, with my compliments."

"I'm so proud of you, Jennie." She was very proud of her youngest daughter who had struggled with making decisions after college.

"You didn't notice but I have two boxes of copies behind the seat. Mr. Mark asked me to drop them off at several businesses in Appleridge."

"Have you thought about offering some of your 'Dear Equestrian' letters to the Chronicle? They were a real hit for the *Ohio Equine Journal*."

"No, I haven't. I guess I could. They're fun to write. Maybe I could reprint some of the letters with permission."

"Did you end up doing the *Tell Us a Story* idea? I didn't see it when I looked through quickly."

"No, we decided to sit on that for a while. I'm still working on the logistics. I have a lot of things ready to try. I don't seem to run out of ideas. Well, except for the Apple Festival parade theme; that one has me stumped."

"What's the parade theme this year?"

"Apple of My Eye." Jennie sighed.

"Oh my, bless their hearts," Ellen joked.

"Oh my, is right."

"Well, I'm sure you'll come up with something for the parade. Get those two teens on the job."

"My thought exactly. We're meeting Saturday night to plan our entry."

Bernice placed their salads on the table. "Here you go, ladies, enjoy."

"Thanks, Bernice, this looks good." Ellen waited for Bernice to leave. "I'll say a quick prayer." They both bowed their heads as Ellen said a short blessing over their food and time together. What Jennie didn't hear was Ellen's silent prayer asking God to always protect her daughter's heart. Ellen didn't know why, but she had a strong urge to hold Jennie tight, and never let her go.

Chapter Eleven

After lunch, Jennie drove her mom home, and then delivered CC copies to the Appleridge vendors. She didn't spend much time at each stop. It was a beautiful fall day and she looked forward to a quiet afternoon, and maybe a short ride on Julep.

Mom seemed happier, and when Jennie asked about the change, she said a daily bible devotion that pops into her email brought everything into the right focus. Ellen promised to forward the devotion to Jennie.

Pulling into the farm drive, Jennie heard her cell phone play music. She stopped Blue Boy and answered when she saw it was Lainie.

"Hey, Lainie."

"Help me, please help me—accident—Shadow—trailer." Lainie was sobbing.

"Lainie, slow down, where are you? Did you call 911?" Jennie's heart was pounding in her chest.

"Yes, 911. Not too far—on the highway near Sycamore Road—Shadow needs a vet. The other driver is still in his car. The jerk ran a stop sign—hit my trailer—doors are jammed—can't get to Shadow—I hear her scrambling." More sobbing.

"Lainie, I'm coming. I'm going to hang up now so I can call Dr. Peterson, ok? I'm on my way and I'm already in Appleridge."

Sobs. "Ok—ok—ok. Hurry, Jennie!"

Jennie hung up and found Dr. Peterson on speed dial.

"This is Jennie McKenzie and I need to talk to Dr. Peterson; it's an emergency!"

"Dr. Peterson is with a client. May I take a message?"

Jennie didn't recognize the voice. Maybe it was someone new. "No, it's an emergency. Interrupt him and tell him it's Jennie McKenzie—now!"

Jennie knew she was being rude but didn't care. She would apologize later. It felt like hours before she heard Dr. Peterson pick up the phone.

"Jennie, who is it?" Dr. Adrian Peterson knew all the horses at Jennie's barn. He hoped it wasn't Megan's horse, Starlight. Later he would be ashamed thinking only about Megan's horse and not the others. He knew how much each of the horses was loved.

"No, it's my friend, Lainie's, horse, Shadow. She's been in a horse trailer accident and they can't get the trailer doors open. Dr. Peterson, she's all Lainie has in this world right now. I know you don't know her but please do this for me." Jennie knew she was pleading, but she certainly wasn't embarrassed.

"Where are they?"

"They're out on the highway west of town near Sycamore Road." Jennie knew Adrian Peterson wasn't a praying man, but she was a praying woman, and she was asking the Holy Spirit to move his heart.

"Ok, I'm on my way. I'll get Bill to cover until I get back to the clinic. Jennie, make sure the fire department is on its way. We're going to need help getting to the horse."

"Ok, I'll call and I'm heading there now."

Jennie called the fire department. The dispatcher assured her they were on their way. Jennie could hear sirens.

She tried to calm herself as she drove to the accident site. Lainie sounded dazed—she was probably hurt. She prayed for the driver of the car, also."

Father, help them, please.

Pulling up to the accident, Jennie gasped. It looked bad. The car must have hit the right side of the truck causing the trailer to jack knife into the truck with the car caught in the crush. The horse trailer was barely upright. It looked like the only thing holding it up was the hitch still attached. The car didn't look good. Jennie prayed the driver was alive.

She parked on the side of the road behind two firetrucks. Two police cruisers blocked the highway from both directions. She grabbed her first-aid kit from the truck seat and ran.

"Jennie, you stay back." One of the officers happened to be a high school friend.

"Tom, I can help with the horse."

Tom motioned her forward. "Be careful. If the horse struggles, I'm not sure that trailer won't tip."

Jennie ran up to Lainie and grabbed her. "Lainie, look at me. Calm down, we'll get her out. Talk to her—keep talking to her.

Lainie only nodded. Because of the tilt to the trailer, the officers wouldn't allow Lainie to climb up to the left window near Shadow's head.

Jennie could see the firemen working on the back door with the Jaws of Life. The right side was smashed. Several men attached ropes to the trailer in an attempt to stabilize it. The firemen already pulled open the car doors and an EMS worked on the driver. Lainie refused to let them look at her, and Jennie knew Lainie would refuse until Shadow was safely out of the trailer.

Finally, the back doors were pried open, just as Dr. Peterson pulled up. With his vet truck, he was motioned up to the front. Lainie squeezed into the trailer before anyone could stop her and ducked under the partition.

"Hey, Shadow, baby. I'm here. We're going to get you out." Shadow was still tied, so she must not have struggled. Any struggle from Shadow would release the rope from the safety ring. Lainie saw blood running down between Shadow's front legs but she seemed to be standing on all four. Her eyes were wide with fright but softened as Lainie rubbed her neck.

Lainie felt someone at her side and saw a vet.

"I'm Dr. Peterson; Jennie called. You ok with me helping your horse?" Lainie nodded. He was already assessing the horse. "It doesn't look too bad. I'm going to give her something to help relax her, but not enough to mask her injuries. She'll be able to walk off the trailer."

Dr. Peterson pulled out a syringe and, talking quietly to the mare, he injected her with Banamine. He noticed the mare was very connected to the girl—if Jennie said her name, he didn't remember. He decided to stay away and let the girl handle the horse.

"Ok, let's see if you can get her to back off the trailer, it may be hard for her."

Lainie seemed much calmer now that she could see and touch Shadow, and there was a job to do. She talked to Shadow, telling her to back while applying a little pressure on the rope. Shadow did what she asked.

Once they were off the trailer, Lainie walked Shadow over to the large grassy berm on the side of the road where Dr. Peterson continued his examination. Blood was running from Shadow's nose and she also had several cuts on her chest.

Jennie stood at Lainie's side. As she looked at Dr. Peterson's face, she felt optimistic. During his examination his face changed from intense concentration to his normal demeanor. He looked up and smiled as he stroked the mare's neck.

"She's banged up. We'll treat the cuts and maybe put a stitch or two in this one." He pointed to a jagged cut on her side. All in all, she faired very well—at least physically." Pointing to her nose, he added, "She probably hit her face during the impact."

Dr. Peterson looked at Jennie. "We'll need to get her out of here. What about your farm?"

"Sure, but how?" Jennie knew Lainie's truck and trailer weren't going anywhere on their own power.

"Get my trailer. Your truck should pull it fine. Are you ok with that idea?" Dr. Peterson glanced over at the other vehicle and saw the EMS working on the driver of the other car. He needed to keep Lainie's focus on Shadow.

"Yeah, I'll go now."

"I'll call Susan. She'll know where I keep the receiver to the hitch."

Jennie gave Lainie a hug and moved quickly to her truck. Adrian watched her go and then turned to Lainie.

"I guess we need a proper introduction. I'm Adrian Peterson, Megan's dad. I think your mare is going to be just fine. I can't say the same thing about your truck and trailer." As he spoke, he motioned for Lainie to walk further away from the accident, and away from the other car.

"I'm Lainie Anderson, and thank you so much for coming. I can't thank you enough. I'm not from here and I didn't know who to call."

"You're welcome and I'm very glad to see minor injuries. You never know what you're going to find with a horse trailer accident." He paused. "I'm going to stitch up her cut while we wait for Jennie. I'll give her a little something to numb the area, and hopefully, keep her relaxed enough to get her on another trailer. That's not going to be easy."

Lainie nodded. She knew Shadow was hurting but drugged just enough to walk onto the Petersons' trailer without a fight. In the future, it would take time and effort to convince Shadow to willingly walk into a horse trailer again. Fortunately, Lainie had the time needed to take it slow and help her best friend.

BY THE TIME Jennie reached the Petersons' farm, Megan was home from school and helped Jennie hitch the trailer quickly. "I haven't done this in years. I'm glad you're here, Megan. You're the expert."

"No problem. I sure hope Lainie's mare is ok." Megan hated to see any animal injured. It was sometimes hard for her to help out at her dad's clinic.

"I think she's going to be fine, but Megan, before we get there, I don't think the other driver is going to make it. The car was a mess and they were still trying to get him out when I left."

"Did you recognize the car?" Megan's stomach didn't feel so good.

"Not really. But the driver looked young."

They were quiet as they drove to the accident scene. Jennie was praying. Megan sat with her head down.

When they pulled up, the state police were directing traffic and motioned Jennie to the side of the road. Two wreckers were waiting, ready to clear the wrecked vehicles. Dr. Peterson was carrying supplies to his truck, and Lainie stood quietly with Shadow.

Jennie opened the trailer doors and waited as Lainie led Shadow up the ramp. The mare hesitated but seemed almost in a daze. Jennie thought maybe Dr. Peterson had given her something to keep her quiet, but she also saw the connection between Lainie and the mare. She would walk into fire if Lainie asked.

"Can you give me a minute to pull a few things out of my truck and trailer? Everything I own is on board."

Jennie nodded. "I know that wrecker service; it's local, and they're good folks. Whatever you can't get, I'm sure we can get later tonight."

Dr. Peterson walked up to the trailer with Megan who had gone over to help him clean up. "I need to get back to the clinic. Are you ok?"

"Yes, we're fine. I'm just waiting for Lainie to grab a few things from her truck. I'm sure they won't let her into the trailer, though."

"I'll stop at your farm tomorrow to check on the mare. Megan, are you staying with Jennie?"

"Yeah, I'll go over and help Lainie carry some things first."

Adrian smiled at his daughter and nodded his head. "When you get Shadow to Jennie's farm, unhitch and we'll leave the trailer there for now. Don't worry about getting it back to our farm. We have nothing to pull it with until we find another truck for you. I don't really want to use the vet truck."

It didn't take long for Lainie to grab what she needed. Jennie talked to Brad Katz, owner of the wrecker, and explained that Lainie would need her clothes and things from the trailer.

"No problem, Jennie." He gave Jennie his card. "Call when you're ready to come over and we'll make sure she gets into the trailer tonight. It'll be in our yard and secure."

"Thanks, Brad, I appreciate your help. The trailer is her home. She'll need everything inside." As Jennie told Brad it was Lainie's home, she realized Lainie needed a place to live and knew immediately she would offer her extra bedroom. Lainie was so worried about Shadow she probably hadn't yet thought about losing her home.

"Brad, do you know what happened to the other driver?" Jennie motioned to the totaled car.

"They brought in life flight. It landed right in the middle of road. He's in bad shape but at least he has a chance."

Father, please give the driver a chance.

ONCE AGAIN, Lainie softly asked Shadow to back out of a horse trailer. She knew the mare was sore and every step hurt.

"Good girl, Shadow; you're fine, girl," Lainie reassured her mare.

"Lainie, bring her into Julep's stall. It's ready." Jennie motioned to the first stall on the left. "We'll make space in the tack room for her things."

Marcy walked into the barn. She had heard about the accident before she left the hospital. "Jennie, I'm not using the second tack closet you gave me for my ponies; give it to Lainie."

"Thanks, Marcy." Jennie loved that Marcy offered.

Lainie looked like she was about to cry again. "Thanks, Marcy. Do you know anything about the other driver? I didn't look in his car. I ran to Shadow and not to him. What kind of person am I?" She was sobbing again.

Marcy walked over and put her arms around Lainie. "You're a good person. You called for help. I think you were in a little bit of shock." Marcy thought she still was.

"But-but-maybe he's dead and I didn't try to help. I called him a jerk."

"You called for help." Marcy's eyes were scanning Lainie for signs of injury. "I think maybe you should be checked over, Lainie. You took a hard hit. Will you let me take you to the ER?"

"I'm stiff but I think I'm ok. I need to stay here with Shadow and I need to get my things."

Jennie spoke up. "I'll go get your things—everything you may need. Megan will stay here and keep an eye on Shadow." Jennie looked over at Megan to make sure that was ok.

"I'll stay here, Lainie. Cassy is coming out soon and we'll both be here." She looked at Jennie. "We'll feed the horses and do the barn chores while you're gone. And here comes Jeremy to help."

Jeremy! Jennie had forgotten her date with Jeremy. She ran out to greet him.

"I heard. What can I do to help?" Jeremy looked at everyone and they told him the plan.

Lainie agreed to go with Marcy to the hospital after they convinced her she needed to be in good shape to take care of Shadow, and she needed any injuries documented for insurance purposes.

JENNIE SHARED everything she knew with Jeremy as they drove to the wrecker yard. "I'm going to invite her to stay with me in the extra room. She's going to need a place to live until she gets another trailer or whatever she decides. She's homeless."

"That's good. She'll need a place to stay, and some friends. With no transportation, I'm sure her clinic will be cancelled, but she'll need to keep working somehow."

"I didn't think about that, but I'm sure she could teach while she's here—if she feels ok. I don't know her situation as far as money and insurance. Maybe we could plan some sort of fundraiser."

"She doesn't seem to be a girl who will accept charity. Maybe she could do a horsemanship demonstration. You know, so she feels like she's earning the help."

"First things first—she'll need a few days to make a plan and I'm pretty sure she's going to be sore tomorrow." Jennie knew when Lainie's adrenaline wore off from the accident she would feel every bruise.

Brad helped Jeremy and Jennie pry open the trailer door to the living area, after they documented everything with photos. The place was a mess. The impact looked like it tossed everything that wasn't fastened down. Cabinet doors hung open with their contents strewn.

"Looking at this, I can't believe Shadow only has minor injuries. Now I know why Dr. Peterson said he would check on her again tomorrow. Maybe he is thinking the same thought."

Jeremy climbed into the trailer with Jennie. "He wouldn't have left if he saw any indication of something more serious, but you never know what will pop up tonight."

As they talked, they started with Lainie's clothes—folding and placing them in the cardboard boxes Jennie still had in her truck after her delivery of the *Farm & Family Country Chronicle* copies. They also used a few Rubbermaid tubs they picked up at Jeremy's house. Tubs that were once filled with all the things his mom saved through the years. The tubs were slowly being emptied as they cleaned out the house.

"I think we can leave the kitchen things for now. I'll search for personal things, and then we'll need to get her tack and equipment. That's pretty important." Jennie felt a little strange looking through Lainie's drawers, but she knew it was important, and in the end, would be appreciated.

"Yeah, tools of her trade, so to speak. To her, the tack and equipment are probably more important than her clothes." Jeremy stood by Jennie ready to help with the equipment, but he was fine with letting Jennie search for personal items.

"If she feels ok, I'll bring her over here tomorrow. She'll need to see everything for herself."

Jeremy looked over at Jennie. "Don't you need to be at work?"

"Nope, Mr. Mark gave us tomorrow off as a reward for this month's issue. Wait till you see my first issue. This morning and then lunch with her mom seemed a hundred years ago to Jennie. "Sorry about our date."

"We'll have our dinner later. It's more important to be available for friends, and I'm glad you were there for Lainie." Jeremy backed out of the trailer door with a full box. When he returned to get another, he had an idea.

"I'm hungry, let's stop and pick up something to take back to the farm—something for all of us. How about Chinese? There's that little Chinese carryout place not too far from here. If we get a good variety, there should be something for everyone, and if no one wants to eat, you'll have leftovers for tomorrow. Hey, do you love cold Chinese food as much as you love cold pizza?"

"I sure do, and I'm hungry so let's get a lot." Jennie realized she was famished. It had been a long time since lunch.

When they finished, Jeremy's SUV was packed. Lainie didn't have her trailer crammed full of things, but it was also everything she owned. The tack and barn equipment took up a lot of space. Jennie was actually surprised at how basic Lainie kept her tack. Most horse junkies were also tack junkies.

THE HOSPITAL EMERGENCY DEPARTMENT wasn't very busy. Once the staff saw Lainie with Marcy and realized she was the other driver in the accident, they quickly brought her to a curtained section. The ER doctor gave her a thorough exam. He was concerned about several large bruises on her chest from the air bags, and the bump on her head. Lainie answered all the questions to his satisfaction, and after giving her medication for pain, he released her to go home. It was then that Lainie realized she didn't have a home. She waited until the doctor left before looking at Marcy.

"I know you don't have a home right now. I think Jennie is already expecting you to stay with her. And good luck trying to tell Jennie McKenzie no."

"I—I—I don't know Jennie well enough. Why would she let me stay with her?" Lainie took a deep breath. "It's enough that we brought Shadow to her place."

"I'm fairly new to Appleridge, but I've learned that it's full of really caring people. Not just pretend caring—real caring. Jennie and the whole bunch of us already consider you a friend."

The nurse, a friend of Marcy's, came in with a prescription for a pain reliever, a little stronger than over the counter aspirin, instructions from the doctor, and paperwork to sign releasing Lainie from their care.

"We're happy to see you doing so well, sweetie. That was one heck of an accident according to the highway patrol."

"Thanks." Lainie didn't know what else to say. She wanted to ask about the other driver but didn't think they would share that information.

They walked slowly out to Marcy's truck.

"I found out the other driver was a high school boy and a life flight took him to Columbus. He's going to live, but has months of recovery ahead. They also think he was on his phone when he ran the stop sign."

Lainie sighed. "I'm glad he's alive. If he was on his phone, it sounds like his injuries are his punishment."

"You and Shadow are being punished, too. I know it could have been worse, but his carelessness comes with a high price for you both."

"I bet you see these things all the time." Lainie stopped and waited for Marcy to answer before she climbed into the truck.

"Yes, too much—way too much." Marcy sighed before she opened her truck door.

On the way to Jennie's farm, both were quiet. Lainie was tired, sore, and depressed. Marcy watched her carefully.

JENNIE HEARD A CHEERY TUNE and she quickly grabbed her purse to find her cell.

"Hey, Jennie, when will you guys be back?" Megan sounded a little anxious.

"On our way now. Is Shadow ok?" Jennie was now also anxious.

"She's fine, but we're getting a little company around here."

"Company? What kind of company?"

"Friends who heard about the accident and are checking on Lainie. Someone named Trina and another lady named Joyce who came with Trina."

"Ok, tell them we're on our way. Have you heard from Marcy?"

"Not yet. Hey, we fed the horses. They're still inside since it seemed to keep Shadow quiet to have horses in the barn. Well, all except Julep; we fed her out in the paddock, but now she's in the aisle making sure all our guests aren't lonely."

"Yeah, that sounds like our girl." Julep was Jennie's horse again but while she was in college, she belonged to Megan. They both loved her. "We'll be there in two minutes; we just turned the corner."

Marcy and Lainie turned the corner behind Jennie and Jeremy. "Lainie, it looks like we have a welcoming committee or it's a party." Marcy drove slowly down the drive to the barn and parked near a couple of other trucks.

Jeremy parked his SUV at the house. "Let's put our Chinese food in the house until we see how many we need to feed." Jeremy hoped not too many. They bought a good amount but not enough for an army.

Walking into the barn, Jennie spotted Trina and another woman she didn't know. She was relieved to see Marcy and Lainie. Lainie looked exhausted. This would need to be a quick party. Standing in the barn aisle, Lainie made quick introductions after Trina cautiously gave her a hug.

"I'm so relieved. When I heard, I was just sick to my stomach. I had to check on you and Shadow. I'm so sorry." Trina looked like she was about to cry.

"Thanks, I'm fine. We're both fine. My truck and trailer, not so much, but hey, they're just things. I'm insured." Lainie tried to sound upbeat, but her heart and body ached. She was so tired but she couldn't ignore these new friends. She could feel their love. They offered more love than people she had known for a long time. She sat down on the bench in front of Shadow's temporary stall.

Trina looked concerned. "Lainie, we aren't going to stay; you look beat. We had to check on you. We'll tell the other gals that you need rest, but it's good, and your sweet mare looks good."

"We're lucky. Dr. Peterson thinks Shadow is going to be fine physically. Mentally—we'll see. It may be a while before she's comfortable in a horse trailer again. I'll give her all the time she needs."

After Trina and Joyce left, they discussed the best situation for Shadow. It was decided that she could stay out in the paddock tonight where she could see the other horses. They turned the other five out into the pasture and then made sure Shadow was comfortable in the paddock with a pile of hay and water.

Jeremy announced, "We have Chinese food up at the house. Come on up for a bite. It's been a long night. Then, we'll carry Lainie's things into the house and get her to bed."

The group thought Chinese food sounded good. The unspoken thought was that after eating, they would help get Lainie's things from Jeremy's SUV, but not stick around.

Conversation flowed as they ate. They didn't realize how starved they were until they took the lids off all the containers and started to fill their plates.

"I have tea in the fridge and water on tap." Jennie offered. "I may have a few root beers; not sure."

Lainie was hungry, but almost too tired to eat. She was quiet. She wasn't sure what was happening. Everyone seemed to assume she would stay with Jennie, but Jennie didn't invite her to stay.

"Lainie, I have a little guest room. As soon as you finish eating, you may want to soak in a bath with Epsom salts while we bring your things inside. I hope we grabbed everything you need tonight. We have your tack, too, and most of your barn equipment."

"Thanks. I don't know what I would have done without you. Thanks so much. I'll try to find a place to stay, but thanks for tonight." Lainie could barely get out the words without crying.

"You're staying here—and for as long as you need. Don't worry. It's what friends do." Jennie's voice was soft but the words firm. "You're staying right here."

"Don't argue with her, Lainie; Jennie doesn't say anything she doesn't mean." Cassy had been quiet most of the evening but spoke up now. "I learned to listen."

The rest chimed in with their warnings to listen to Jennie.

"Wow, you guys, am I really that bossy?" Jennie was only half kidding. The nodding heads and smiles indicated that they were only half kidding, as well.

"I hate to break up this party, but we need to unload my SUV, and Lainie needs rest. Can you two stay and help?" Jeremy looked at Megan and Cassy. They nodded yes. "Marcy, I know you probably have an early shift tomorrow. You get on home."

"Jeremy James, I swear you're getting as bossy as Jennie." Marcy loved teasing Jeremy. "But I'm going to listen because I do have an early shift and a long day." Marcy waved and was out the door.

Jennie helped Lainie up the stairs and started the water for a hot bath. Jeremy carried cartons up into the spare room.

"Jennie, stay here with Lainie. Megan, Cassy, and I will put everything in the barn. We'll just stack it in the tack room for now." Jennie nodded. "And then I'm going to go home, ok?" She nodded again and walked over for a hug and kiss.

"Thanks. Let's talk tomorrow." Right now, Jennie couldn't remember what they needed to talk about. She just knew they needed time to talk.

"I'll let the girls go out first and then close the gate." Jeremy always felt better knowing Jennie didn't need to walk down the drive to close it herself.

"Thanks. I don't think I told Megan and Cassy thanks. Will you tell them for me?"

"Yes, sure will." And with that he was out the door.

Jennie was upstairs when Lainie got out of the tub. She helped her find something to sleep in and then made sure she was in bed before turning out the light.

"I'll leave a small light on in the bathroom. We can hang up your things tomorrow. Ok?"

Lainie nodded. She already looked half asleep. "Thanks, my friend."

Chapter Twelve

he next morning, Lainie could hardly move. Every muscle of her body ached, especially her chest. It hurt to breathe. She noticed Jennie was already up and tried to dress quickly. Ouch, ouch, ouch. Bending to put on her socks caused her to wince. She would need to get her prescription filled today.

Lainie walked down the stairs slowly—one step at a time. As she entered the kitchen, she saw a note on the counter near the back door.

Lainie, I'm out in the barn. I'll be back as soon as I feed. I'm not sure what you want for Shadow so I'll just give her a flake of hay for now. Jennie

Before Lainie could find her boots, Jennie was back in the house.

"She's fine but moving a bit stiffly. She was hungry and tore into the hay. That's always a good sign." Jennie finished her report. Why don't we eat a bit of breakfast and then I'll help you out to the barn to see her for yourself."

Lainie sat down at the table. She wanted to be a good guest, but she was anxious to see Shadow.

"I know you're anxious to see Shadow, so is cereal ok?" Jennie reached for the box.

"Do you have toast and peanut butter?" Lainie asked. "That's all I need."

"Sure do. You're a girl after my own heart. I like peanut butter on a granola bar." Jennie put the cereal away and reached for the peanut butter instead.

They ate quickly and walked to the barn slowly. Jennie could tell Lainie hurt.

"Did they tell you what to expect today?"

"Yes, I have a prescription to fill. The doctor said I would be really sore, especially from the air bags. He was right."

"I'm off today. We'll go into town to the pharmacy. You can tell me what to do and I'll put your things away."

"No, I'll help. It helps to move a little." Lainie did think moving helped. "Did you happen to grab the ration balancer from my trailer?"

"Yeah, we brought as much as we could. We'll need to take my truck to get the hay and anything else we missed." Jennie laughed. "Jeremy didn't really want the hay strapped to the top of his SUV."

Lainie scooped some things into Shadow's bucket for her breakfast. She was relieved to see her hungry and eating her hay. Shadow seemed to be moving better than she was.

They turned the herd out in the pasture and put Shadow in the paddock. They moved Lainie's tack into Marcy's empty tack closet, and found places for the other tools. With that job finished and all the equines happy, Jennie and Lainie walked back to the house.

"Do you need to rest or are you ready to tackle your things upstairs?" Jennie moved around the kitchen, straightening up a few things.

"I don't want to totally disrupt your life. If you need to be someplace, I can get things sorted."

"I know you can. I don't need to go to the office today, but I do have an interview later this afternoon. Do you want to take care of our errands first, and then I'll leave you alone to unpack this afternoon?" Jennie could tell Lainie needed some time alone.

"That would be good. I need to call my insurance company. I filed a report last night but didn't speak to anyone. I have good insurance. That's something I learned from my parents. After I make that call, could you take me to the horse trailer and then to the pharmacy? I called the clinic organizer while we waited at the hospital. She was very understanding. I don't know if she'll reschedule or not. I'm not sure what I'll be doing. I guess I'll take one day at a time."

"One day at a time is good. First, you need to take care of yourself and Shadow. Everything else will wait."

"I've never been good at waiting." Lainie thought maybe she would soon learn.

WITH ERRANDS FINISHED, Jennie left for her interview. She was meeting with the Apple Festival Committee—or at least with several on the committee.

Lainie sent an email to the Follow the Leader program explaining her situation, saying she would not be attending the instructor gathering in a few weeks. Heck, she didn't know where she would be in a few weeks. She was thankful for Jennie's help, but she hated being dependent on anyone.

Lainie finished hanging up her clothes in her temporary room. She stacked the boxes and tubs and put them in a corner of the closet. She would need them when she moved—somewhere. She decided to walk out to the barn and check on Shadow. The pain reliever was helping.

Before she reached the barn, her cell phone rang and Lainie grabbed it out of the holder on her belt. "Lainie Anderson."

"Well, hello Lainie, it's Brock Rodgers." Lainie wished she would have looked at the display before answering but she thought it would be the insurance company.

"Hello, Brock." She said nothing more and waited.

"Sorry about your rig." Before Lainie could say thanks, he continued, "I have a note saying you aren't attending the instructor gathering. I'm calling to make sure you know attendance is mandatory."

"I know, but I don't have a truck, trailer, or a horse. Shadow has been injured." Lainie couldn't believe the gathering would be that informative.

"Like I said, I'm sorry to hear about your rig, but you have time to get them replaced. That's why you have insurance."

"But Shadow, I can't leave Shadow right now." Lainie hated to sound like she was whining. She knew she needed to present confidence or Brock would tear her apart. He hated whiners.

"Like I said, get everything replaced, and get here in time for the gathering. I have several nice horses on the ranch right now. I'm sure we can replace your mare easily. She isn't anything special." Brock laughed and finished the call with, "See you in a few weeks, Lainie, or your contract will be terminated."

Lainie was speechless. She barely caught the reference to her contract because she was seething at Brock's callous talk about Shadow. This from a man who makes his living convincing the public he loves horses.

Terminate my contract—you jerk. Do me a favor and terminate it now. I'll leave and you'll think it was all your idea.

She knew right then that she couldn't continue to represent the program. She wanted to escape while she still had a shred of integrity intact.

Lainie put her phone back on her belt and continued her slow walk out to the barn. Shadow nickered when she walked into the paddock.

"Hey, sweetie, I sure hope you don't hurt as much as I hurt." Lainie stroked her neck and gave her the peppermint she had in her pocket. She took a deep breath. She needed to make a plan.

Yes, Brock, you're right. Everything can be replaced—including you and your program. He didn't have a patent on good horsemanship. Lainie wasn't even sure if he could spot good horsemanship if it kicked him in the face. That made Lainie laugh—the thought of a good kick to Brock's pretty boy face.

"Shadow, you're the best mare around. We'll show Brock what a good partnership can do, won't we, girl?"

Shadow searched Lainie for another peppermint. Lainie decided to grab her notebook and—where was her notebook? She felt like crying. Silly, crying over a notebook. The enormity of the accident finally hit Lainie square in the face, but a second later, she found herself thanking God for keeping both her and Shadow safe from serious injury, and for friends like Jennie,

Jeremy, Marcy, Cassy, and Megan. To Lainie, they were the best friends she never had.

God, am I supposed to stay in Appleridge? That was a pretty dramatic way of stopping me from leaving. Please, God, please heal the boy who hit us. And, oh yeah, I'm sorry for calling him a jerk, but I'm definitely not sorry for calling Brock Rodgers a jerk. Amen.

WHEN JENNIE RETURNED home, she found Lainie sitting on a bench in the barn, writing notes.

"Hey, Jennie, I hope you don't mind. I found this note pad in the tack room. I can't seem to find mine."

"No problem; I probably have them stashed everywhere. I'm a habitual list maker." Jennie sat down beside Lainie. "Are you feeling better?"

"Yeah, I put my things away. The lockers are really neat. I'm going to steal that idea if I ever have my own barn."

Lainie filled Jennie in on her conversation with Brock. "I think there's a clause or something in the contract about nothing being owed if Follow the Leader chooses to end my contract, but if I choose to end it, I have stipulations to follow. I'm going to pretend I'm devastated at the possibility and somehow get them to kick me out. It may hurt my reputation a little, but I think it's my best plan."

"Wow, what arrogance. It's as if they're so wonderful no one in their right mind would ever think about willingly ending their association with Follow the Leader." Jennie shook her head.

"That sort of sums it up, doesn't it?" Lainie shifted slightly, trying to get more comfortable.

"It does. So, are you going to teach on your own? Maybe stay in Appleridge?" Jennie put her hands together like she was pleading for the right answer.

"I'm thinking about it. I really like it here. I need to decide because it will make a difference in how I spend my insurance money."

Jennie was curious and asked, "How so?"

"I don't think I would need to spend money on a large living quarters in my trailer if I don't travel constantly. I would still like some sort of weekend package for short fun trips, but I wouldn't need what I had, and if I don't get as large of a trailer, I won't need the larger truck. I know one thing—I'm buying my new trailer from the same company."

"I don't blame you. That trailer protected Shadow in the accident. It may have saved her life." Jennie had mentioned the same thing to Jeremy.

"The company advertises all their safety features—which is why I bought it in the first place. It wasn't inexpensive." Looking out the door at Shadow, she added, "But worth every penny."

"Hey, we took a lot of pictures. Maybe they could feature you in an ad, and also give you a good deal on a new trailer." Jennie was always thinking ahead.

"That's a thought." Lainie really did think it was a good idea, and maybe a neat way to promote herself as an independent instructor, too. It sure wouldn't hurt to be in an ad campaign stressing the importance of safety while traveling.

Lainie looked at Jennie. "I'll try to figure this all out as soon as possible and get out of your way. I'll never be able to repay you for helping me, but I'll try."

"Enough said about repaying me. Friends help friends and I consider you a friend. I believe you would do the same for any of us." Jennie looked up to see a truck pull in the drive. "That looks like Dr. Peterson's truck."

Lainie stood up. "He said he would check on Shadow, but I wasn't sure when."

Both Lainie and Jennie walked out to greet the vet when he parked beside the barn.

"How's the patient today?"

"She seems to be doing a lot better than me." Lainie smiled. "I can't thank you enough for coming out to help us yesterday. You didn't even know me."

"Well, I know Jennie, and she would never ask for a favor unless it was important."

They walked to the barn where Lainie grabbed Shadow's rope halter. Dr. Peterson asked a lot of questions as he examined Shadow. When he finished, he looked satisfied.

"I think this mare is going to be just fine. What a trooper." He rubbed his hand down Shadow's neck. "Anything I can do for you while I'm here? What about the other horses?" He looked at Jennie.

"I don't think so, but if you give me a minute, I can check records." Jennie went into the tack room. "The ponies are due for Coggins soon, but I don't want to say go ahead without Marcy's permission."

"No hurry. She's probably going to ask for Coggins the next time she needs a health certificate. Doesn't she have a competition next month?"

179

"Yes, and I'll check with Cassy when we make that appointment. It's nice to have everyone on the same page."

Dr. Peterson looked at Lainie. "Megan says you teach horsemanship with a program similar to what she studied."

"Yes, the Follow the Leader program founded by Brock Rodgers. Brock and JJ used to be friends. Megan and I have compared notes and I think they both have wandered from their original mission."

Jennie was surprised Lainie was being so candid with Dr. Peterson—probably because they have something in common—no love for cowboys with huge egos trying to be millionaires instead of staying true to their mission.

"Yeah, Megan's experience this summer was a real eye-opener. You'll have to get Megan and Jennie to tell you the story about JJ and Julep."

"I will. I guess I'll have time to stick around and hear it, finally." Lainie added, "Knowing JJ, I'm sure it's an interesting story. I could tell a few stories about Brock. I'm ready to leave the Follow the Leader experience behind. I want to help people and horses, not make Brock a millionaire."

"Are you thinking about sticking around Appleridge?" Jennie's mind was making huge leaps as she followed the conversation. "Are you looking for a barn to lease? I think you could do quite a business in this area."

Dr. Peterson looked over at Jennie. His mind was also making huge leaps. "We need to talk when I have more time. I have an empty barn with a separate drive onto the property. Megan keeps Starlight here because she needs a horse herd and Megan enjoys being around this human herd. It's a shame to have a nice barn stand empty. Do you want to talk?"

Lainie's eyes were bright. "I'm definitely interested. When are you available?"

"How about Sunday afternoon? I'm on call, so, barring any emergency, I'll be home. Jennie can bring you out around two or so." They both looked at Jennie to see if she was on board with that idea, and she nodded yes.

Lainie gave Dr. Peterson her cell number, just in case he needed to cancel.

"I'll see you both on Sunday."

After the vet left, Lainie looked at Jennie. "Ok, spill it; what's the barn like? Is there an arena?"

"Yes, there's a small arena perfect for lessons, but you couldn't have a large group clinic like you had at Trina's farm."

"Small groups and individual lessons are good. I'm not a fan of the large clinics, but I needed to teach as many people as possible at each stop. It was a money thing. How big is the barn?"

"It's a really cute barn, about this size, four stalls, tack room, wash stall. One side has an enclosed area for hay storage attached and the other can be used for a run-in shelter for the horses—really nice." Jennie had a sobering thought, and her smile faded.

"What's wrong?"

"Hmmm, I was just thinking if you lease the barn, Dr. Peterson may want Megan to move Starlight home, and if Megan leaves, Cassy will take Treasure."

"Wait—I'm not interested in getting into the boarding business. I guess I couldn't stop Megan from bringing her horse to her own barn, but that will definitely need to be discussed. Of course, I need at least one horse to keep with Shadow. Oh, Jennie, I don't want to hurt you. Maybe I don't need to meet with Dr. Peterson on Sunday. There must be another place available."

"I'll be ok if they move. I hope they don't, but it's ok. Don't give up a chance to have a great location for your business. I'm sure I'll find other boarders easily, maybe Sam. You don't know Sam, but he's our farrier, and I've known him forever, and maybe I'll get a driving pony, or maybe Jeremy will want a horse again." Jennie knew she was rambling, but it was hard to be hopeful for Lainie and not worried.

"No, I'm not going to take the lease if it means all this mess. No. I thought about asking Trina if I could teach from her farm. See, I have lots of ideas."

They agreed to see what terms were offered and then go from there. Both vowed silently not to hurt the other.

"Lainie would you be ok here alone for dinner tonight? I have salad stuff in the fridge. Jeremy is taking me out to dinner. I hate to leave you here, but I think he has something important to talk about." Jennie was a little embarrassed asking, but she and Jeremy did need privacy to talk.

"Sure. I'll be fine. If you let me borrow your truck, I'll go into town and pick up a few things at the store. I don't want to eat you out of house and home."

"Yeah, you can borrow the truck. If I give you money, would you also pick up a few things on my list?" Jennie was out of milk, cereal, and bread—the basics.

"Give me your list. I'll just pick up everything. Don't worry about money. Consider it a downpayment for my room and board." Lainie didn't want to take Jennie's hospitality for granted.

And Jennie knew it was sometimes important to take help when offered. Most people were givers, not takers. At least the people she enjoyed.

"Ok, I'll take you up on that offer. I only have a few things on the list." She glanced at her phone to check the time. "Let's feed these munchkins, and then I'll get a shower."

They fed the horses together. Lainie wanted to learn the routine so she could help out when needed. Like tonight, she thought. It would be nice if she could say, "Don't worry, I'll feed tonight." But maybe Jennie liked to feed horses as much as she did. It was never a chore. She thought maybe Jennie didn't think of it as a burden, either.

"I'm going to stay out here and do some massage therapy on Shadow. Anything I should do before going up to the house?"

"No, just let the herd out. If Shadow is doing well, would you like to test her in the herd tomorrow?"

"Yeah, that would be good. She isn't a herd leader. It's funny but she usually buddies up to the herd leader. She's clever that way. She gets all the protection and none of the responsibility."

"Hmmm, Julep's our leader. It'll be fun to see if she attaches herself to my mare." Jennie checked the barn and was satisfied she was leaving it in order. She trusted someone as experienced as Lainie, but it was her habit to always scan the barn before she left for the evening.

"I'll leave the truck keys on the kitchen counter with my list. The house key is on the same ring. Please close the front gate when you leave. I know it's a pain to get out of the truck to close and open the gate, but I feel better when it's closed. Don't worry about locking it, but make sure it looks like it's locked. Ok?"

"Yes, I certainly will; you and Jeremy have a nice evening."

Jennie ran up to the house. Wow, she couldn't believe she met Lainie barely two weeks ago and here she was staying in her extra room, keeping her horse at the barn, and borrowing her truck. It seemed strange, but it also felt right. She was glad she was in a position to help. What a blessing!

JENNIE DIDN'T KNOW where she and Jeremy were going, so she didn't know how to dress. She decided to try a dressy casual look, or as much as her wardrobe would permit. She needed to take time to shop. She hated to shop unless it was at a tack store. She didn't think riding pants would be considered dressy casual, although the equestrian look was hitting all the stores, and she would be authentic. Jennie showered and dressed in gray pants and a white linen blouse. She would add a classic navy blazer that her mother sewed back when she was in high school. It still looked great. Classic clothes never go out of style.

Jennie was just cleaning out her purse when Jeremy knocked and walked into the kitchen. "For a minute there I saw the lights on in the barn and thought you forgot, and then I remembered Lainie was here and probably in the barn."

"She's giving Shadow a massage, and then she's taking my truck to the store. I think she was relieved to have some alone time." Jennie knew from experience. She lived with two roommates while in college and they always made sure to give each other space occasionally.

"Are you ready? Your chariot waits." Jeremy swept an imaginary hat off his head and bowed.

Jennie grinned. "Yes, kind sir."

Once in the SUV, Jennie asked, "And where is my chariot taking me?"

"We are going to an imaginary castle on the top of an imaginary mountain."

"Hopefully, we aren't eating imaginary food because I'm starved." Jennie played along.

"No, you'll get real food—really good food. We're going to The Country Inn in Richburg. I thought it would be a nice place to enjoy some quiet time."

"Wow, nice atmosphere, good food, and great company."

They chatted casually on the thirty-minute trip. Jennie found it easy to talk to Jeremy, but she didn't feel obligated to talk. Sometimes they were quiet. Nothing felt forced. She couldn't imagine what Jeremy wanted to talk about and couldn't decide if she would bring up the subject of Bert. It didn't seem quite so important now after the last two days.

They were seated on the left side of a huge fireplace. It was just cool enough to have a fire, and the restaurant's windows were open to the evening breeze.

"Don't look at the menu prices. I know it's hard for you to spend more than ten dollars on a dinner, but please get what you want tonight. Ok? The seafood is awesome."

When the waitress returned, Jeremy ordered a bacon scallop appetizer. "I know you like it, and I also know you won't order it."

"I guess you're on to me, Jeremy James."

"Yes, the boy with two first names IS on to you."

"I wasn't going to bring that up, Mr. James." Jennie paused. "This is fun. I hope I don't get spoiled."

"Spoiling is good once in a while." More than once in a while, thought Jeremy.

When the waitress brought the appetizer, they ordered their dinners. Jennie ordered shrimp with vegetables and rice and Jeremy a nice big steak.

After the appetizer and dinner salads, Jennie was already full.

"My eyes may have been bigger than my stomach. I'm full."

"No problem; eat what you want and then take the rest home. I'm sure it will taste good tomorrow."

Jeremy cleared his throat. "I wanted to have some private time to talk about our future. I know we haven't been together long, and I've never really told you how I feel, but I love you. I told myself not to say it, yet, but I need to make some important decisions about my life, and all I know is, it's important you know that my decisions will be based on what is best for us—you and me together." Jeremy couldn't read Jennie's face, so he added, "Is this too much pressure? Am I rushing you?"

Jennie finally spoke. "I wasn't expecting this, but I feel the same. I want to be in your decisions. I've been thinking about life after you leave seminary, and it worries me a little. I don't want to lose you and I don't want to leave Appleridge. And I don't want to make that decision now. Not yet.'"

"I'm not asking you to make a decision, but I need you to be a part of mine." When Jennie nodded a yes, Jeremy continued, "I'm not sure the ministry is the right path for me. I don't see myself pastoring a congregation. I want to help people find faith.

I'm trying to figure out how I can do that and not pastor a church."

Jeremy took a drink of his ice tea before continuing. "Sam and I went to dinner—gosh it seems like forever ago, but it was actually just a few nights ago. Sam needed help. He said I could share this with you, but not anyone else. He got into a bit of IRS trouble and wanted advice. He needed to find a good accountant and didn't want to ask Belinda, because he was embarrassed. He didn't feel he was good enough for someone like Belinda."

"I certainly hope you set him straight on that idea." Jennie sat up in her seat.

"I did. He called Belinda and they're good. But the really neat thing was sharing my faith with Sam and telling him God thought he was good enough. That's what I want to do, help people find faith. Help people find faith while helping them with life challenges."

"Doesn't a pastor do that?" Jennie wasn't sure what Jeremy was thinking.

"Yes, they do, but they also deal with church politics and church building funds."

"You would be good at those things," Jennie encouraged.

"Yeah, I think so, but I also think I need to explore some more options."

Jennie felt nervous all of a sudden. As if Jeremy was going to announce something difficult. "What options?"

"That's just it, I'm not sure. I thought maybe I should study law and become a Christian legal advocate, but I'm looking for something more personal. I just don't know."

"What do you need from me, Jeremy?" Jennie was pretty sure Jeremy was trying to tell her something but couldn't quite say the words.

"I need you to believe that you have a place in my life while I'm searching."

"Ok." Jennie didn't know what more to say.

"I'm thinking about delaying school next semester and doing a six-month mission trip in Appalachia."

"Where, exactly?" Jennie was relieved he didn't say someplace like the Middle East. That seemed selfish but it's what she thought.

"I'm not sure yet. I was looking into places overseas, but when I read about the poverty in our own country, I felt a call."

Jennie hated the idea of Jeremy leaving Appleridge for six months, but she also knew what it was like to be confused about the future.

"I understand feeling called. Do you think this will be your life's work, or is it time away to pray and discover your life's work?"

Jeremy simply said, "Yes."

"And if it is your life's work, how do I fit into the picture?" Jennie wanted to be totally honest. Their relationship would depend on his answer.

"I want to use it as a time of spiritual renewal and time to discover my direction. The only thing I'm absolutely sure about is my commitment to you. Whatever I decide will depend on us."

"Jeremy, I'm not saying I wouldn't move away from Appleridge. I don't want to, but I won't say definitely no. I also don't want to follow you in your work and give up my work. I'll support you and love you, but I won't give up on me. Does that make sense?" Jennie's voice was soft but firm. She didn't see herself as someone who would follow her husband and totally give up her dreams.

"It makes perfect sense. I don't want to turn you into a second me and lose you. Even if I became a pastor, I wouldn't want being a pastor's wife to become your entire life. I know that's what most congregations expected in the past, but those times are changing—and for the good."

Jennie relaxed a little. "Are you saying you see marriage in our future?"

"Yes, do you?" Jeremy certainly hoped so. He was sharing his heart with the one who already had his.

"Yes. I hoped so. I thought we were going in that direction."

"Jennie, I'm in love with you, with us. I know we aren't ready to take the step into marriage yet. I have to know my calling before I can ask you to commit to a future with me. Can you give me this time?"

"I can give you time. I also need time. And I think we need to be very clear on what will happen if you choose the mission field, or, I should say, if the mission field chooses you."

"If the mission field chooses me, I won't fight God." Jeremy felt he owed Jennie honesty as hard as it was to say.

"I won't fight God, either, and I trust that he'll help us through a tough decision."

"I want to ask you to marry me now, tonight, but I don't think that's fair. What I do want to ask is—can we make a promise to one another? Can we promise to love and be committed to our relationship, and to plan a future together? And to pray that God shows us a path that won't require either one of us to live a life we don't want to live? I know that sounds strange. We're always taught that marriage is give and take, and that if we love someone, we should be willing to sacrifice our dreams for our partner. But I think that's a terrible way to start a marriage, and a certain way to spoil a marriage. I would give my life for you, but I won't give away my passion and calling, and you shouldn't, either. God doesn't want us to give away our passions, he wants to use our passions for his kingdom, and if one of us gives away our calling to follow the other, I don't think we'll be following Jesus."

Jennie sighed. Jeremy was pretty smart about relationships with both people and God. "I've never heard anyone preach that message but I believe it's a message of truth."

Jeremy reached into his pocket. "I would love to put an engagement ring on your finger tonight, but I know it wouldn't be the right time."

He opened a little box and took out a beautiful ring with three dainty but bright sapphires. "This was my mom's ring. I read that sapphires represent trust and commitment and are often given when loved ones are separated for a long period of time. I thought this would be appropriate. Jennie, I pledge my love and commitment. I pray we can be together in marriage someday."

"Jeremy, I promise to trust you and stay committed to our love. I also promise to trust God's plan for our lives. Like you, I pray God's plan is a lifetime together, but if it isn't, I accept whatever his plan may be."

Jeremy placed the ring on Jennie's finger and they both sat silently, thinking, knowing that tonight they committed their relationship to each other, and to God.

It was late when Jeremy dropped Jennie off at the farm. He walked her to the door but then pulled her to the swing seat on the back porch.

"I'm going to talk to my advisors tomorrow and make some decisions. I wouldn't leave until after the New Year. Sarah and I have decided to sell Mom's house. We don't want it sitting empty and I don't see myself living there all alone. We're each keeping a few things. I was wondering if I could store a few things down in your basement. Sarah doesn't have much room at her place."

"Sure, I have room and the basement stays surprisingly dry for an old house. Are you keeping furniture?"

"I'm keeping my bedroom furniture and my mom's hutch. I was surprised Sarah didn't want the hutch because it was our grandma's. I guess because she already has an antique cupboard. I forget what they're called, I think it's a Hoosier cabinet."

"I could put your bedroom furniture in my extra room. The basement stays dry but I don't think you'll want your mattress in the basement for any length of time." Jennie's face felt hot. It may seem old-fashioned in this age, but she was embarrassed talking about bedroom furniture with Jeremy.

Jeremy witnessed Jennie's blush but didn't say anything. He thought it was really sweet, though.

"We'll have time for logistics once I find out where I'm going and when I leave. I probably won't get home much. I don't think you get vacation time with this type of mission."

He kissed Jennie goodnight, turned to leave, but stopped. "Hey, Jennie, I'm sorry about not telling you about Bert."

Jennie had forgotten about Bert. "Oh, Sam told you? I'm sorry he had such a sad ending. He was a great horse. I'm also sorry for the family. I'm sure it broke their hearts, and yours, too."

"I was going to tell you later but later was too late. It wasn't that I didn't want you to know. It was just too long and sad of a story for that moment."

"I understand, and I wasn't mad. Well, at first I was upset that you didn't explain, but then I realized it was a hard story to tell."

"I can't leave without another kiss."

Jennie agreed.

Chapter Thirteen

ennie didn't think anyone would notice the sapphire ring, but, boy, was she wrong. The next day, Lainie commented on how pretty it was, and asked if it meant something special. Jennie didn't want to share everything, so she decided to call it a promise ring. It didn't get past Cassy and Megan, either. She gave the same short explanation to them when they gathered Saturday evening as planned.

Jennie invited Lainie to join the group. Lainie thought the parade planning sounded fun and she also hoped to talk to Megan about the farm. Well, maybe not. She decided to be careful with what she said in case Dr. Peterson hadn't shared anything with his family yet. She didn't have to worry because Megan brought it up immediately.

"Hey, Dad said you were going to consider leasing our barn. That's pretty cool. He also said I didn't have to move Starlight. That won't hurt your feelings, will it?"

Wow, thought Lainie, her new friends had no problem sharing their feelings. She decided open communication was a good thing. It certainly took the guess work out of relationships.

"No hurt feelings. I understand and I really don't want to board horses. I'll need to have another horse, though; Shadow can't be by herself."

Both Cassy and Megan said in unison, "Sam! Sam's looking for a new place for Sadie."

"Oh yeah, Jennie told me about Sam. That's a thought and having a farrier on the premises would be a plus." Lainie added, "But we're getting ahead of ourselves. I don't talk with your dad until tomorrow."

"Hey guys, here's Marcy. She has the food." They all met Marcy at her truck to help carry in the pizza, pop, plates, cups, and napkins.

"Hey, we need to keep picnic supplies out here somewhere. I almost forgot to bring plates and cups, but had time to run to the store while I waited for the pizza. Let's eat!"

They pulled the camp chairs from the tack room and sat in a circle in the barn aisle. There wasn't too much chatter at first because they were busy stuffing their faces with pizza. When they finally slowed a little, Marcy looked at Jennie and said, "Wow, new ring! Special reason?"

Cassy and Megan shouted, "It's a promise ring!"

Jennie was glad the horses were in the pasture. This party was getting rowdy.

"Ok, friends, yes, it's a promise ring. We aren't ready for an engagement, but we are in a committed relationship." Jennie wanted to take the attention off her ring and her relationship with Jeremy. "Now, let's get busy; we have a parade entry to plan."

Marcy spoke up. "The parade theme is Apple of My Eye. I looked up the expression and it means a person treasured. Actually, a person you treasure. Maybe like when you give someone a promise ring." That comment caused a lot of chuckles. "Sorry, Jennie, I couldn't resist." Jennie caught the humor and waved for her to continue. "I thought maybe we could turn the carriage into a treasure box."

Cassy was excited. "Really neat, and those riding in the carriage would be the treasure. But how will we dress? Some of us will be walking and we'll need to be treasure, too. I guess we could all dress in gold, and maybe pass out chocolate coins, but that isn't cheap candy."

They all thought for a moment, then Lainie spoke up. "I would like to join you, if that's ok?" There were nods, fist bumps, and smiles all around. With the hearty welcome from the group, she continued, "We'll need to bring apples into the mix somehow, don't you think?"

"That would be pretty—gold decorations with red apples, or gold decorations with red and green apples. But how do we make it all come together?" Jennie's creative mind was blank. She hated not having ideas as they usually came to her easily.

They all sat quietly thinking. Cassy jumped up. "I got it. The carriage is a treasure chest and we could dress in something easy like black and wear apple masks. You know, a big apple with the middle cut out for our faces. We could have some sort of gold accessories; not sure about that yet. The masks would be colorful apples and we could laminate them."

"I like it. It shows we are the apple of each other's eyes and we are the treasure." Marcy really did like it. "It needs to be colorful and shiny and fun to see, even if everyone doesn't get the theme idea. I'll braid the ponies' manes and have them looking really sharp. I could braid in gold ribbon and little red decorative apples—if I can find them."

Jennie spoke up, "I like the idea of wearing black, because we probably all have things in black. Maybe we could make gold sashes that say something like Miss Apple of My Eye or for Jeremy it will be Mr. Apple of My Eye. Parades always have queens with sashes."

"Now we're getting somewhere. I'll volunteer to make the apple masks." Megan already had a few ideas in mind.

Cassy looked at Megan. "Do you think we could make the sashes? All we need is wide ribbon, glue, and glitter."

Megan gave Cassy the thumbs up sign. "The craft stores actually have glitter glue." Megan saw that she needed to explain. "The glue already has the glitter so all you need to do is write with the glue—very easy-peasy."

"I'll work on ideas for the carriage but I'm sure I'll need help." Marcy didn't think she was very creative but she was good at making things once given an idea. "I'll definitely need help with the ponies, and lots of prayers that Riley will stay clean after he gets his parade bath." They all laughed—Riley was well known for his love of dirt.

"Ok, Cassy and Megan are making the masks and sashes. I guess that leaves Lainie and me to help Marcy make the carriage look like a treasure box." Jennie thought a second. "We'll look at pictures and go from there. It will probably be cardboard attached to the carriage and decorated to make it like a treasure chest."

"That's easier said than done." Marcy joked. "Hey, it's getting late, and I'm working tomorrow, so I guess we can start looking at pictures and collecting supplies. Girls, don't spend your own money on the supplies. I'll bring out some cash to get us started."

"Maybe we could all chip in and create a fund?" Lainie suggested. "I'll donate twenty to start.

"I can do that." Jennie agreed. Looking at Cassy and Megan, she added, "Don't worry about cash. I'm pretty sure you're going to do most of the creative work."

Marcy quickly added, "It was my idea, so I'll cover the parade entry. I wanted to be in the parade with the ponies and I'm just thrilled I'll have partners in crime to share the fun and lend a hand."

The party broke up with everyone picking up empty plates, cups, and pizza boxes. Then they folded up their chairs and stowed them in the tack room. After saying goodbye to Cassy, Marcy, and Megan, Lainie and Jennie walked to the house.

"You didn't know what you were getting into when you decided to hang around with this gang." Jennie loved her gang.

"No, but I love it. I want to be a part of this gang when I get my own barn, too."

"I'm glad you feel comfortable going our separate ways during the day. It's nice to have help around here, but it's also nice to know I don't need to entertain you. I guess you're sort of stuck without transportation, but if you need to go anywhere, just ask. I'll either say, hey, I need to go there, too, or go ahead and take the truck."

"Thanks. I like space on occasion, so I thought maybe you did, too. I'm going to teach a few lessons at Trina's barn this week and she offered to give me a ride while you're at work, if needed. She also offered to help me out when I shop for a new truck and trailer. It's barely been two weeks, but it feels like I've known you guys forever. I definitely don't want to wear out my welcome."

"I don't think that's going to happen because we're going to communicate. Just like now—I'm going to take a shower and then read in my room. I'm getting up for early church. You're very welcome to go with us. We'll go to the Petersons' in the afternoon, unless you want privacy, and in that case, I'll either stay here, or visit with Mrs. Peterson while you and the Doc conduct business. How's that for communication?"

"Very good, thanks. I'll take a bath after you're finished in the bathroom. May I use the Epsom salts again?"

"You may," answered Jennie.

"And—I'll be happy in my bedroom, making more lists, and reading. I would love to go to church, but Trina is picking me up. I think she likes going with a friend." Lainie hoped going to church with Trina didn't hurt Jennie's feelings.

"That's nice; I'm glad Trina asked. Hey, I have an extra house key. Let me get if for you before I forget." Jennie walked into the former living room, currently outfitted as her home office, and found the key in her desk drawer. Lainie followed.

"I like your workspace, Jennie. It's a nice room."

"I didn't need a dining room because I like eating in the little nook in the kitchen. I thought, why not use this room as an office? I like the low windows. I can even watch the horses if they're in the side pasture."

Lainie yawned. "I'm heading upstairs to organize a few things. Let me know when the bathroom is available."

"I will." Jennie looked around. "I'm finished down here. I'll lock up the house and get upstairs. It's been a long day. I think I can smell myself and it doesn't smell nice. Oh wait, I forgot, I left a load of towels in the dryer. I'll get them first."

"I'll get them. You go ahead."

"Thanks. If you want to fold them, use the kitchen. The basement isn't terrible, especially for an old house, but it's not my favorite place, either. Someday I'm going to move the washer and dryer upstairs."

"Where would you put them?" Lainie stood near the basement door.

"Well, the upstairs bathroom is huge. I think a smaller stackable set would fit nicely in the corner. Like anything, it's the money that dictates when and how." Jennie wasn't whining, she was just stating a fact. "Anyway, thanks for getting the towels."

It wasn't long before both Jennie and Lainie were bathed and relaxing in their rooms. Jennie prayed—thanking God for Lainie's safety and for the resources to help her friend.

Lainie was just learning to talk to God. She thanked him for her friends and asked what she ever did to receive so much kindness. She wasn't sure where the next thought came from, but she heard a little voice in her head.

Share what you've been given.

An idea was slowly starting to take shape. Lainie drifted off to a comfortable sleep.

THE NEXT MORNING, Jennie and Lainie somehow finished the barn chores, and were ready for church in record time—actually, with a little time to spare.

Waiting in the kitchen, Jennie leaned on the kitchen counter, watching out the window for Jeremy.

"There's your ride, Lainie. Trina is in the drive and turning her truck around. Hey, ask Trina if she wants to meet Jeremy and me for lunch again. If not, that's ok, too. It's not like we have many choices in Appleridge on Sunday, but I thought The Café had a good brunch last week."

"I did, too. It was good. I'll check with Trina and we'll catch up with you after church." With that, she was out the door.

Jennie decided to wait outside for Jeremy. She locked the house, and before she could take a seat on the porch, Jeremy arrived. She motioned for him to stay in the car, and she would walk down the drive and shut the gate. He didn't have any trouble understanding her sign language.

"You look great." Jeremy reached over and took her hand.

"Thanks, I clean up really good."

"You sure do—especially for a horse girl." Jeremy loved kidding with Jennie. She could always give it right back on most days, but not today. Today she looked serious.

"You know how we talked about a future and how we don't really know God's plan for our lives? I thought maybe we should make sure we're on the same page about a few things after marriage. And we both want marriage, if possible."

"Ok, what are you thinking?" Jeremy didn't think they had enough time for that sort of discussion, but he was willing to give Jennie a chance to share what she obviously had on her mind.

"Well, what about a family? Do you want children?"

"Yes, definitely. Do you?"

"Yeah, good so far." Jennie thought he would want children because he was so good with his nephew.

"What else is on your mind, Jennie girl?"

"Could you see yourself living at the farm? How about a horse? Do you want a horse again? Are you ok with me always having a horse?"

"I can't see you without a horse." Jeremy was being serious but smiling at the same time. "I can see myself with a horse, or maybe a driving pony. I'm getting pretty attached to driving Riley and Stuffin."

"I'd like to have a driving pony, too. Hey, maybe we could get a pair. Drive a pair and also drive them separately."

"And they could also provide pony time for our future children."

"That sounds like a good plan." Jennie loved the way Jeremy followed her thoughts.

"Anything else? I'm doing pretty good, two for two." They were near the church and wouldn't have much time to finish this discussion.

"Well, we already know the importance of our faith in a good marriage. I think we're good there." Jennie thought a moment. "That's it—faith, family, and horses. I think I've covered everything on my mind. You'll get your chance after church."

"I don't have anything right now. Faith, family, and horses covers it for me, too. Don't forget friends. I have a few hobbies. I like to read, play golf, and I enjoy some online gaming with friends from college. I don't suppose you would have a problem with any of those things. At least if I promised not to make you play golf or play on my Xbox?" Jeremy knew the answer. Jennie often read while he played and didn't seem to mind.

"No problem. I think it's good to have some free time once in a while." Looking at Jeremy's face she quickly added. "No offense, but Lainie and I discussed that very thing last night. We give each other personal space but still enjoy doing some things together.

"Oh, that was a pretend sad face?"

"It was good, wasn't it?" He was trying to keep his sad face, but the corners of his mouth refused to stay down. "I know what you mean. Everyone needs time to be by themselves. It's a time to rest. I think hobbies only become a problem if they put their hobby before helping their spouse. You know, like if I went with friends to play golf but never gave you free time to do what you wanted to do. I guess that's not a big problem until the kids arrive."

"It's like the church message a few weeks ago—about finding happiness in serving others. I know Pastor wasn't necessarily applying it to marriage, but I can see how it would be important in a marriage." Jennie thought so, anyway.

"I think so. It's funny, but we live in a world that teaches us to take care of ourselves first, but really, that isn't what God calls us to do, and I don't think that's where we find true happiness. If we found happiness putting ourselves first, there wouldn't be a need for so many self-help books."

Jennie nodded. "Yeah, you're right."

"We better hurry. Church is starting."

They ran from the parking lot to the front doors of the church, holding hands and laughing. Jeremy opened the big door and Jennie stopped to straighten her clothes before walking inside. It was hard for her to keep the huge smile off her face, but she didn't need to worry. In this church, smiles were always welcome.

LAINIE FOUND TODAY'S service just as good as her first week. She loved the music. All her life she thought church music was a little boring, but not here. Today they were raising the rafters. She smiled when Jeremy and Jennie walked in during the first song. They sat three rows up, at the other end from Lainie and Trina. They didn't seem embarrassed to walk in late, and no one turned to give them a reproaching glare for being late. Instead, they got smiles.

The message was about being generous with your time, talents, and gifts. Well, thought Lainie, it was certainly obvious that her new friends understood and lived that message. She was surely on the receiving end of their generosity, and, yes, it was such a wonderful blessing in her life. It felt good, and it gave her strength.

After church, Jeremy and Jennie waited to talk about lunch. Lainie had already asked Trina and discovered Trina had planned a lunch at her farm.

"Hey, guys, do you want to join us for lunch again?" When Jennie and Jeremy nodded, she continued, "I have a lunch planned out at the farm, if you're interested. I like cooking, and I never get to do much unless my friends visit. Can I interest you in a crock pot full of soup, freshly baked bread, and an apple pie?" Trina knew from the sparkle in their eyes they wouldn't say no.

Jeremy spoke up first, "You had me at homemade soup." He looked at Jennie.

"Me, too, it sounds perfect."

"Ok, meet you out there in a few minutes." She turned to leave.

"Wait, can we bring anything?" Jennie didn't know what, but she could always stop at the store.

"Not this time. Just bring your appetite." Trina and Lainie both waved bye and left the church. Trina wanted to get home and pop the bread in the oven to warm before her guests arrived.

WITH LUNCH OVER, Jeremy leaned back in his chair and patted his stomach. "That was delicious. You're a very good cook. I'm not sure I can handle a piece of pie right now, but it looks delicious."

Trina got up to clear the dishes and Lainie helped. She motioned for Jennie to stay seated with Jeremy. "We can visit a while and then have it later, if you aren't in a hurry. I know Lainie has an appointment at two but it's only twelve-thirty now."

They walked out to the porch overlooking a pasture and the barn. Trina had several rocking chairs and Jeremy sat on the porch steps.

"You have a beautiful place here." Jeremy turned to tell Trina.

"Thanks, I love it." She didn't offer more, but Jennie wondered what brought her to Appleridge. She decided to ask a few questions. She was interested.

"Do you have a large boarding business?" Jennie didn't want to press too much. She would be able to tell how much to ask based on Trina's answers.

"I have six boarders. There are eight stalls in the barn, but boarding horses is more a labor of love than a big money maker.

I enjoy the boarders I have, and I can do most of the work my-self, especially when the horses have plenty of pasture time. Any more horses and I would need to hire help, and that would defi-nitely steal any profit I make. I'm pretty careful about who I bring to the farm. My main business is hosting clinics and events. You host for a few days and then the work goes home until next time." She laughed and looked at Jennie. "I noticed you only have four boarders; is it a source of income?"

"Yes and no. It's a little extra income if I'm careful. It helps pay for my horse, Julep, and I enjoy the company. I want to give really good care, and when you buy nice hay, and feed plenty of it, it's hard to come out ahead. The cost of hay is my biggest ex-pense. I thought about hosting clinics, but I'm not really set up for one yet." Jennie loved her boarders, but it was hard to keep the fees down and make a little profit.

"I have ten acres in hay and I split the crop with a farmer who bales all over the county. I give them use of my land, and they use their equipment and labor. It's a pretty good deal." Trina continued, "Depending on the number of cuttings each summer, I have plenty to feed my barn. Sometimes I have a little to sell, too."

"I'm interested if you're selling. I'm always looking for hay. I can't store enough for the entire year." Jennie knew she would need to build some sort of hay storage eventually. It was always less expensive to purchase hay in the summer, or better yet, right out of the field when it's baled.

"I'm done for this year, but I'll keep you in mind for next year." Trina motioned to the barn. "I see we have some activity down at the barn. It's a beautiful afternoon." She looked at

Lainie. "Maybe you could come back after your appointment. The girls were thrilled with what they learned last week, and I'm sure they would love to work with you again today."

When Lainie didn't answer right away, she apologized. "I'm sorry, Lainie, it sounds like I'm trying to take advantage of you. The girls don't expect free lessons every week. They can pay something. Maybe not Follow the Leader prices, but you shouldn't teach for free, either."

"No, its fine, I was just thinking about offering lessons in the area. I wouldn't mind clients here at your barn, if you're agreeable, but I should pay a barn fee if I teach here."

"Heck, I would just be happy if you were here helping my boarders. It makes my life easier if humans and horses are communicating." She waited a moment, then said, "I'll tell you what, if you teach a clinic here, I'll charge a fee. If you're only teaching my boarders, no fee; after all, they already pay to keep their horses here at the farm. Opening the farm for an instructor is a perk. Or at least should be."

"It's a deal." Lainie felt like she was already establishing a business in Appleridge. She couldn't help but be nervous about meeting with Dr. Peterson. I was hard for her to pay attention to the conversation. Her thoughts were somewhere else.

Jeremy had been quiet during the conversation. "I think I could handle a piece of that pie now. I don't want to miss my chance."

"Sure thing. How about everyone else? Who wants pie?" Trina was already on her feet and standing by the door.

A chorus of me, me, and me followed. Who could turn down apple pie? They followed Trina into the house, ready to grab their pieces.

There wasn't much talking as the friends ate. There was only the sound of smacking lips and a yum here and there.

"This is great, Trina. The whole lunch was delicious. Thanks so much for this treat." Jennie couldn't imagine putting the last bite in her mouth, but she couldn't imagine leaving it on her plate, either. It was too good.

After they practically licked their plates clean, Trina collected them for the dishwasher. She seemed a little embarrassed with all the compliments.

"I love to cook. It was my pleasure. Thanks for the company."

Lainie, Jennie, and Jeremy walked out to the SUV. They were quiet—either too full to talk, or too focused on leasing a barn.

"I'll drop you both off but won't stay. I'm going to my sister's house. I promised Daniel I would throw a football with him and take him to the Dairy Queen. You're going to your mom and dad's tonight, right?"

"Yes, we're reviving the Sunday night supper tradition after a short break." She turned to look at Lainie in the back seat. "My mom calls it Sunday night supper. We gather for a simple meal and a bit of catch up. You're welcome to come, Lainie."

"Oh thanks, but I don't want to invade your family time." She really didn't.

"You're going to have to meet my family sooner or later, but I warn you, my sisters are not horse girls, my nephews are wild toddlers, but my brothers-in-law are pretty skilled with tools, so it's all good."

"Well, that's certainly enticing, but I guess it depends on what happens in the next few hours. I may be busy planning my future." Lainie was very optimistic. "I think I'll be fine staying at your house. I want to meet your family, but maybe not tonight. I bought a few of my favorite things at the grocery. I'll find something to eat later, although I can't imagine eating another thing. I'm really stuffed."

"Yeah, that pie hit the spot. It was so good but I'm too full. I could take a nap, but I know it's better to keep moving to help it digest."

They arrived at Jennie's farm. Jeremy kissed Jennie and gave Lainie a hug. "It's been a pleasure, ladies."

It was only one-thirty. The girls went into the house to use the bathroom and freshen up a little. Jennie decided to change into jeans. Lainie was already wearing jeans so she was comfortable.

"Do you want me to stay with you or leave while you talk to Dr. Peterson? I'm ok either way."

"I want you to stay so we can talk about it later, and feel free to ask questions. You know the area, and the Petersons, and may think of things that I miss."

The Peterson farm was only a couple of miles as the crow flies, so they arrived a few minutes early.

As they drove into the farm lane, Lainie spied the barn sitting in front of the house and to the right. "Oh, my, it's really cute. And I love the arena."

"Yeah, I hung out here a lot during high school, Megan's sister, Belinda, is my best friend. There's an old barn in back of the house, and it's been fixed up as a really cute storage place, and the main floor is used for gatherings. They tried not to change the look. It's neat but wasn't the best barn for horses. You'll see. The separate drive to the barn makes it an ideal barn to lease. Students won't be near the house and it even has a little half-bath in the barn and a full bath in the upstairs apartment. Heck, I've always wanted to live there." Jennie was enjoying the look on Lainie's face. "Belinda and I stayed out in the apartment on occasion. It was fun. Everything is in one room. Well, except the bathroom; it's private. It's not big, but I bet it's bigger than your horse trailer living quarters."

Jennie parked Blue Boy and they walked to the house.

"Come in, ladies." Dr. Peterson greeted them at the door. "Susan, this is Lainie." He introduced his wife.

"It's so nice to meet you, Lainie, I'm sorry about your accident, but what a blessing that you and your horse will heal." Susan gave Lainie a hug. "Sorry, I'm a hugger, and now you're one of my girls like this one with you. She's like another daughter." Susan gave Jennie a hug, holding on a little longer. "Come on in the kitchen, our favorite meeting place. Do you girls want anything?"

Both Jennie and Lainie explained they were fine and still stuffed from Trina's lunch. Dr. Peterson, never one for small talk, spoke up. "Let's walk on out to the barn. We can't discuss what you haven't seen."

On the walk to the barn, Lainie finally found her voice. "From what I can see, I love it. The arena is perfect. Not too big, not too small, and the barn is cute."

"Wait, Lainie, don't say anything more, Dr. Peterson will up the price." Jennie was teasing, but Lainie's face showed that she wasn't so sure. She glanced at Dr. Peterson and was relieved to see him smiling.

Jennie loved seeing Belinda's dad so relaxed. That was a huge change for him. She knew it had something to do with his trip to South Carolina, meeting Dr. Bobby Gray, and rescuing both Megan and Julep, but she wondered how the experience made such a huge change in a father who was usually detached and demanding. It was like he discovered how much he valued his family.

They walked through the barn and then upstairs to see the apartment. "I love it; it's perfect. Let's talk money."

Dr. Peterson loved Lainie's ability to get right to the point. "Ok, we can lease it on a monthly basis, or whatever length you desire. You will need to have insurance to cover you and your students. I would like all students to sign a liability waiver for the farm. We will lease the barn and five acres, nothing near the house, and students should stay here and not approach the house. You'll be responsible for mowing the pasture, but you may use my tractor. It's small and easy to use. What do you think so far?"

"Good so far. I already have insurance for students and myself. It's required by Follow the Leader."

"Actually, that's the only concern I have—your connection to Follow the Leader. I put Brock Rodgers in the same pot as old JJ, and that's a very black pot."

"Dr. Peterson, I understand. I plan on severing my tie to Follow the Leader, although that isn't public knowledge yet. There won't be any advertisement for the program by the time I officially open for lessons."

Adrian seemed pleased with that answer. "What about boarding horses? Megan doesn't want to leave Jennie's farm. You'll need another horse, but will you board as part of your business?"

"I don't want to operate a boarding barn. My focus is education. I have a teaching degree and taught elementary education for two years. I'm a skilled instructor. That's my focus. I may board one horse to keep with Shadow, but it would need to be someone recommended by you or Jennie. I also may buy a nice pony for lessons ff I can find a nice lesson pony, and that's a whole other topic."

"How about leasing the barn, apartment, and five acres of pasture for six hundred a month?" Adrian was ready to make a deal.

"I would say that's a steal, Dr. Peterson. It's worth a lot more."

"Yes, but can you get a business started and pay more?"

"It would be hard."

"I thought so. I want this to work and I'm getting six hundred dollars a month for a barn that has been sitting empty, plus I'm getting my pasture mowed. I can't complain. But, to be clear, I don't know what will happen when Belinda finishes school. I'll only guarantee a lease until that time."

"I understand, and if all goes well, I'll be ready to purchase my own farm by then."

"Good, let's shake, and I'll have my lawyer draw up a simple lease with everything we discussed. Now, I'll leave you ladies here to explore. I have a football game to watch."

They said goodbye and waited for Adrian to leave before grabbing hands, jumping up and down, and trying not to scream.

Jennie spoke first. "I'm so excited for you. You have a place to live and a barn. Can you pay six hundred? It's more than worth it, but still, that's a lot of money when you're just getting started."

"I have a little bit saved and good insurance on the truck and trailer. I'm a little embarrassed to share this, but the truck and trailer are paid for, and I don't have school debt or any other debt. Well, unless Brock Rodgers tries to sue me."

After seeing Jennie's surprised face, she continued, "Mom and Dad paid for college. They didn't want to mess with writing checks every month, so they gave me a set amount each year, and it was plenty. I paid my tuition and banked the rest. I worked at a stable near the college and lived in an apartment over the barn. Not as cute as this one but it worked. I was driven to save every cent and buy Skippy. You know that didn't happen, but I left school with a degree, no debt, and enough money to study with Brock, and that wasn't cheap. And, I still had enough to buy my truck and horse trailer."

"Wow, that's impressive." And Jennie was impressed. She motioned to Blue Boy. "Tell me about it on the ride home."

The word *home* was one Lainie seldom used. She smiled; that would soon change. "I worked hard but I also know I was fortunate my parents paid for college. They never asked where I lived, and they never visited. I guess they thought I had enough money to afford something really nice, so they didn't care."

"They never visited?" Jennie thought that was sad, but she also realized it was probably why Lainie wasn't eager to meet her family. She didn't know what it was like to have good family time together.

"It was actually good they didn't visit. It may have foiled my plan." She never had much connection with her parents, so she didn't miss seeing them during college. "I went home a few times, but they were always off somewhere on most holidays."

Jennie was determined to change Lainie's idea about family as soon as possible. She and Jeremy, Trina, Cassy, Megan, and Marcy would become Lainie's family.

"Everything looks like I could move in tomorrow."

"Yeah, it looks like Mrs. Peterson came up here recently and gave it a good cleaning. She probably did it as soon as Doc mentioned you were interested."

"Do you call him Doc to his face?"

"Oh, no, it's always Dr. Peterson. When Belinda and I were younger we called him, Herr Doktor, because he was always barking orders. Then we shortened it to Doc. It seemed a little nicer."

"He seems really nice."

"Well, yes, he is very nice and a very good vet. He doesn't bark out orders anymore. He's mellowed quite a bit."

"Hey, I'm looking at trucks this week. As soon as I have transportation, I'll get out of your hair."

"You've only been with me a few days. I'm not that bad, am I? Jennie knew she snored at night, but she didn't think she was a bad roommate.

"It's been great and I'm truly thankful." Lainie fought to be independent, but she didn't know what would have happened without Jennie's help.

"And I'm truly thankful for all your help yesterday. What a blessing to have you do all the trimming while I mowed."

"I'm pretty good at weed eating. Anyone who does an internship with Brock Rodgers knows how to handle a weed eater."

"I thought you were there for horsemanship?" Jennie remembered Megan telling her about all the work she did at JJ's ranch. "I guess JJ copied that idea from Brock, too."

"I'm sure he did. Free labor is pretty attractive. You wouldn't believe some of the jobs I've done while supposedly learning horsemanship. That's probably why Brock is so miffed about anyone missing the instructor gathering. We always work on what he calls team projects. It means we all work at his place and he likes to call us a team."

"Well, anyway, I'm thankful for your help and glad it was offered."

Lainie thought helping someone because you wanted to be helpful sure felt a lot different than being ordered to help.

They both went to the barn to feed the horses. It didn't take long and Jennie needed to leave for her parents' home and Sunday night supper. She hoped Grandpa would be there. She hadn't seen him in a week, and that was unusual.

Lainie opted to stay out in the barn for a while. "Have a good time, Jennie; I'll see you later. I've got a lot of planning to do." And she did.

Once Lainie was back in the house she opened her new laptop computer. This would be a fun night to work on plans for her new business and her new barn. She decided to send another email to Follow the Leader, notifying the organization she was unable to attend the instructor gathering. She was praying they would kick her out and end the contract. She needed to remember to put on a good act if Brock should happen to call again.

Chapter Fourteen

The next week proved to be busy for everyone. Jennie returned to the Chronicle office ready to work on the next edition. Lainie found a new truck she thought was perfect. With insurance money in hand, she paid cash. Finding the horse trailer would be more difficult. She wanted the same brand of trailer as before and they were hard to find used. If her business took off, she would consider purchasing something new.

Jennie asked Sam to stop out at the farm so she could introduce Lainie. Lainie would need a farrier for Shadow, and possibly for students. Jennie laughed, thinking Sam would definitely be on the approved boarder list for Dr. Peterson. She also thought Sam would probably appreciate a lower boarding fee than he was currently paying. If Sam moved Sadie to Lainie's barn, she wouldn't need to buy another horse—at least not right away. That meant Sam was really doing Lainie a favor.

When Jennie explained the situation to Lainie, she agreed and figured out what feed and hay would cost and named an amount that would just barely cover the expense. It felt good to help Sam just as all the others were helping her. Lainie decided that generosity was contagious. She knew what it felt like to be in an organization where everyone was just looking out for self. It wasn't good. Being with people who were generous with their time, money, and friendship was a true blessing. Lainie wanted to be that kind of person, and that kind of teacher.

Once Lainie was in possession of her new truck, she moved her things into the barn apartment. Sam was moving Sadie Thursday night and promised to pick up Shadow and bring her, also. Lainie couldn't wait. She thought about asking Jennie to bring Shadow using the Petersons' horse trailer still parked at her farm, but Sam offered, and that made everything easy, plus Shadow was happy in her temporary herd.

Lainie purchased hay, feed, shavings for the stalls, and a few other items for the barn. She was thankful Jeremy and Jennie rescued her buckets, rake, broom, and other small things from the wrecked trailer. She didn't need to purchase those things. The apartment had a day bed in the corner, a chair for seating, and stools at the counter bar for her meals. It also had a small refrigerator and stove. She didn't need much—it was perfect. She would use the same sheets and towels from her travels in the horse trailer, but eventually, she would put more thought into decorating. Right now, she was more interested in setting up the barn and preparing for students.

Lainie decided to form an LLC and officially name her business Lainie Anderson Horsemanship, but for advertising she would use Lessons with Lainie. She would get a sign made and place flyers in the feed store.

Brock didn't call, but she received an email asking for a mailing address and the Petersons gave her permission to use their address. Several days later she received a certified letter officially ending her association with Follow the Leader. She knew many of her friends would be shocked when it was announced at the instructor gathering the following week. She also knew several would call and want the scoop, but Lainie decided to stay positive and simply say she found a wonderful opportunity in Appleridge. No need to share the whole story. Lainie would always value the time she spent with Follow the Leader and the skill it added to her horsemanship. Traveling on the road had started to wear thin a long time ago, and she couldn't blame that on the program, or on Brock. It felt better to focus on the positive, and maybe, just maybe, this was God's plan.

With the festival and parade scheduled for the upcoming weekend, Jennie's barn was a beehive of activity. They painted cardboard and used zip ties to connect the shapes to Marcy's marathon carriage, turning it into a treasure chest. Megan and Cassy finished the sashes and masks. They were all very pleased with the results and couldn't wait until Saturday afternoon.

Lainie decided to enter the parade driving her truck with signs on both sides, and maybe a few fall decorations like straw bales, mums, and scarecrows in the bed that could be seen with the tailgate down. She decided to ignore the theme. She didn't consider herself a float and wouldn't be judged. Well, maybe she would add a basket or two of shiny apples—just to get in the spirit of the day. She wanted to introduce Lessons with Lainie. She could make signs that said, *Become the Apple of Your Horse's Eye.* That would be cute.

Mrs. Williams was very disappointed that Megan refused to ride on her golf cart. Feeling bad, Megan and Cassy invited Mrs. Williams to Jennie's barn to visit as they worked on the decorations. She was thrilled when Lainie asked her to ride in her truck and throw candy out the window. Lainie also promised that Moose could ride with them.

Moose, a gentle giant of a dog, lay in the barn aisle beside Mrs. Williams's chair. Watching the love Mrs. Williams had for her dog, and the way he laid at her feet, Lainie decided to visit the local animal shelter and find a nice farm dog. Maybe not quite as large as Moose, but she wanted to find one that could be a nice companion. She wasn't afraid to live alone, especially with the Petersons nearby, but sometimes she did get lonely.

The next evening, both Mrs. Williams and Jennie's grandpa sat in the barn aisle watching them work. The girls enjoyed hearing their banter. Grandpa was a little older than Mrs. Williams, but they were long-time friends.

"Well, missy, you are sure looking as young and beautiful as you did in high school. You haven't changed a bit." Jennie looked over at Grandpa. Was he flirting with Mrs. Williams?

"Now, Charlie, you and I both know we're showing our ages, but I thank you for the compliment, nonetheless." She actually did look younger when she smiled.

"You always were one of the prettiest girls in Appleridge, Lizzie. Of course, these young ladies sure give you some competition."

Mrs. Williams laughed. "They are a pretty bunch, that's for sure, and so very creative. Why just look at this carriage all decorated up like a treasure box."

"Mr. Gantzler, I'm decorating the bed of my truck. Maybe you and Mrs. Williams could ride back there in chairs, throwing candy." Lainie thought maybe Mr. Gantzler wanted to be in the parade, too.

Megan spoke up quickly. "And Cassy and I can make you sashes to wear to look like ours, or maybe yours could say, *Keeping our Eye on Appleridge.*

"I love that idea, Megan." Jennie looked at the two seniors. "What do you think?"

"Why that sounds like fun. How about you, Charlie, are you interested in a parade?" Mrs. Williams looked as coy as a teenager.

"I am, but only if Moose also wears a sash. I bet he keeps his eyes on Appleridge."

It was settled. Cassy and Megan took out their supplies to make three more sashes, and Lainie added a few things to her list of supplies needed for the parade. What fun. She couldn't wait.

Lainie offered to take Mrs. Williams and Mr. Gantzler home. "I need to stop at the grocery, so it's not out of my way." It wasn't very late, but both seniors we're ready to turn in for the night. They left after hugs for the girls and promises to find something black to wear.

After they left, Cassy said, "They're so cute. Do you think they're interested in spending more time together?'"

"I'm not sure, but I've never seen my grandpa flirting with a woman before, so maybe something is happening. I guess we'll just have to see how they behave in the parade." Jennie also knew the entire town of Appleridge would be buzzing after their parade debut. That's the way things get started in a small town.

"He called her Lizzie. I never knew Mrs. Williams had a first name." Megan added quickly, "Well, I knew she had a first name, but I didn't know what it was."

"I think it's Elizabeth, but I've never heard anyone call her by her first name, either. Lizzie is so cute for a name. Did you see her blush?" Jennie was sure she saw the color rise in Mrs. Williams's wrinkled cheeks, and it wasn't what her grandma would call rouge, either.

After Lainie left, the others finished quickly and put away their supplies. They were quite pleased with themselves and the parade entry.

Marcy spoke as she brushed off her jeans. "I think that's everything unless Lainie wants our help decorating her truck. I'll pick up a few fall things to add to whatever she brings. I could always set them by the door to my apartment after the parade. I haven't had time to decorate at home yet."

"We can't forget the candy. We'll need lots of candy but someone else will have to store our cache!" Cassy knew she couldn't be the keeper of the candy. "I don't trust myself, and I don't think you should trust Megan, either."

"No, don't trust me, and I know Jennie has a sweet tooth, so Marcy, I guess that means you. Can we trust you with the candy?" Megan was serious.

"Oh, the things I do for my friends." Marcy raised her eyes to the sky. "If it's not open, I'll be ok, but maybe you could just bring it with you on Saturday?"

They agreed to each pick up a couple of bags of Halloween candy sometime between now and Saturday—and not to open any of the bags.

LAINIE DROPPED off Mrs. Williams at her small house near the ball fields and Mr. Gantzler at his apartment, then drove to the grocery store. She saw Jeremy walking to his SUV as she climbed out of her truck.

"Hey, Jeremy," Lainie called, getting his attention.

Jeremy pushed his cart in her direction. "Lainie, I thought you ladies were at Jennie's tonight finishing up the parade decorations."

"We were. I needed a few things at the store, so I dropped Jennie's grandpa and Mrs. Williams off and here I am."

"Did you finish the decorations? Why were Mr. Gantzler and Mrs. Williams at Jennie's?" Jeremy thought Charlie probably just wanted to visit.

"Just to visit, and Megan was trying to get Mrs. Williams involved because she thought her feelings were hurt when she didn't want to ride on her golf cart in the parade. They're both going to ride in the back of my truck and throw candy."

"They'll love that. I think they went to school together, way back when."

"Yeah, they did. They were funny teasing each other and reminiscing about the good old days."

"Hey, Jeremy, you always seem to have a nice way of helping people understand the important things in life. May I ask you a question? Or, should we meet another time?" Jeremy already felt like a friend to Lainie, but she didn't want Jeremy to think she was trying to make their friendship anything more, so she added, "I don't mind sharing my thoughts with Jennie. It's been busy at the barn, and since I moved into the apartment, we haven't had any time to talk much."

"Sure, what are you doing tomorrow? I'm going out to Jennie's."

"Well, Sam is moving Shadow for me tomorrow night. Maybe you could come out to my new place? It wouldn't matter if he was there to hear our conversation."

For a brief moment, Jeremy thought about Lainie and Sam at the same barn. "I promised to have dinner with Jennie; how about if we come out after dinner?"

"That would be perfect. I'll buy something for dessert." Lainie really didn't like to cook much but she loved ice cream.

"Ok, see you then. I'll call if Jennie made other plans."

"They said goodbye, and as Jeremy loaded his groceries into his SUV, he chastised himself for the brief but disconcerting thought he had about Sam and Lainie. Lainie was a very attractive girl with a great personality, but Sam loved Belinda, and they both seemed to be honest people.

Jeremy called Jennie when he finished putting groceries away. They talked for a long while. Jennie was very excited about the parade and the fun of decorating the carriage. She filled Jeremy in on her grandpa and Mrs. Williams.

"He called her Lizzie; it was so cute." Jennie couldn't help sharing her grandpa's flirtation with Jeremy.

"Lizzie, wow, it'll be hard to call her Mrs. Williams knowing that." Jeremy couldn't quite see himself calling Mrs. Williams anything but Mrs. Williams. "She's a nice lady, though. She's always been very kind to me and brought several good casseroles to the house after Sarah and I lost Mom."

"Yes, she's a nice lady. Funny, I never wondered about her life much. I don't remember Mr. Williams."

"Me, either, but I think I'll ask around, just because I'm curious."

Jeremy told Jennie about seeing Lainie at the grocery store and her invitation to talk. "Are you ok going over after dinner tomorrow? She said Sam may be there. I guess he's picking up Shadow tomorrow."

"Yes, and I'll try to get home from work early, if possible. The office has been crazy, but fun crazy." Jennie was feeling a little stressed at work, but she didn't want to complain. Complaining never helped her feel better. Besides, it always made little things grow into large things.

"I'm home tomorrow, but I have a paper to write. Hey, you wouldn't—"

Jennie cut him off before he finished. "Very funny; no, I'm not doing your homework, Mr. Jeremy James."

"Just kidding, I love to get a rise out of you." Jeremy could hear the smile in her voice.

"I better hang up so I can get my rest—and you can start on that paper."

"Ok, sweet dreams; love you." Jeremy didn't think he would start a paper tonight. He would go to bed and start fresh tomorrow. His sweet dreams would be all about Jennie. He wouldn't think about a possible relationship between Lainie and Sam, other than a relationship between good friends. Jeremy didn't know why he couldn't get the strange thought out of his head, but he sure was going to try. He didn't care for making assumptions, especially wrong assumptions.

AS JENNIE WALKED upstairs to her bedroom, she wondered about Lainie and Sam. Maybe her suggestion for Sam to board Sadie at Lainie's barn wasn't such a great idea. No, she thought,

Sam loves Belinda, and the Petersons were just up the lane. It wasn't fair to either Sam or Lainie to make the wrong assumption. But still, Jennie's prayer list would be long tonight. She would start with asking God to help her mind her own business and let him take care of everything else.

Chapter Fifteen

ennie rushed home from the Chronicle to finish her barn chores. She wouldn't have much time to spend in the barn tonight. She spotted Lainie's new truck parked at the barn. She was sad to think this would be the last evening that Lainie and Shadow would be at her farm, and she prayed a quick prayer that Lainie's business would be booming soon. But she also hoped Lainie would have time to stop by for a visit from time to time.

Jennie rushed into the house and changed her clothes. Just as she started her walk out to the barn, Sam pulled into the farm with his horse trailer. She waved and continued walking.

"Hey, Lainie, I'm glad I made it home before you left. I wanted to make sure this was not a goodbye, but a see you later."

"It's definitely a see you later." Lainie didn't want to stop seeing her new friends. "Shadow and I enjoyed our stay, but now it's time to get our new life started, and you're a huge part of our new life." Lainie never had many close friends, but Jennie was becoming a very good friend. "I already tempted you with ice cream tonight."

"Yes, you did!" Jennie laughed.

"Hi, Sam, do you have sweet Sadie in there, too?" Jennie motioned to the trailer.

"Yup, she's ready for her new home. She didn't get too much pasture time at her old barn. She'll enjoy more freedom at the

Petersons', oops, I mean Lainie's barn." Sam looked a little red in the face.

"You're right, Sam, the barn does belong to the Petersons. I'm only borrowing it for a while." Lainie thought it was cute that Sam was embarrassed. She could tell he was trying to make a good impression. He seemed shy on the several occasions they met.

It didn't take Lainie long to load Shadow into the trailer. After spending hours and hours helping Shadow become confident walking into a horse trailer again, today everyone witnessed the result—a horse in a horse trailer accident that learned to trust again. It was probably one of the biggest challenges Lainie had ever faced with a horse. Shadow was terrified, but Lainie slowly built her confidence. Jennie watched several sessions at night, and she also knew Lainie did quite a bit during the day while she was at work.

"I'm so impressed. I watched you patiently introduce tight spaces, and then the trailer, to Shadow. I learned quite a bit by watching you with your girl. You really are a skilled horse-woman."

"It was nice Dr. Peterson told you to park their trailer here, and then agreed to my using it for practice. I'm very proud of my brave girl."

"You should be," Sam said. "I admit, while I was driving over here, I wondered if we were in for a marathon trailer loading night."

"I think trailer loading a horse is one of the most important skills for anyone to learn. Well, that, and how to teach a horse how to stand quietly for the farrier." Lainie looked at Sam.

"I sure agree with you on that, but you wouldn't believe how many horses find it difficult to stand quietly on three legs."

"Sure. When you think about it, lifting and holding one leg takes away their ability to flee if anything should attack. In their world, they think like that. I'm not sure why people skip that step, but horses need to learn how to trust having their leg held up—and also how to balance on three legs."

Lainie didn't want to climb up on her soap box while the horses were waiting in the trailer. "I'll save the rest of my thoughts for later. Let's get these girls to their new home. I'll follow."

Jennie waved as they pulled out of her drive, first Sam with his horse trailer, and then Lainie in her new candy apple red truck.

Jennie went up to the house to check the vegetable soup she started in the slow cooker that morning. She would put garlic bread in the oven and maybe shred some cheese to add to the soup. It was an easy dinner and she hoped it tasted good on this nice fall evening with her favorite friend.

JEREMY LEANED BACK in his chair and patted his stomach. "That was good soup. I better stop eating like this or I won't be in very good shape for my mission trip."

"Have you learned anything more?" Jennie took their bowls to the sink, as Jeremy picked up the placemats and breadbasket.

"I've narrowed my choices down to two organizations that lead missions into Appalachia. The school has been involved with both. One seems better suited for a six-month mission. My advisor suggested giving both a try on short-term trips before I sign on for six months. I think that is a pretty good idea."

"That does seem like a good idea. If you take the whole semester off school, you could actually take a bunch of different trips in different areas."

"I could. And, if we sell Mom's house, it will help fund the time away."

"And the rest of your education when you decide what you want to do."

"Yes, that's true."

They finished cleaning up the kitchen and prepared to leave for Lainie's barn.

"Do you know what Lainie wants to talk about?" Jennie was curious.

"No, but I think it has something to do with her newfound faith. She said Sam could stick around, so it must not be private."

LAINIE HAD FOUR CHAIRS set up in the barn aisle when they arrived. Sam already sat in one and was watching Shadow and Sadie graze side by side in the dusk.

"It looks like introducing Sadie and Shadow was pretty much a non-event." Jennie motioned to the two mares grazing contently.

"Yeah, they danced around a little but nothing much happened. They seem pretty happy." Sam got up to shake Jeremy's hand as he talked.

"Hey, Jennie, will you help me bring down the bowls of ice cream? What do you guys want to drink? I have water and water."

"I think I'll have water. What about you, Sam?" Jeremy sat down.

"Why I think water is fine for me, too."

The girls laughed.

Lainie called out, "Four bottles of water coming right up along with four bowls of ice cream."

As they enjoyed their ice cream, dusk turned into evening, and Lainie turned on a battery lantern Jennie remembered saving from the wrecked trailer.

"I didn't want to turn on the bright barn lights, if this is ok."

"Good idea, less bugs." Jeremy finished his ice cream and sat the bowl on the concrete floor by his chair.

"Ok, I'll get started. Jeremy, you're pretty good at this God stuff. It's all new to me, so I have questions."

Jennie noticed Sam looked a little uncomfortable as he sat quietly.

"I'm not an expert but what do you want to know?"

Jennie looked at Jeremy and smiled. This was right up his alley. He loved sharing his faith. She finished her ice cream and relaxed into her chair to enjoy the conversation.

"I never attended church until a few weeks ago. My parents don't believe in God. In fact, they make fun of all the silly people who believe in such a myth. They call those silly people uneducated and gullible. To my parents, education is what gives a person worth."

Lainie glanced over at Sam because he made a noise that sounded like air escaping through his teeth.

"Sorry, I didn't mean to interrupt, but I've been ridiculed by people like your parents my entire life. They also look at appearance and associate lack of money with ignorance."

"I know, Sam, I'm sorry." Lainie patted his arm. "I went to college and after teaching at an elementary school for a few years, I became an instructor for the Follow the Leader program. Needless to say, teaching wasn't considered an honorable profession, and teaching horsemanship wasn't even in the ballpark."

"You feel like you're a disappointment to your parents?" Jeremy said it but already knew the answer.

"Yes, I know I am."

"What did they say when you chose elementary education as your major in college?" Jennie was curious. "I think teaching is one of the most noble careers. How could your parents value education, but, yet, look down on teachers?"

"I know it doesn't make sense. Talk about ignorance. They thought I would continue with school and teach at the college level. That was acceptable, at least if I was determined to be a teacher."

No one said anything, so Lainie continued. "I love teaching. I love teaching children and I love teaching horsemanship. Sometimes I get to do both by teaching children about horses." She grinned and they saw the joy.

"I've not led a good life—not terrible, but not good, either. I've always tried to be honest and I protected my integrity but wasn't too picky about inviting a cowboy to spend the night in my trailer. I was lonely." Lainie avoided looking at the faces. She didn't want to see judgement.

"Lainie, look at me." Jeremy said softly.

Lainie looked and she didn't see judgement. She saw compassion.

"All of us here have done a few things in life that weren't our best moments. Why this girl here used to make fun of my name." Jeremy didn't look at Jennie, but he motioned with his thumb.

"Lainie, I'm not trying to make fun, but I am trying to make you smile."

Lainie smiled and continued. "I talk about people. I complain about people. I've been angry with my parents, and unhappy and lonely. I was only happy with my girl, Shadow."

"You said was—and now?" Jeremy is very astute, thought Jennie. He's a good listener.

"I arrived in little Appleridge and a friend invited me to church. I go, and to my surprise, I like it. The pastor prayed a little prayer for those who wanted to accept Christ. I'm pretty stubborn, so I didn't surrender my heart during the prayer, but I thought about it. It was the first time I sat in a church for something other than a wedding or baptism for a friend, and something happened to me. I can't explain how the message touched me, but it felt so personal.

Lainie took a drink of water. "Then I hang out with you guys, and find nothing but kindness and generosity. I thought, how does that happen? What's with these people? So—I prayed that prayer and asked God for help. And when I was so scared during the accident, I remember calling to God, and the next thing I knew, Jennie was on the phone, and Dr. Peterson came, and Shadow somehow escaped serious injury. And I'm so very thankful."

"God is with us always, Lainie, and he will turn something bad into something good, but I also want you to know, believing in God doesn't make life perfect. We still suffer hardships and loss. The difference is God is always by our side helping us through those times of loss and trouble." Jeremy paused, glanced at Jennie, then at Sam, and back to Lainie.

"I understand, Jeremy, and I felt him by my side during the accident. I think that was the first time he felt real. I'm learning to be more thankful. I don't get angry as quickly. Follow the Leader sent a certified letter basically kicking me out of the program. Yes, it's what I wanted, and even though they're saying terrible things about me, I don't feel the need to explain my side or to bad-mouth the program. I value everything I learned in the program. I'm fine. The old Lainie would have been breathing fire!"

"I'm happy for you." Jennie could see the honesty on Lainie's face. "Now what happens?"

"I'll get my business started. I'm so thankful for this barn and apartment. I feel a tug to reconnect with my parents. I'm afraid to tell them I'm a Christian. But I'm more afraid not to tell them. I've received so much peace and joy and want them to have the same peace and joy. I've been reading the bible the pastor gave me, and it says Jesus died on the cross to pay the price for my sins. They won't believe they have sins, let alone believe Jesus went to the cross because he loves them. I want my parents to believe in God, but I'm afraid that will take a modern-day miracle."

Sam was hanging onto every word. He looked at Jeremy, waiting for his response.

"Wow, what an awesome testimony, and, you're right, it's hard to explain the peace and joy people receive when they accept Jesus as their savior. Life is good for many nonbelievers, but with Jesus, life is amazing, because God is amazing. As Christians, we acknowledge our sins, but we won't suddenly become perfect. Life won't suddenly become perfect, either. But God will be by our side in good times and in bad times. His power and grace are more than enough. And because we're thankful, we want to honor God with our actions. We aren't trying to change to earn our salvation. We've already received God's perfect gift."

"Ok, explain that, please." Lainie didn't understand everything Jeremy shared.

"People think they can earn their salvation, or their way into heaven, by doing good deeds. That's impossible. We can't be good enough. But when we believe God loves us, we have a desire to show God's love with our actions. We want to love others as he loves us. We didn't earn his love, and that's called grace. As Christ followers, we're also called to love and offer grace to others. That's what you're experiencing with Brock Rodgers and your parents. A lot of things have happened to justify your anger. You may never forget those bad things, but you can be thankful for the good things, and also extend grace. Does that make sense? I'm not sure if you realized it or not, but I think you have found forgiveness."

"You mean I've been forgiven?"

"Yes, and you have also forgiven others."

"A few friends from the Follow the Leader program have asked if I'm going to sue the kid who caused the wreck. I'm so thankful, I can't possibly sue anyone. They can't understand. All they see are million-dollar signs. The insurance company would probably settle quickly for a large chunk of cash. A month ago, I would have sued just to punish him for his carelessness. Now, I get on my knees and thank God for saving me and my Shadow from serious injury. Hey, that's funny—me and my Shadow."

All four laughed and then sat quietly thinking. Lainie was thinking about everything wonderful happening in her life. Sam was thinking he wanted to learn more about having a relationship with God. He certainly felt peace from the prayer Jeremy shared the other night. Jennie was thinking about Jeremy and what a gift he had for sharing God's message in easy-to-understand words. Jeremy was praying and thanking God for giving him words to share.

"What happens next?" Jeremy wanted to hear her thoughts.

"I need to talk to God more. I guess I'm what I heard someone call a baby Christian, and I have a lot to learn."

"Yes, talk to God, but you're learning quickly. We're all learning. Life is one big learning experience."

"Thanks." Lainie hesitated and sat up straight. "Now—I'm going to be honest about a few thoughts I'm having, and I certainly don't want to offend any of you, because I treasure you as good friends. Even you, Sam; we just met, but I know we'll become really good friends."

Jennie noticed Jeremy sitting back in his chair and waiting. She was puzzled by his expression. It looked guarded.

"Well, here goes—I don't want to turn my business into a boarding business, but I will need to have a companion for Shadow." She turned to look at Sam. "I know you're here for now, but I question the wisdom of this choice. I don't want to give anyone the wrong idea, especially the Petersons. I've never met Belinda, but I've heard enough to figure out she is a pretty special person in your life."

Now Lainie turned to look at Jennie. "And I know you love your boarders, and I don't want to ruin what you've worked hard to establish, but—"

Jennie sat up. "But?"

"Once I get my lesson program started, I want to also start a performance team of young riders using jumps and other obstacles. I think both Megan and Cassy will enjoy such a program, and maybe enjoy being mentors to the other girls who would trailer in for lessons and practices."

"You want Cassy and Megan to move here?" Jennie was trying not to get angry. How dare Lainie!

"I think it will happen eventually, and I also think Sam should move Sadie to your barn."

Jennie sat saying nothing. Her mind was busy—sorting through what was said and what was innuendo. Did Lainie think Sam would cheat on Belinda with her? That was pretty arrogant. But didn't she think a similar thought—even if she shoved it out of her mind?

Jeremy watched Jennie. He could almost see her thoughts by watching her face. Sam sat with his head down. What was he thinking? Did he also question the situation? Would he be more comfortable at Jennie's?

Lainie watched all three. She felt like crying. Maybe she should have kept her big mouth shut. She wanted to do the right thing. She didn't want to hide what she thought could happen.

She didn't want to lose her friends because of any misunderstanding. She was sure the young girls would love hanging out at her barn, because they would ride with other young girls. She was also sure no matter how innocent her relationship with Sam remained it would eventually fuel small-town gossip.

"Wow." Jennie lowered her head. It seemed like forever before she looked up and continued. "I have to admit, my first emotion was anger. Fortunately, I'm getting better at thinking before I speak." Jennie noticed that Lainie looked like she was about to cry. Jeremy had a grin on his face. What? And Sam just looked uncomfortable. "And I also admit, I wondered those things myself."

Sam looked up. "Me, too. I'm not so sure I should be the only male at a barn full of teenage girls."

"I don't blame you for not wanting to deal with a barn of teenage girls," Jeremy was quick to add.

"I'm thinking ahead. There isn't any need to make any changes right now, but, eventually, I can see a few issues. This is my first night here at the barn with Sam, and when Dr. Peterson drove by slowly, Sam looked uncomfortable."

Sam nodded. "Lainie, you seem like a nice girl, but I love Belinda."

"But that's the whole point. Sometimes how the world perceives a situation often hides the truth. Don't get me wrong, I don't think I'm so wonderful you wouldn't be able to resist my charms. Goodness, no. But I also think the world may not believe the truth."

She turned to face Jennie. "And I know the girls love being at your farm. But I also know they are good riders who would love being challenged. They could trailer here for lessons and activities, and that is what will happen for a while. But how long will that happen before Dr. Peterson and Megan start to think it would be so much easier to have Starlight here on their own farm?"

"And, Cassy will follow. I understand. It's ok." Jennie did understand. She hated the thought of losing Cassy and Megan, but she understood the truth in Lainie's words.

Jeremy leaned forward in his chair. "That would be a good time for Sam to move Sadie to Jennie's, and I've been thinking about getting a horse again—us old folks could hang out at Jennie's place."

Jeremy's comment was just the right comment to make everyone comfortable again.

"Thanks for being honest, Lainie. It was uncomfortable for a while, but honesty is always better than dancing around the truth." Jennie waited for the others to comment.

Sam didn't say anything. He was thinking about how he almost lost Belinda by being afraid to share his trouble and thoughts honestly. He certainly learned a lesson about trust and truth. Belinda's recommendation for an accountant had worked a miracle. The tax bill was straightened out and his business or reputation hadn't suffered. Maybe the accountant didn't work the miracle. Maybe it was God loving him a little bit and teaching him how to love himself.

"Thanks for being honest. I'm happy to have Sadie here to keep Shadow company, but I'm in agreement a move to Jennie's farm may be a good idea—for many reasons."

"It's getting late. How about I end this evening with prayer? Everyone ok with that idea?" Jeremy reached for Jennie's hand.

Heads nodded and then bowed. Holding Jennie's hand, Jeremy reached for Lainie's on his left. The others followed, reaching for hands.

"Father, I thank you for this time together with friends sharing ice cream and truth. We love you, and we thank you for all the wonderful things you're doing in our lives. Help us to always be honest and truthful. In your precious name we pray. Amen"

"Thanks for the ice cream and stimulating conversation." Jeremy looked at Jennie and she nodded.

"Honesty is hard." Lainie walked toward Jennie to give her a hug.

"It is, but you did good, girlfriend. It didn't hurt too much." Jennie added, "You care. Some people say things that hurt and call it being honest. I don't think that's the same thing."

"I don't think so, either. Being honest isn't an excuse to blurt out hurtful things." Sam hadn't said much but he wanted to add his thoughts. "Growing up, people said cruel things to our family and pretended they said those things because they wanted to help. Maybe that's why I keep so much bottled up inside—although I'm learning the difference, thanks to my friend here." He shook Jeremy's hand. "But that's a story for another time. I still need to unhitch my trailer. Did you pick out a place for me to park? I forgot to ask if that's ok." He looked at Lainie for an answer.

"Yes, it's perfectly ok. I thought a good place would be over there along the fence, on the gravel. That's where I'll park my trailer. That is, when I get another trailer."

BOTH DEEP IN PRIVATE THOUGHTS, Jennie and Jeremy didn't speak until they reached Jennie's farm.

"If you want to drop me off at the gate, that's fine."

"My mother would never forgive me if I didn't see my girl safely to her door." He glanced at Jennie. "Are you ok?"

"I am. I see the wisdom in what Lainie shared, and I would enjoy Sam and Sadie here at the farm. Are you serious about looking for a horse?"

"I am."

Jeremy walked Jennie to the door, gave her kiss and a hug, and said, "Good night, sleep tight, don't let the bedbugs bite."

She answered, "And if they do, hit them with a shoe, and they'll go away, half past two."

"Ah, so your parents said that, too?"

"Yup, my dad did. Only I thought bedbugs were make-believe."

"I'm sure you have nothing to worry about. I'll shut the gate."

Chapter Sixteen

arade day! The ponies gleamed, the carriage was transformed into a treasure chest, and they were ready.

"This is going to be so much fun!" Cassy could hardly contain her excitement. Dressed in black, she couldn't wait to wear her sash and apple hat. They decided to create apple hats instead of masks. It wouldn't be fun to scare the horses or small children. For good measure, all the sashes and hats were stowed safely in Marcy's truck.

"Is Jeremy picking up Mrs. Williams and your grandpa, Jennie?" Marcy was getting anxious to load the ponies.

"Yes, but he's bringing them to the parade line up instead of here. Lainie's going to meet us there, too."

"I can't believe Lainie's new truck is candy apple red. It's perfect." Megan wanted to get in the conversation. She was also looking at trucks and trying to find something nice but used—very used. Megan was envious.

"We're entered as one entry. Lainie will lead, we'll put Megan and Cassy next, walking and throwing out candy, and then I'll follow with the ponies and carriage. If you and Jeremy could walk beside the carriage, one on each side, it would keep the crowd away and you would be able to get to the ponies' heads quickly if needed." Marcy thought the ponies would be fine in the parade, but she also knew the Appleridge Apple Festival parade drew large crowds.

They all agreed. Marcy had a good plan.

Jennie added, "Lainie's going to get there early and save a good spot to park the horse trailer—someplace quiet and away from most of the activity. The parade starts in the park, travels into town, around the square, and ends up back in the park."

"I drove there yesterday to see the layout. It looked like there was plenty of room for parking."

"Yes, they block off an entire area for parade participants. Belinda and I used to ride the horses into town for the parade. Do you remember, Megan?"

"Yeah, and I did it a few times with Julep. Some of the 4-H kids met at our farm and we rode into town for the parade together. It was fun, but the ride home always seemed longer."

"Ok, ready? Let's get the ponies loaded and head downtown. We don't want to rush." Marcy wanted to get moving.

"Good idea. Mom said she would meet us for a tailgate. I think she and Megan's mom are bringing food." Jennie knew her mom enjoyed being involved.

Megan nodded in confirmation. "Yeah, she had to hide the cookies from Dad. I'm not sure when he turned into such a cookie monster."

The carriage was already stowed in the horse trailer and the ponies loaded easily. Jennie gave the three mares, Treasure, Julep, and Starlight each a flake of hay out in the paddock. "Here you go, girls, we don't want Riley and Stuffin to have all the fun."

Megan and Cassy climbed into the backseat of Marcy's truck and Jennie settled in the front passenger seat.

"I guess age does have its privileges."

"Jennie, you old people can have the front seat," Megan teased.

Cassy said, "Hey, do you think maybe next year we'll ride Treasure and Starlight in the parade?"

"Let's make it a goal." Megan answered.

Jennie decided to test the waters with her next comment. "Lainie wants to form a little performance team. Maybe she'll have a group in the parade next year."

"I would love that. I told my mom about Lainie and she remembers when Lainie competed as Elaine Anderson. If I continue to keep up my grades, she said there may be money in the budget for me to take a few lessons—if I can get Treasure over there somehow. Hey, Megan, maybe we could go together. Hurry up and get a truck to pull your trailer."

"I've only messed around jumping a horse, but I have always wanted to learn. I'm in."

"Why do you have that grin on your face, Miss Jennie?" Marcy thought something was up.

"I don't know, I guess it all sounds like fun. I'm probably too old to join Lainie's group, and Julep is getting older so I don't want to jump her much, but I would like to learn from Lainie. I've never ridden very much in an English saddle."

Marcy gave her a look that said I'll get you to spill the beans later when we're alone.

Jennie changed the subject. "Jeremy is thinking about getting a horse. He said one that will ride and drive."

"I knew I liked that boy, and I think we could teach Julep to drive." Marcy kept her eyes on the road but she could sense Jennie's smile.

Jennie turned to look at the girls in the back seat. "We have a lot to look forward to, don't we, gang?"

"We sure do." Cassy reached forward and gave Jennie's braid a little tug.

Pulling into the park, Marcy spotted a red truck in the far parking lot. "I bet that's Lainie."

"Yeah, there's Mom and I see Jeremy's SUV beside Mom's car. It looks like we have our own little corner.

Marcy pulled past Lainie and then expertly backed the trailer into the spot on her right. She opened the doors of the trailer but decided to leave the ponies inside happily munching hay for now.

Jeremy and Lainie decorated Lainie's truck while Jennie's mom, Ellen, and Megan's mom, Susan, arranged a picnic on a table next to Ellen's Enclave. Mrs. Williams and Grandpa sat in camp chairs supervising the scene with Moose lying quietly at his mistress's feet.

"Hey, sweetie," Jeremy whispered as he kissed Jennie's check.

Megan opened the side door of Lainie's truck for a peek. "I love the smell of a brand-new Silverado. But didn't you have a Ford before?"

"I did, but this one was on the lot and they gave me a good deal. I guess my loyalty lies with the best deal."

Ellen spoke up. "Not at our house. Our loyalty lies with GM because they put food on our table for over thirty years." Ellen's words sounded harsh but she smiled and winked.

"Besides, as a GM retiree, my dad gets a good discount." Jennie felt the need to clarify.

"We may need to take advantage of that discount someday." Jeremy could tell by Jennie's blush he needed to explain. "Mrs. McKenzie, Jennie and I aren't officially engaged, but we have a committed relationship and see marriage in our future."

"That makes me happy. Her dad and I welcome you to our family." She walked over and gave her maybe-someday future son-in-law a motherly hug.

"Congratulations, you guys. You make a great couple." Lainie stopped decorating to give both of her friends a hug. "Now, let's finish up this job so we can eat some of those snacks calling us over there."

"When Jennie told me what you were doing, I dug out a few things. Here's a rug remnant for the bed of the truck and I brought some mums I had sitting on my front porch." Ellen motioned to the plants. "I'd like those back, though."

"No problem, Mrs. McKenzie; thanks." Lainie climbed up into the truck to roll out the rug, and then reached for the straw bales Jeremy handed up to her. They added the mums, two baskets of apples, and two sturdy chairs for their seniors. "I love these chairs."

"Jennie's dad makes them."

"Yeah, and come to think of it, I don't have any at my barn yet."

"Well, daughter, Christmas is just around the corner, you know."

"I guess I'll need to make sure I'm good."

Jeremy couldn't resist. "Good luck with that!"

And Jennie didn't resist giving him a little punch in the arm.

"How much candy do we have?" The candy hadn't been far from Cassy's mind, but she didn't open her bags.

All the bags of candy they each donated made a huge pile and a good assortment.

"I found a few inexpensive tote bags with pictures of apples. I think I have six bags."

"Nice! They're perfect for our theme." Jennie took the totes and lined them up on the tailgate of the truck. Then they took turns dumping an assortment of candy into each tote bag.

Megan lifted a bag. "I think we have plenty of candy. These are heavy."

"The truck looks great. All we need to do is add our seniors." Ellen added quickly, "But not yet; first, you have time to sit and eat a little lunch."

"JENNIE AND JEREMY, it's time to hitch the ponies and I welcome your help. You, too, Lainie, I'll need help with the carriage."

"Sure, Marcy, glad to help." Jeremy walked to the trailer with Jennie and waited for instructions. Lainie followed after she took one last look at her new truck all decorated for the parade. She couldn't wait to add the Lessons with Lainie magnetic signs she had made for each truck door.

Riley backed off the trailer first and Jennie reached out for the lead rope. Then Stuffin backed off the trailer and Lainie grabbed the little mare's rope. Moose got up and was very interested in the ponies, but he didn't bark. Jeremy went inside the trailer to help Marcy roll the carriage down the ramp. It was tricky, as most of the good places to grab were covered with cardboard zip-tied to the carriage, turning it into a treasure box.

"It looks like our decorations survived the short trip. I wasn't sure if Riley would reach forward and try to eat the cardboard. He does that sort of thing on occasion." Marcy loved her pony and her laughter told the story. "I'll get their harness."

Normally, the ponies stood quietly while Marcy harnessed and hitched them to the carriage, but in a strange environment, and in this situation, with the excitement of the parade, she wanted someone at their heads during the entire process.

Once hitched, she handed Jeremy a helmet. "Do you mind riding on the back step while I take them out for a little warm up?"

Of course, he didn't mind.

As they drove, Marcy shared her plan. "During the parade, I want you and Jennie to walk beside the ponies and be ready to go to their heads if anything gets too exciting. I hear this parade brings huge crowds, and when candy is being thrown, sometimes kids jump out into the street."

"Sounds good—we'll have Cassy and Megan walking near in front, too. The four of us should be a good human fence."

The ponies seemed good, so Marcy turned them back to the trailer area. She could see the parade organizers starting to line up the various units. Lainie looked their direction and motioned that she was moving her truck into place. Mrs. Williams and Mr. Gantzler were already seated in their places of honor, wearing their sashes with huge grins.

The Appleridge Festival Committee knew how to organize a parade, and today was no exception. The parade volunteers were old hands at their jobs and gave great directions. They understood when Marcy indicated she needed to take advantage of an empty area to allow the ponies to move but would be ready to get in line quickly.

It was time. The first parade units started down the street. The horses were usually last. It took a while before Lainie started to inch forward in her truck.

Please God, help me to drive well, and not dump our two seniors out of their chairs by braking quickly. Amen.

The prayer helped. It was almost like she heard God say, *I'm here with you on this fun day, daughter. Relax and enjoy.*

The day was brisk and sunny, the crowd happy and huge. Cassy, Megan, Jennie, and Jeremy threw out candy to delighted children. They noticed some children forgot to scramble for candy because they were enthralled watching the beautiful ponies. Those were the children who had a touch of horse fever.

Jennie smiled. *All you parents would be smart to feed that horse fever. Yes, it's expensive, but not as expensive as a teenager in trouble.*

Lainie saw several people point at her sign and wave. She waved when she saw Trina. She should have invited Trina to ride in the truck with her. The parade was moving slowly so Lainie motioned for Trina to climb in the front seat. To her surprise, Trina did.

"Hey, friend, I'm glad you could join us."

"Thanks, Lainie. I was standing with some of my boarders, but they gave me a little shove and said, we'll see you later. I love your new truck."

"So much has happened. Do you want to grab dinner tonight and I'll fill you in on everything?"

"Sure, that sounds fun."

The parade lasted about an hour. They didn't run out of candy until they turned the last corner—perfect timing.

Back at the trailer, Ellen and Susan helped the seniors down from the truck so Lainie could assist with the ponies.

"These guys are awesome. I couldn't believe how calm they were around the crowds, with firetrucks and balloons. Oh my!" Lainie stroked Riley's neck in admiration.

"They are solid citizens, but as you know, it doesn't happen easily or quickly."

"No, it doesn't, and if I can get my students to understand the best training is getting out there and putting in the time, well, I think that's the best lesson I can teach."

"I think that's true about horses and other things, as well. It's called walking the walk." Grandpa walked up to the group. "Thank you for inviting me to join you today. Ellen is going to drive me and Lizzie up to the festival. We're going to eat a funnel cake and sit and listen to music."

"We loved having you and so did the crowd." Jennie noticed the parade watchers seemed to enjoy seeing the two seniors together. She was sure it would be big news at the Bake & Shake on Monday.

"I'm going to head back to the farm with the ponies. Is anyone going back up to the festival later this evening for the big concert?"

"I'll follow you home. I think Jennie and I are going back after she feeds the horses. Is anyone else?"

"Trina and I are going to eat dinner somewhere and catch up. Maybe we could meet you guys at the concert?" She glanced over at Trina. "But first, I think I'll grab a shower."

"Oh boy, I need a shower, too." Marcy fanned her hands like she couldn't bear to smell herself.

"And me, three." Jennie shared. "What about you?" She looked at Jeremy.

"Why? Do I stink?" He pretended to smell his armpits.

"No, you never stink—much. Except when you're so stinking cute."

It was agreed. Everyone would shower, eat, and meet up as a group for the big concert and dance to close out the evening. The Appleridge Apple Festival was always a fun weekend, and this year, it was a memory to treasure.

Chapter Seventeen

riving to the Chronicle office on Monday morning, Jennie knew she had a great article about the festival. She spent most of Sunday afternoon working on the piece. Several personal stories gave it a nice touch. Mr. Mark was pleased with her work on the festival special supplement and she wanted him to be as pleased with this article, as well.

Father, thank you for this wonderful weekend spent with friends and family. Sometimes I wonder why I've been so blessed, and then I remember what Grandpa teaches—it's important to thank you for all our blessings and not worry about what may or may not happen. So, Father, I thank you. Thank you for being with Lainie and for bringing her to Appleridge. My prayer is for Sam, Marcy, Megan, and Cassy to also feel your love and receive your joy. In your name, I pray. Amen.

As Jennie ended her prayer, Lainie was also saying a little prayer of her own. She was very thankful for the support of her friends and for the calls she was already getting about her lessons. Everything seemed to be falling into place. What did she do to deserve such happiness?

She remembered Jeremy saying that God didn't stop bad things from happening. Maybe she shouldn't be so happy? Maybe she should expect something bad to happen? She didn't deserve all the good things coming her way. But she also remembered Jeremy saying that we didn't receive happiness because we deserved it; we received it because God loves us and he would always be by our side through both the good and the bad times. Boy, she sure had a lot to learn about being a Christian.

HANK PULLED OUT HIS PHONE. He was seething with anger. If Brock Rodgers thinks he'll get away with his latest scam, he's crazy. Hank would rally the troops. If he got enough people on his side, they could file a class action lawsuit. He still couldn't believe the news revealed at the instructor gathering. Every instructor would now be required to pay ten percent of their earnings to Brock or lose their license, and this was in addition to the yearly licensing fee. It wasn't their fault old Brock lost his shirt on his latest venture. Why should they make up the money he lost on another one of his crazy schemes?

If they protested, they would lose their license, and be required to pay a huge penalty. It was crazy and Hank was sure it wasn't legal. Those terms were not in their contract and wouldn't stand up in court. Brock figured none of the instructors had enough money to fight a court battle, and he was probably correct. But a class action suit may be possible if he could find a lawyer willing to take the case—and Hank decided to lead the charge. A class action would tarnish Brock's reputation, and for a man earning a living convincing the public he was of good character, a bit of tarnish would be very damaging.

Hank couldn't and wouldn't pay those huge fees, but he also knew he wouldn't be a Follow the Leader instructor much longer. Win or lose, Brock would make sure any instructor who protested would be finished in his program. He would make up some big lie, saying he got rid of all the bad instructors. It would be a tough journey trying to build a teaching business after leaving Follow the Leader. It was a losing situation for everyone. Hank found it strange that Brock didn't see it would be a loss for him, as well.

Hank thought about Lainie. According to the rumor mill, she was kicked out of the program because she couldn't attend the instructor gathering. He also heard about her accident. Lainie was out of a job, a truck, and a trailer. He bet she would be interested in sticking it to old Brock Rodgers. He wondered if she heard about Brock's latest threat to take back all the rescue horses he parceled out to the instructors. He would steal them back and then sell them to pay his debts. Wasn't Lainie's horse, Shadow, one of those horses? He thought so. He would definitely give Lainie a call.

LAINIE'S MOTHER, CONSTANCE ANDERSON—and never called Connie, leaned her head back on the head rest of her Mercedes. Never in a million years had she suspected Herbert of being unfaithful. They never had an extremely warm relationship, but they supported each other in their work. Wasn't that what you did in a marriage? Two people working toward a common goal, with their goal being success in their chosen careers. They never argued. She supposed it would be difficult to argue when they spent so little time together. In a way, they were nothing more than roommates. How was she supposed to know Herbert was looking for something more? She certainly didn't remember him showing any sort of affection—at least not in years. Her husband may be a doctor, but she was the lawyer in the family, and she would make sure her marriage ended with satisfactory financial arrangements. That certainly was a silly thought; they both were successful, and often her income was higher than Herbert's. They would have an amicable divorce, divide the property, and go their separate ways. Herbert wouldn't be alone. He had his girlfriend and her teenage sons. That certainly hurt. Herbert never wanted to spend much time with their own daughter, Elaine, but now he was going to help raise this woman's sons.

She was alone. She wished she had a good friend's shoulder to cry on, but, no, she never had time for friends. She thought about her daughter. She hadn't spoken to Elaine in ages. Occasionally, she looked Elaine up on the internet and followed her career teaching some sort of horse thing—somewhere. Constance had no one. She had a great career but nothing else. Her co-workers were certainly not her friends. She never needed or wanted their friendship, but now, with the loss of her marriage, she found herself wishing she had paid more attention to her daughter.

LAINIE HUMMED as she finished grooming Shadow. After a long break due to the trailer accident, this was their first ride and she wanted to take things slow. She needed to bring Shadow back carefully—physically, mentally, and emotionally.

She was so thankful for everything happening in her life. The sun seemed to shine on her every day. She already had six students and word was spreading. Life was good.

Her faith would soon be tested but Lainie didn't know.

TRUSTING TRUTH

JEREMY'S DRIVE HOME from Columbus was fueled by a million thoughts. His advisor helped him plan three mission trips during the spring semester. All were in Appalachia. She suggested something international, also, and he promised to give that idea some thought. He was surprised to learn a semester of mission trips would actually earn some credit in school, and he would also take a few other classes. He wasn't sure if he wanted to continue in seminary, but if he did, the earned credit was good. He also learned about career possibilities leading mission trips. He found the information interesting and wondered what Jennie would think about being married to someone taking off for weeks at a time. If he followed that career path, he would remain in school and become a pastor who led mission trips.

LAINIE FINISHED Shadow's after-ride grooming and took her to the pasture to graze with her new friend, Sadie. She would grab a quick bite to eat before teaching three lessons this afternoon. She loved her new students, and having students haul their horses to her place was certainly nicer than driving to different barns for lessons, although she promised Trina she would teach at her barn one afternoon a week. Lainie wanted to help out her friend, and, after all, without the invitation to teach the Follow the Leader clinic at Trina's barn, she wouldn't have found a new home in Appleridge.

She jogged up the stairs to her barn apartment and grabbed her phone from her back pocket when she heard it make a noise. She looked at the display. Hank? What does he want?

"Hey, Hank, it's been a while."

"Hey, Lainie, yeah, how are you? I heard about the accident."

254

"I'm good and feeling very thankful both Shadow and I are fine. It was a pretty bad accident. A high school kid was texting and ran the stop sign."

"Wow. I also heard old Brock kicked you out of Follow the Leader."

"You heard right. I'm no longer a Follow the Leader instructor." Lainie was tempted to tell Hank the whole story, but something told her to be very guarded.

"Well then, let me tell you what happened at the instructor gathering. There's a bunch of us planning a rebellion."

Hank spent a few minutes sharing the scoop from the gathering. Lainie listened and was very thankful none of this news affected her new life.

"So, Lainie, are you in with us?" Hank waited.

"I'm already out of Follow the Leader, Hank. I'm not sure what you want from me. I mean, I feel for you all. It's a bad situation."

"We want to band together and stick it to old Brock. If we stick together, we may be able to force him to pay damages."

"Like I said, I'm already out, and I'm trying to move on and start my own teaching business."

"Come on, Lainie, don't you care? Wouldn't it feel good to stick it to the big guy?"

"I do, I really do care, but I don't want to stick it to anyone. I've changed. I'm learning how to live a different life." Lainie thought this was the moment she should share her new faith but she held back. She wasn't ready.

"Don't get all goody-goody on me now, girl. The next thing you're going to tell me is you found God or something."

"I'm not a goody-goody but I'm trying to live better." She paused. "And, ok, yeah, I've been going to church and I'm learning what it means to be a Christian."

She heard Hank whistle.

"I don't know what to say—I was just joking." Hank figured it was time to bring out the big bomb. His news would change Lainie's mind.

"You need to listen carefully, because I'm not joking now. Brock has threatened to take back all the rescue horses he rehomed with instructors, and wasn't your Shadow one of those horses? I bet losing your mare will change your little church girl tune."

Lainie felt a stab of fear so huge she could hardly breathe.

Hank jumped on the silence. "I bet that changes things, right?"

"I need to go. Give me time to think, ok?"

"Sure, church girl, but don't take too much time. Brock is desperate for cash and I get the impression he doesn't care who he hurts trying to dig his way out of a huge hole."

"I'm not sure what I'm going to do, but he's not taking Shadow."

"Oh, I'm pretty sure what you'll do—you'll fight with us. Should I count you in?"

"Give me time, ok? You just dumped this on me." She was getting angry—angry at Brock, angry at Hank, and angry at herself for getting angry.

"Sure, talk to you later, but don't wait too long. We need to plan our attack."

Lainie pressed stop and threw her phone on the kitchen bar.

Well, God, here it is—the bad times. Are you still by my side? I need you, I can't lose Shadow, please don't let Brock take Shadow.

Tears ran down her cheeks and she wiped them with the back of her hand.

Father, I believe in you.

She did, she felt a presence and she felt peace.

Please show me what to do next. I need your help. Amen

She couldn't lie. She was worried. But she also felt hope. Was that what God sent in times of trouble? Was it hope?

Lainie washed her face. She wasn't hungry but she was ok. She would go out to the arena and prepare for her first student of the afternoon. Every student and every horse deserved her best—and that's what she would give—her best.

JENNIE RETURNED to her desk in the corner with a grin on her face. Mr. Mark was thrilled with the article on the Appleridge Festival and the sneak-peek of the next edition of the Chronicle. He loved Sherilynn's preview of the new website, and Charlie reported several new advertisers. So far, the new look was being noticed.

She glanced over at Sherilynn's desk and saw the same silly grin on her face.

Good for her; she works hard and she keeps this train called the CC on track.

Jennie glanced at the time. Instead of starting a new project at her desk, she decided to shut down her computer and leave a few minutes early. As Mr. Mark liked to say, it'll come out in the wash, and since she spent most of Sunday afternoon working on her articles, Jennie thought this was wash time.

"I'll see you later, Sherilynn; I'm leaving for the day. I'll be in tomorrow and then I'll be out interviewing on Thursday and Friday."

"Thanks for letting me know. Have a good night."

Jennie zipped her jacket as she walked to her truck, Blue Boy. There was definitely a nip in the air tonight. And with the time change next week, it would be dark before she arrived home most evenings.

She started the truck. Before she pulled out, she glanced at her phone. No call from Jeremy but there was one from Lainie. She listened to the message. Lainie needed to talk. Instead of returning the call or sending a text, she decided to make a quick stop at Lainie's barn. In her mind, it was still called the Petersons' place but it was slowly becoming Lainie's place.

Lainie's last student was in the arena when Jennie parked. She motioned to Lainie that she could wait until the lesson was finished, and then leaned up against the fence to watch. The student was a good rider. Lainie had barrels in the arena and a few other obstacles. The horse cantered around the obstacles calmly and his person was smiling. It must have been a good lesson.

Lainie had a nice calm presence in lessons which seemed to help both riders and their horses build confidence. The lesson finished and Lainie instructed the rider to cool down her horse before loading him into the trailer for the trip home. The student's mother greeted Lainie and asked a few questions Jennie couldn't hear, but from her expression she seemed pleased with Lainie's answers. Lainie walked over to the fence.

"Hey, thanks for stopping by. You got my message?"

"Yeah, I'm on my way home and thought a short visit would be nice. I haven't seen you for a few days. It looks like lessons are going well."

Lainie hesitated just long enough to puzzle Jennie. "Yes, lessons are going really well but I have something else going on. I need advice." She glanced over at her student untacking her horse. "If you have time, let's wait until my student has her horse loaded. It shouldn't take long."

"Sure. Hey, I hear Megan and Cassy signed up for your group lesson on Saturday. Megan's cast comes off this week but she still doesn't have a truck. I promised to lend her Blue Boy to pull the trailer."

"That's what Megan said. Thanks for helping her out. This will be their first Saturday session. So far I have five girls signed up."

"It's some sort of synchronized riding?"

"That's the end goal. First, I'll have to get them all riding well. Actually, they all ride well; I just need to get them to all ride well together. It's usually the horses that set that timeline."

"It's always the horse that sets the timeline, isn't it?"

"You're correct." Lainie waved as the truck and trailer pulled out.

Jennie waited.

"I got a call from one of my Follow the Leader friends. Apparently, Brock Rodgers needs money and he's charging instructors crazy fees."

"But you don't work for Follow the Leader anymore."

"I told Hank, that's my friend, I wasn't interested in joining their cause. He wants to get a group together and file some sort of class action breach of contract. He thought I would love to stick it to old Brock."

"But you don't because you've moved on?"

"I think what I actually said was—I'm not interested in sticking it to anyone because I'm trying to live a different life."

Jennie nodded her approval. "And he didn't like that answer? And let me guess, he thinks you're now a goody two-shoes? Although I'm not sure where that expression came from—I may need to do some research, but, sorry, go on."

"I told him I was trying to live my life as a Christian—although he didn't believe it."

"Ok, that's good—it sounds like a great response."

"Thanks. But then he said Brock was in deep financial trouble and he was going to take all the rescue horses he rehomed with instructors and sell them to get quick cash."

Jennie didn't know where this story was going, but she felt a sudden pain deep in her stomach and was barely able to ask, "Was Shadow a rescue horse?"

"Yes."

They were both silent, just staring at each other, eyes watering.

Jennie was the first to speak next. "Ok, we'll fight. He won't get Shadow. We won't let it happen. And just so you know, it's perfectly fine for Christians to fight for what's right. And you will not fight alone."

Lainie couldn't hold back her tears. "Thanks; knowing my friends will fight with me helps. But how is that different than Hank wanting me to fight for him?"

"Where is Jeremy when we need him? Ok, I'll give it a stab—from what you described, Hank is fighting to stick it to Brock. Hank wants revenge. You're fighting for your mare. A mare that you took in good faith on the promise she would have a good home. Did you get any sort of paperwork?"

"I haven't had a chance to look yet, but there wasn't a bill of sale, because there wasn't a sale. I didn't pay for Shadow—not in cash. The verbal agreement was I would take over her care and training and give her a forever home."

"Which you did and are doing—you are fulfilling the promise."

"Yes."

"What about a transfer on her registration papers?"

"I couldn't get an official transfer because she was a rescue. The AQHA doesn't require DNA so I couldn't use DNA to prove she was in the registry. I looked up the name we were given, and the details match, but I couldn't get duplicate registration papers without the signature of her last known owner. I haven't tried to contact the last known owner yet. I think I'll give it a shot. He may not want the AQHA to know he didn't do an official transfer of ownership as required. I'll do more research, but since I don't know how she ended up a rescue horse, I'm sort of afraid of digging too deep."

"I understand. It's scary." Jennie reached out to give her friend a hug. "It's going to be ok. We'll help. I hate to suggest this but maybe it's time to give your mom a call?"

"I'm desperate enough to risk getting beaten down by what she may say. I'll call tonight."

"Call me later if you need to talk. I'll be praying for you, Shadow, and your mom."

"Thanks. Just talking to you has helped. I'm not sure how I went so long without good friends."

"Can I share this with your other good friends? We'll get Jeremy and Trina started praying."

"Yeah, tell Jeremy, but I'll call Trina. I want her to hear the whole story from me."

"Good idea. Love you, girlfriend."

TRINA LISTENED to Lainie's story and sighed. "Oh my, I'm so sorry to hear this. You don't need this worry."

"No, I didn't need this worry but here it is. I'm going to call my mom. We haven't spoken in over a year but she's a lawyer, and I think I'm being nudged to call."

"You think you're being nudged?"

"Yeah, a little nudge from Jennie, but I'm also feeling it from something else."

"My prayers are with you. Call if you need to talk or come on out to the barn. The girls love their lessons, and that's all they talk about."

"Thanks, I'll be out on Friday as planned."

Lainie hung up and then sat on her day bed preparing for the next call. Life is funny, she thought. Here she was about to call her mom, the infamous Constance Anderson, and ask for help saving Shadow even though her mom was responsible for taking away Skippy, the first horse she loved. Her mom broke her heart and now she was going to ask for help so her heart wasn't broken again. It's crazy and probably a waste of time but she couldn't ignore this strange sort of nudge.

God, are you nudging me? Well, if you are, please stick really close 'cause this could hurt.

"Elaine, is this you?"

"Yeah, hi Mom, it's me."

"It is good to hear from you." *Was that her Mom saying it was good to hear from her?*

"Are you ok?" *Her mom just said ok?*

"Yeah, I'm good, but I want to talk to you about something." *And she hasn't corrected me for saying yeah and I said it twice.*

"Honey, I need to talk to you, too." *Did her mom just call her honey?*

"Ok, I'm listening."

"I thought I would come visit you so we could talk. I have some news to share and I would like to see you."

"You want to come see me? What about work?" *What about all your European trips?*

"I need to get away and I am thinking about taking a short sabbatical. I am not sure yet, but I do want to visit you. Where are you now?

"Well, I'm actually not too far. I'm in Appleridge, Ohio."

"Are you still teaching people to ride horses?"

"Yes, that and so much more. I teach people about horses."

"That is nice honey. I am very anxious to see where you live." *Was that a second honey? Who took her mom and replaced her with this nice lady?*

"I would love to see you, Mom, but I live in an apartment above a barn I lease. You may need to find a hotel. I don't think you're a barn sort of girl." Did she just hear her mom laugh?

"You are correct—I am not a barn girl. I will get a hotel. Does Appleridge have a five-star?"

This time Lainie laughed. "No five-star in Appleridge and probably not in Richburg, either, but I think you'll find a nice hotel in Richburg, and it's only fifteen miles from Appleridge.

"That is fine. I will call my travel agent tomorrow and ask her to find something nice. I would like to visit this weekend if that fits your schedule?"

"Yes, it fits. Just call and let me know when to expect you and I'll make sure to arrange lessons around your visit."

"Thank you, Elaine, and please do not worry, I would love to watch you teach."

"Ok."

"Well, I look forward to my visit. I have missed you, Elaine. Bye now."

"Bye, Mom."

Lainie hung up the phone, amazed. Her mom missed her? She wanted to visit? This had to be what Trina called a *God thing*. There was no other explanation.

It wasn't until much later that Lainie realized her mom wanted to visit, but there was no mention of her dad.

Chapter Eighteen

*L*ainie checked her closet again. Didn't she have anything nice to wear except jeans and boots? Clothes were strewn across her day bed, but nothing felt right for lunch with her mom.

Enough! It is what it is and Mom will just need to accept the truth. Her daughter doesn't wear designer clothes. Her daughter doesn't like designer clothes. Her daughter is an Ariat, Goode Rider, and Irideon sort of girl, although those tack store brands can also be pricey. Of course, not near as pricey as designer. Anyway, this daughter always has a mess of blue jeans thrown in for good measure. Deal with it, Mom!

Lainie chose her newest jeans and a light sweater. She dressed before hanging up shirts and folding jeans, clearing her bed. She was meeting Constance Anderson for lunch in Richburg, but just in case her mom wanted to see the apartment, she straightened and cleaned. The barn was already good. Horse girls were like that—they enjoyed cleaning barns and only tolerated cleaning an apartment.

She added comfy canvas shoes and brushed her hair with care. She looked good—healthy and happy. She actually looked forward to meeting her mom. If she was totally truthful, she needed to admit she looked forward to eating lunch. To save money, she didn't eat at nice restaurants very often.

Lainie spied her mom as soon as she walked into the restaurant. Mom was standing beside her table and waving. Wow, so uncharacteristic of Constance, but it felt good just the same. She motioned to the hostess indicating her party was inside and walked past the other waiting diners.

"Hi, Mom, it's good to see you."

"You look wonderful, Elaine, it is good to see you, too. Please sit down. I hope you don't mind. I already ordered a little appetizer."

Lainie looked at the antipasto tray. "It looks great and I'm hungry—and thirsty." She glanced around and the waiter was immediately at her side. This was a good restaurant.

"May I have both water and a Diet Coke with cherries, please?"

The waiter nodded and left to fill her request.

"Mom, I forgot to ask about Dad when I was on the phone. Is he here? That's stupid, obviously he isn't here. How is he?"

"That is what we need to talk about and I will just be blunt. Your father has a new family. He wants a divorce."

"Oh, Mom, I'm so sorry. And you didn't know?" Lainie reached over the table to touch her mom's hand. Constance seemed surprised, but then covered Lainie's hand with her own.

"I had no idea he was unhappy. We just lived life and worked hard."

"Are you going to be ok?"

"I am. We have agreed to split our property amicably. We both have good careers so financial arrangements are satisfactory. I have asked for a six-month sabbatical, just to get away, clear my head, and not be in the house when your father moves out; however, it has been suggested I should retire instead."

"Oh, Mom, I'm so sorry." Lainie didn't think her mom would like leaving work. Wasn't she only in her fifties? *Shame on me for not remembering my mother's age and when was her birthday, anyway? I'm as bad as my parents.*

"I am thinking about retirement from the law firm. I may enjoy something else for a while. I thought about teaching."

Lainie's fork clattered to the table. "Sorry—that surprised me."

"I thought it would. I can't explain anything right now. I only know I felt a strong desire to connect with you and to make amends, and then you called. I haven't been a caring mother but please know I care. I came to ask for forgiveness. Your father and I did a few things that hurt you terribly."

"It's ok. I'm fine." *Can't? Did her mom just use a contraction?*

"No, it's not fine. I tried to convince myself we had your best interest at heart. But I don't believe that lie myself so I won't ask you to believe it, either."

"That's true, Mom; when you sold Skippy, it hurt. It still hurts but I forgive you. I've learned a little bit about forgiveness recently. And just so you know, I found Skippy, and he's happy and with the same family. That takes the sting away."

"Thank you—I was not expecting forgiveness. I expected anger."

"When you're ready, I'll explain. But we should look at the menu. I think our waiter is getting anxious about our order."

"You may be correct. I think I am having the quiche of the day and a salad."

"Yum, me too; spinach is my favorite."

Constance looked at the waiter and he was immediately at their table. They placed their orders and relaxed.

"I'm enjoying our lunch. We could never do this before. Why?"

"I am not sure, honey. I think it is because I never tried and I am so very sorry."

"Maybe I didn't try, either. I was so angry about Skippy and a few other things. I pretty much shut you out."

"I truly am glad Skippy is in a good home. He was a good horse. Your father and I believed the trainer when he convinced us to sell Skippy and buy a horse to take you to the Olympics. Looking back now, I realize he was just looking for a huge commission, or whatever you call it when a trainer finds a horse."

"I think it's called a finder's fee."

"How are you, Elaine, really? You look good. You seem happy but you called for a reason."

"I'm happy. I have a new life in Appleridge with good friends. I left the Follow the Leader program and I'm happy about that, too. I have a horse I love. Her name is Shadow." Lainie took a breath and explained the situation and her worry about losing Shadow.

"I took one horse away and I will do everything in my power to make sure you do not lose the second horse you have loved. I promise, honey. We will fight, and I am a good attorney to have in a fight. This Brock will not know what hit him."

Constance leaned back in her chair with a smile on her face.

"I can tell you love a good fight, and I'm very glad to have you on my side. I'm not interested in making Brock suffer—I just want to protect Shadow."

"We will. When would be a good time for me to come over to your place to plan our strategy? I took several weeks off. I have never taken time off without planning a major trip. I actually drove here. I think I may make reservations at a bed & breakfast in Amish country and enjoy some rest and relaxation on the way back to Philadelphia."

"Wow, I'm impressed. Good for you." Lainie liked this new Mom.

"I have my notebook computer and I will start researching some similar cases. Can you meet with me tomorrow?"

"Yes, I'm teaching at my friend, Trina's, barn tomorrow afternoon. Why don't you come to Appleridge, we'll get lunch, and then you can go with me to my lessons? That is, if you're interested in watching me teach."

"Do you have an address for the GPS?"

Lainie gave her the address to her barn. "I'm leasing the barn and apartment from the Peterson family. Dr. Peterson is one of the local vets."

After lunch, Lainie walked out of the restaurant, still chatting with her mom. She was surprised to get a goodbye hug. It felt good—really good. And it also felt good to have one of the best lawyers on the east coast taking her case.

Thank you, Father!

She loved her mom for not talking badly and blaming her dad for the divorce. *I don't expect Dad to call, especially since he has a new family now. But if he does try to connect, I know I want a relationship with him, too, if possible.* As she recently learned, a person can never have too many people to love.

WHEN CONSTANCE ARRIVED at Lainie's barn, her daughter almost didn't recognize the lady in nice jeans. *When did Mom start wearing jeans?*

"Wow, Mom, you look totally hot in those jeans! And I mean that in a good way."

"Thanks, honey, I forgot how comfortable a nice pair of jeans could feel. I may get more."

"I'm taking you to the Café for lunch. It's a nice little place."

"Appleridge looks very quaint."

"It is, but the best part is the people. Just wait until you meet my friends."

Lainie was a little disappointed they didn't meet anyone she knew at the Café, but her mom seemed to enjoy her lunch.

On their way to Trina's barn, Lainie explained how she met Trina, and also explained that she went by the name of Lainie instead of Elaine.

"I will try to remember to call you Lainie."

"No worries, Mom."

At the farm, Trina took Constance under her wing, so to speak. "You go on, Lainie; your students are ready. I'll take good care of your mom. We'll sit in the shade under the pavilion."

"Thanks, Trina." She waved quickly and went to meet her students for the afternoon.

"Would you care for anything to drink, Constance? Let's go up to the house and we'll find something. We won't miss too much. Lainie is teaching three lessons today, I think."

Constance sighed as she walked into Trina's home. "Oh my, this is so nice and warm. It's like a little retreat."

"Well, it's my retreat. Thank you."

They filled glasses with ice and tea, and Trina filled a small thermos for refills later. They both took theirs unsweetened.

"You must not be originally from the south since you did not sweeten the tea?" Constance always noticed little details.

"I'm pre-diabetes, so no sugar with my tea."

"You are smart to take control now."

"Thanks; adult-onset diabetes seems to run in the family. I decided to do whatever I can to avoid the need for medication." Trina's mom was a diabetic.

On their way to the pavilion, carrying their drinks, Trina stopped to introduce Teresa.

"Constance, this is Teresa; she coordinates some of the clinics here at the barn. Teresa, this is Constance Anderson, Lainie's mother."

"It's so nice to meet you, Constance. We adore Lainie. I was surprised to hear she left Follow the Leader. I'm sure she didn't make the decision lightly. I've heard rumors that Brock Rodgers isn't always the man he appears to be to his followers."

"I am learning a bit from Lainie. She adores the program, but I gather this Mr. Rodgers is rather difficult."

Trina remained quiet. She would keep the details Lainie shared in confidence.

"I didn't meet Lainie until this year, when she taught the clinic here at Trina's farm, but I've followed her for years."

"How did you follow her?" Constance asked.

"The organization used to put out a nice magazine and being a fan of the program, I read them religiously. Lainie was featured fairly often. I also saw her at several of Brock's demonstrations."

"They stopped printing the magazine?" Trina finally found a safe way to join the conversation.

"Rumor has it the program is having financial problems. Brock isn't touring, either."

"What sort of articles mentioned Elaine—I mean Lainie? Sorry, I have always called my daughter Elaine."

"Well, both are beautiful names." Trina spoke up quickly.

"They are, and I think the early articles mentioned she competed under the name Elaine Anderson. There were also articles on each instructor who took a rescue horse as a forever horse, and Follow the Leader followed their journeys with the horses for several issues. I remember how beautifully Lainie wrote about her journey with her rescue horse, Shadow. She shared wonderful insight into Shadow's behavior."

Constance sat up and put her ice tea glass in the holder on the arm rest of her chair. She tried to appear casual.

"Do you happen to still have the magazines? I would love to read them, and I promised to return them when I'm finished."

"I do—I saved them all. I'm what you'd call a huge fan of the Follow the Leader program."

Trina sat with her mouth open. Obviously, Lainie had time to share the Shadow situation with her mom. Wasn't her mom a lawyer? Wasn't she a really well-known Philadelphia lawyer? Trina had a feeling Brock Rodgers was about to be taught a lesson he wouldn't soon forget. She couldn't wait to see how this scenario played out.

Chapter Nineteen

Constance Anderson couldn't wait to sink her teeth into Mr. Brock Rodgers. He sounded like a bully and she didn't like bullies. She would talk to Lainie's Follow the Leader friends, especially Hank. She didn't think there was a need to follow up with any type of class action suit. She would apply a bit of pressure and get the bully to back down and pay up. It didn't sound like he had the funds to pay much. Of course, there are other ways for him to compensate the instructors.

She surprised herself. She enjoyed meeting Lainie's friends and watching her teach lessons. Why in the world did she wait so long to spend a little time with her only child? She was practically salivating over the opportunity to defend this small group of instructors. She shook her head. How could this happen? How could she change so much so quickly? It was hard to believe only last week she sat in the hospital parking lot, crying, all alone. And now she sat in blue jeans—even though they were designer blue jeans. Looking in the Mercedes mirror, she saw a tinge of pink across her cheekbones and a little dirt under her French manicure. She spent the whole day at a barn watching horses—and it was fun.

BACK AT HER HOTEL, Constance showered. Wrapped in a luxurious robe, she pulled her small notebook computer from her briefcase—time for a little research. She would also call this Hank person before driving back to Appleridge. Lainie's friend Jennie was hosting an impromptu potluck at her farm. Apparently, Lainie's friends wanted to meet her mother.

She couldn't remember the last time she attended a potluck—the parties she attended or gave were always catered. Constance paused, a memory tickling her thoughts. Her last potluck was in law school. A group of friends met to study and everyone brought snacks. They ended up with quite a few trays of brownies. Constance smiled—amazingly her face did not break.

Closing her laptop, she leaned back. This case would be almost too easy, but somewhat enjoyable. She was helping her daughter. This was not a case of helping a greedy developer grab more properties, or fighting a wealthy husband trying to cheat an unsuspecting partner. And it felt good. The pro bono work felt good, too, although she did not clear it with her law firm. The same law firm that suggested she was ready for an early retirement. Maybe she was ready for retirement—retirement from loneliness, from greed, from catered dinners.

Constance picked up her cell phone and found the number Lainie had given her for Hank. Dialing the number, she wondered how well Hank knew Lainie.

"Hey."

"Mr. Hank, I am sorry I do not know your last name. This is Constance Anderson, Lainie's mother."

"Oh, yeah, Mrs. Anderson, Lainie left a message. Thanks for calling."

"And your last name is, young man?"

"Mumberg. It's Horace Mumberg. Please just call me Hank, ok?"

Constance smiled. Oh my! "I understand, Hank. As Lainie shared, I am an attorney in Philadelphia and I am willing to help you fight the injustice perpetrated by Mr. Brock Rodgers."

"Huh?"

"I'm going to stick it to Brock." Did she just say that out loud? Goodness.

"Yeah, ok, I got it."

"While I'm not licensed to practice law in Iowa, I will research the case and ask one of my associates in Iowa to actually file—if necessary."

"If necessary? I think it's really necessary."

"Of course, Hank, but it may not be necessary to file a case. I suspect Mr. Rodgers will fold quite easily once he understands you have legal representation—excellent representation, if I may be so bold."

"Ah, Mrs. Anderson, I don't have much money, that's why I need to fight. I can't pay Brock and I can't pay you."

"I understand, Hank; this work is pro bono."

"Pro what?"

"Pro bono means I will donate my services."

Hank said nothing for a few seconds. "Thank you, Mrs. Anderson, and thank Lainie, too."

Constance asked the cowboy a few more questions, and when satisfied with the information, she pressed off her cell. Hank seemed like a nice young man, but Horace Mumberg was quite a name. She certainly understood Hank taking a nickname and wondered if Hank or Brock made that choice. For that matter, perhaps Brock was also a nickname. How interesting.

Glancing at the Cartier adorning her wrist, Constance decided to dress for the party. There was time for her to stop at a little deli she noticed while driving through Richburg. Perhaps she would find something nice to take to the potluck. She didn't want to arrive empty handed. She would bring food and plenty of information to share with Lainie and friends.

LAINIE JOGGED down the steps from her apartment when she saw her mom's Mercedes turn into the farm drive. Motioning for her mom to park, she grabbed two folding chairs and put them in the truck bed.

"Hey, Mom, you look nice."

Constance wore the same jeans from earlier today but had changed into a gauzy white shirt with a light sweater.

"Thanks, honey; I'm having fun trying out a different look with some of my old things."

Lainie was sure nothing in Constance's suitcase was very old but she liked the look.

"What do you have there?" Lainie motioned to the box.

"I stopped at a little deli in Richburg and found these delightful brownies." She didn't want to admit the brownies brought back a few memories.

"Yum, they look great. Thanks, Mom, the gang will love them. We all love chocolate and we love sugar."

"I suppose it's easy to burn off calories when you ride horses and work outside all day."

"Yeah, so far, it has been easy for me." *Yup, a few contractions were definitely sneaking into Mom's speech.*

"You do look healthy. You glow." *Wow, two nice compliments from Mom. I really love this new Mom.*

"I'll drive. Your car will be fine parked here. I haven't gotten my new truck out much. I've been teaching quite a few lessons. I'm so thankful my business is off to a great start."

"They certainly love you at Trina's, and I loved watching."

Constance was sincere. She did love watching the lessons. And she did notice how the students adored her daughter. She also enjoyed talking to everyone as they watched. It felt so good to be kind. She was not always kind, but kind was a good feeling, and she wondered how she ever forgot how good it felt.

There was already a crowd on Jennie's back porch when Lainie pulled her truck into the drive and parked. She waited for her mom to walk around the truck and they approached the group together.

"Mom, these are my friends. Everybody, this is my mom, Constance Anderson." Lainie proceeded to name each friend and gave a brief explanation of who was who. Her mom repeated each name and asked a little question. She was a real pro at meeting new people, and her friends enjoyed the attention.

"I'm hungry, so if Jennie's ready, I'll say grace and we'll eat." Jeremy looked over at Jennie.

She nodded and said, "I invited Sam and he has a few late appointments so he said we shouldn't wait for him."

The group formed a circle and held hands. Constance appeared uncomfortable but joined the circle.

"Father, thank you for this time with friends and bless this food. We invite you to our gathering with thankful hearts. Amen."

That was short but sweet, thought Constance—and not painful at all.

The group chatted as they went inside the house to fill their plates. Constance noticed the food was nicely arranged on an old table in the eating nook. This was a casual affair but certainly charming with the blue metal plates and red bandana napkins. The plastic utensils were in a cute basket. She looked around for something to drink and was surprised to find a selection of sparkling water and ice tea. She wouldn't whine about the lack of wine. Silly me, she thought, and I'm never silly.

Jennie had several tables arranged on her back porch and everyone brought a chair —no one needed to balance a plate on their knees. They had seven in their group tonight—Jennie, Jeremy, Megan, Cassy, Marcy, Lainie, and Constance.

Dinner conversation evolved around the recent Appleridge Apple Festival parade.

"Mom, I wish you could have seen our entry. It was so neat. You'll get to meet Marcy's ponies later—and all the horses living here at Jennie's farm."

"Mrs. Anderson—" Marcy started.

"Please, everyone, call me Constance. Well, all except you, Elaine, you stick with Mom."

"Ok, Constance, would you enjoy a carriage ride this evening?" Marcy took every opportunity to share her ponies.

"Why, I would love a carriage ride."

"Then it's settled. Enjoy dinner and then we'll hitch the ponies."

Lainie took a few minutes to share her latest news. "Jeremy, you said that my life as a new Christian would be good, but bad times were sure to arrive. Well, they arrived." She glanced at her mom and noticed a puzzled expression, but not an angry expression.

Lainie explained about Brock Rodger's threat to take Shadow. She could tell by the expressions on her friends' faces that Jennie hadn't shared her news. She couldn't tell for sure, but she may have shared the news with Jeremy, and that was fine.

"My dad is pretty good at holding a dishonest cowboy's boots to the fire. He was amazing this summer when I found myself in trouble in a similar program." Megan was very proud of her dad and how he handled JJ at the Double J Ranch.

"I agree. He saved both Starlight and Julep." Jennie walked over and put her arm around her young friend.

"I'm not sure if some of you know my mom is an attorney—a very good attorney. She's going to fight on behalf of all the Follow the Leader instructors and keep Brock from stealing Shadow and the other rescued horses."

Jennie noticed that Constance nodded in agreement. She looked confident. Not smug, exactly, but very sure of herself.

"Do you think it will be a difficult battle?" Jennie had to ask.

"I don't think so. I recently learned about a helpful bit of evidence." She looked at Lainie but didn't explain further. "I'm researching a few things now. I won't be able to file the case in Iowa, but I'll find an associate, if needed. I don't anticipate a need to actually go to court. Brock will fold."

Lainie couldn't wait to hear about this so-called evidence. Her mom seemed very confident and that was reassuring.

"What sort of evidence?" Megan wasn't shy about asking.

"The truth, young lady, and if you can prove the truth, that is all you need."

Megan knew she was getting the brush-off but Lainie's mom wasn't being rude.

"Megan, that's the same question I wanted to ask." Jennie noticed her friend seemed a little embarrassed.

"Megan, are you the Megan who lives on the farm Lainie leases?"

"Yes, ma'am."

"Well, it is a lovely place."

"Thank you. You'll have to walk up to the house and meet my mom while you're here."

"That would be lovely. I would love to meet her, but I don't want to invade the privacy of her home. Maybe we will meet at the barn?"

"I'll let her know you're in town and would love to meet her."

"Thank you, dear."

"Well, Miss Constance, are you ready?"

The friends got up and walked their plates into the house. Jennie rinsed each before placing them in a sink of warm sudsy water. They sat the glasses on the counter next to the sink.

Still chatting, the group adjourned to the barn. Megan and Cassy walked into the paddock to get Riley and Stuffin, Lainie and Jennie went to the horse trailer to get the carriage, and Marcy went to the tack room to grab the harness. Jeremy noticed a bewildered look on Constance's face.

"You can wait right here with me." He reassured Constance. "They'll have the ponies groomed, harnessed, and hitched before we can settle our supper."

Constance was intrigued. What cute little ponies. They weren't scary like a big horse. She walked over to see everything up close, as Marcy explained each step.

Lainie walked out of the tack room with a funny-looking hat.

"Here, Mom, helmets are required at Fawn Song Farm, and helmets are required at Lessons with Lainie, too."

Constance gave a brief thought to her hair and then placed the helmet on her head. Lainie helped to adjust the chin strap. It was not too bad.

Marcy climbed into the carriage and sat on the far right. Lainie helped her mom find the step and get settled on Marcy's left.

"Walk on," Marcy asked the ponies and they responded.

"I'm so thrilled Mom wanted to go on a ride. I can't believe she agreed but I'm thrilled she did."

Jennie looked at Lainie. "So, everything is going well with your mom?"

"I can't believe how well. It's like you said—a miracle."

"Miracles happen all the time."

"I agree with Jennie; miracles happen all the time. We just don't notice." Jeremy continued, "Remember when we talked about God taking bad things and turning them into something good? Maybe he is taking this very bad situation with Brock and turning it into something good for you and your mom."

Lainie nodded in agreement.

"Your mom isn't anything like I thought she would be." Jennie didn't expect to like Constance.

"She isn't anything like I thought she would be, either, and that's the miracle." Lainie scanned the pasture for the carriage and could see her mom and Marcy chatting away as the ponies trotted. Constance Anderson's face spoke happiness.

"Mom is leaving tomorrow and spending a few days at a bed & breakfast in Amish country. She doesn't seem to be in any hurry to return to work. She says she'll work on the Follow the Leader case at the bed & breakfast. I never, and I repeat never, remember Mom being this casual and relaxed."

"What about her firm in Philadelphia?" Jennie had heard horror stories about large law firms and how they expected a certain number of billable hours from their associates.

"Mom's a partner, but according to her, not well liked. She mentioned a possible retirement, but I don't know what she would do without her work. Her work has always been the most important thing in her life." There, she said it. It's what Lainie believed, although she had never thrown the accusation at her mom.

"I think maybe things are changing for you and your mom. Give it time." Jeremy patted Lainie's arm and then walked to the barn door as Marcy navigated her team of ponies into the paddock. He waited to help Constance down from the carriage.

"Oh my, that was so wonderful. Thank you, Marcy." Constance Anderson's face was flushed, and when she removed her helmet, her hair was smashed, and she didn't care.

She tentatively reached out to pat Riley's neck.

"Here, Mom, stroke his neck like this—they like a nice stroke instead of a pat."

Megan and Cassy helped Marcy unhitch and unharness and tied Riley and Stuffin in the aisle for their grooming session.

"If you want to put the ponies in their stalls, we'll bring them all in for their supper." Jennie nodded when Cassy and Megan motioned to the three mares waiting at the pasture gate. The mares were convinced Riley and Stuffin were getting something they should also get.

With all the horses in stalls and munching on hay, Lainie introduced each one to her mom, and explained what type of horses they were, who owned them, and the disciplines they enjoyed.

"Everyone has a horse but you." Constance looked at Jeremy.

"For now—I'm getting horse fever and Sam's promised to keep his eyes open."

Marcy walked up. "I'm keeping my eyes and ears open for a horse that rides and drives."

"That would be very tempting. First, I need to complete my mission trips and figure out what God is calling me to do in life."

Constance noticed God was being mentioned a lot in this group and wondered about this God who seemed so real to her daughter's friends, and apparently, to her daughter, also.

"Mrs. Anderson, I hope you'll join us for church tomorrow before you leave."

"Now, Jennie, you can call me Constance."

"Hmmm, I'm not so sure about that; it seems disrespectful."

"Give it a try."

"Ok, Constance, will you join us for church tomorrow before you leave?"

Constance looked at her daughter. "Do you attend church?"

"I do. I started here in Appleridge. I can honestly say it's changed my life. Well, these people standing here changed my life, because they've shown me a different way to live."

Constance did see something different about Elaine. She was happy. She was not as guarded as she normally was when they were together.

"I'll attend church with Elaine and I would love to invite all of you to brunch following the service. I'll make reservations at an inn I found."

DRIVING BACK to Lainie's apartment, Constance pondered her decision to attend church. She supposed she was still trying to make amends with her daughter. It was working. Elaine was thrilled.

"Do you want to meet me here tomorrow, Mom, or do you want me to pick you up at your hotel? I don't mind."

"Please don't make a special trip to Richburg. I'll meet you here."

Lainie noticed a contraction or two continued to slip into her mom's sentences. *Funny!*

"Your friends are very nice."

"They are. They've shown me what true friendship looks like. You looked like you were having a blast on the carriage ride."

"I certainly was. Marcy is amazing. Does she also have a job?"

"She's an RN at the local hospital. She works in the emergency department."

Constance was impressed and asked, "And the two young girls—Megan and Cassy?"

"Megan is a senior in high school, and Cassy is a freshman at Richburg College. They're getting to be really good friends, and both are my students."

Constance nodded her head but remained quiet—thinking. "I surmised Jeremy and Jennie are a couple?"

"Yes, Jennie has a promise ring. They're waiting to see what God has planned. Jeremy attends seminary in Columbus and next semester he is going on mission trips to Appalachia. I know you probably think that's odd, right?"

"Odd, no, but interesting, yes."

"Mom, two months ago, I would think it all very odd. But being here and experiencing the changes in my life, well, I'm very interested in what God has planned for my life. I can feel him—I can feel his love."

"You can feel his love?"

"And I can feel his love in you." Lainie held her breath.

"Why in me? God is not in me. I am very sure."

"I think he is. He knows you but you don't know him."

"You never knew your grandparents, Elaine. They were vowed atheists—or agnostics; I'm not sure where they aligned themselves."

"Were they happy? Were they kind? Did they show love? Did they have joy?" Lainie could go on and on.

"I wouldn't say they were happy. They didn't show love and I didn't see much joy."

"But you wanted to be like them?"

"I'm not sure if I wanted to be like them or if I didn't know any difference. I was taught the more education I received, the more I would know about success and life."

"And that's what you wanted for me, too?"

"Yes."

"But it wasn't enough, Mom. There's so much more."

"Yes." That's all Constance could squeak out before Lainie reached across the front seat of the truck, now parked at the farm, and hugged her mom like she never wanted to let go.

And her mom hugged back.

CONSTANCE GLANCED around the church sanctuary before service started—wearing a simple navy suit and low heels. Lainie wore new jeans and boots. Trina was in a jean skirt. Jennie wore capris. It was an interesting mix of attire. She felt slightly overdressed until she saw several women three rows ahead wearing suits. She was fine. She was always very confident dressing in every situation, but today she felt like a fish out of water. She was experiencing many things out of her normal— fun with her daughter, jeans, horses, boots, potlucks, and now church. If she had friends, they would be amazed. She smiled at the absurdity of that thought. She didn't have friends. She wanted friends. Friends like Lainie's friends.

Lainie glanced at her mom, saw her little smile, and smiled back.

Constance enjoyed the music. The musicians were very good. She was surprised. The pastor walked out in his khaki pants and polo shirt. That was interesting. She thought church leaders wore robes. But how would she know what to expect, since she had no experience in this sort of thing?

The pastor began his message. He looked at Constance and smiled. She smiled back. Did Lainie tell him anything? He was entertaining, while at the same time, serious. He talked about a man named David and his affair with Bathsheba. They had a son from the affair and the son died. God still loved David and blessed them with another son, who became the next king. God loved him after his affair? But the son died. Did God punish David?

Constance had a million questions. She never knew the bible was so juicy.

Lainie could tell her mom was intrigued. She would ask the pastor if he had a bible for her mom. She led her mom to the door.

"Mom, this is Pastor Shearer."

"Thank you for joining us today." The pastor held out his hand.

"Thank you."

As if reading Lainie's mind, Pastor Shearer reached behind him, found a bible on the table, and presented it to Constance. "Would you like to have a bible? It's a nice translation."

Constance tried to appear nonchalant. "Why, thank you." She took the book carefully, as if it held magic.

Walking to the truck, she asked, "Does everyone get a bible?"

"I'm not sure how he knows who would like a bible, but he does. He gave me one on my first visit."

"I was surprised to hear the story of King David. I read an archeological article several years ago about King David. I didn't realize his story was recorded in the bible."

"There's a lot of history to support the bible. It's all new to me, but I'm learning."

"Yes, it's very interesting."

"Thanks for inviting my friends to lunch in Richburg. We'll go back to the farm to pick up your car and I'll ride over with you. Jeremy, Jennie, and Trina are riding together. They'll have room to take me home."

Constance treated the group to brunch at The Country Inn in Richburg. The food was delicious and the conversation enjoyable. She would hate to leave in the morning. Her time in the country was most pleasant. She would return. Now it was time to get back to work. She had a very important case to build against a bully named Brock Rodgers.

Chapter Twenty

"T hat was so much fun!" Megan dismounted and un-fastened her riding helmet. "Thanks, Miss Lainie."

"Miss Lainie?" Lainie made a funny face.

"Mom said I should call you Miss Lainie when I'm with the other students. It's a respect thing, you know."

"Thank you. And thank you both for leading the charge, so to speak. You both raised the bar."

Cassy glanced at Megan. "Thanks. It's nice to get back into some serious work. Treasure and I have been a little lazy this summer."

"I'm sure your first year in college is taking up a bit of time. You and Treasure have a lot of potential. Maybe we can squeeze in a few shows and events this year?"

"That would be so awesome!"

"What about you, Megan? Starlight seems like she is going well."

"She is, I'm pleased, but we're stretching it a bit with this group. I don't have much jumping experience." Megan thought she was doing ok. Not as well as her friend, Cassy, but fine for starting a new horse.

"I'm pleased to have you both as students. You'll make me and my lessons look good."

The girls walked their horses to the trailer. It was time to un-tack and load them up for the trip to Jennie's farm.

"Megan, this is your place. Do you ever think maybe we could keep our horses here? I love Jennie, but all the fun is here, and Lainie's going to build jumps in the pasture. What do you think?"

"I heard Dad say something about giving Lainie permission to build permanent jumps last night. I don't want to hurt Jennie's feelings, and what happens when I start college next year?"

"We could still keep the horses here. I'll have three more years and you'll have four. That's a really long time."

"Lainie needs at least one horse to keep Shadow company; having two more wouldn't be too many. Sam could move to Jennie's. I think he would like that better. He seems uncomfortable around all the lessons."

"Now that's an idea. Then Jennie would only need to find one more boarder to take our places."

"I think Dad would like the idea. He didn't want to get back into the horse business, but it would be Lainie's business, not his. And I don't think she would object since he's giving her a good deal on the barn and apartment."

"And Jeremy said he may get a horse. But I don't think Jennie would make Jeremy pay board. Do you?"

"No, but he and Sam sure would be good help around the place. I'll ask Dad what he thinks." Megan knew her dad would be fine with the idea as long as Lainie was there to take care of the barn and horses.

"It's just a thought. But, yeah, ask. We could always stay in touch with Jennie and Marcy. I really like them both."

"Even if they are old farts?"

"Stop it! I didn't say that, Megan!"

"You didn't need to say it because we both thought it."

The girls laughed. They thought themselves very funny.

"They sure do talk about God a lot."

Megan didn't answer right away. "Yeah, they do. But it's fine."

"Yeah, its fine but I never hear you talk about God. Do you go to church?"

"I go with Mom, and Dad goes with us sometimes. He seems to go more now. He's changed."

"My family never went to church. But my parents are good people." Cassy suddenly felt the need to defend her parents.

"You don't have to go to church to believe in God." Megan struggled with how to respond. She wanted to share her thoughts with Cassy without judging. She didn't like people who judged in the name of religion. "If people believe in God and want to invite him into their lives, they seek out churches to be with like-minded people."

"So, why do you go to church?"

"I like our church. It's a great place. Even if I don't share my faith boldly, I'm learning more about having a relationship with God."

"Maybe I'll go with you and see this for myself." Cassy hated to be left out of anything.

"Meet me tomorrow at the 9:30 service. That's the service with a great band. I'm not real fond of organ music."

"What kind of music does the band play?" Cassy loved most music.

"You know the music Lainie played as we rode today—did you like it?" Megan loved riding to music.

"Yeah, it rocked. I've never heard it before. I love riding to music. It's pretty cool."

"That music is by Toby Mac. He's a Christian artist."

"Are you telling me you listen to this Toby Mac in church?"

"We sing stuff from a lot of Christian artists. There are some great groups out there. I've got a bunch on my phone." Megan suddenly realized she was more into her faith than she realized.

"I'm surprised we were riding to a Christian artist. I noticed the words were nice and there wasn't any of that nasty stuff, but you actually hear that music in church?"

"Yup—cool, right?"

Cassy didn't answer. She was thinking.

Megan pulled the truck and trailer into Jennie's drive. "Let's unload the horses and then I'll park the trailer."

"Sounds like a plan." Cassy was also forming another plan in her head. Maybe she would check out church.

JENNIE LEANED FORWARD and listened to Jeremy describe his plans following Christmas.

"You're taking four two-week trips, one every month starting in February, and still taking spring semester classes? You'll be exhausted!"

"I know. And I'll be away from you."

Jennie answered, "That part makes me sad."

"I need to find my calling."

"You know your calling—you have a calling to lead people to God. It's the where and how you need to find." She smiled a reassuring smile. "I'll be fine. Go and do what you need to do. I support whatever you choose."

Jeremy sat down beside Jennie and gathered her into his arms, just holding her, saying nothing.

"Will you promise to miss me?"

"Of course, I'll miss you, silly Jeremy James."

Jeremy knew Jennie was fine if she could tease.

"I can't imagine a Jeremy James who wasn't being authentic and true. I can't. You have to do this or you won't be you. You won't be the Jeremy James I love."

Jeremy simply nodded. He usually had something to say about everything, but at this moment, he couldn't think of a thing that could get past the little lump in his throat.

LAINIE LOOKED at her phone and answered quickly. "Hi Mom, did you make it to the bed & breakfast?"

"Yes, I'm here and enjoying a few days of rest, relaxation, and doing quite a bit of thinking."

"Thinking about our case?" Lainie prayed her mom had good news.

"Of course, about the case, but also about my life and the changes I need to make."

"You've already made quite a few changes—all good, I think."

"Thank you, honey. I enjoyed our visit. I find it hard to think about going back to my life in Philadelphia but I suppose I must."

"You have time to work out a few things. Take it slow."

"I have a wise daughter. I have never been impulsive, but I have tasted happiness, and I see changes in my future."

"I understand more than you know. Once you taste happiness, it's addictive. What's your plan? Other than saving my sweet Shadow, that is?" Lainie certainly didn't want her mom to forget the fight for Shadow.

"Don't worry, sweetie. I don't see a fight. The case is quite simple. I will need to decide if it is time to start a new career. Your father and I will sell our house and divide the property. I will find a new place to live, but that will depend on what I decide about my work."

"Those decisions are huge. My prayers are with you."

"Thank you, dear." *Mom likes my prayers. Oh, thank you, Father.*

"You'll be ok financially?"

"I will. Your father and I will both be fine. I may downsize quite a bit and live more simply. I feel a strong need to shake loose from a lot of baggage."

"Don't change too much, Mom. I love you exactly the way you are—right now."

"What a wonderful thing for you to say, honey. I love you. Bye for now."

"Bye, Mom."

CONSTANCE RETURNED her phone to the purse lying on the dresser. She loved talking to her daughter. Their conversation made her feel like being more social. She decided to go downstairs and meet the other bed & breakfast guests during the afternoon social hour. She was pleased with her research and would make her first contact with Mr. Brock Rodgers in the morning. A phone call should clear up any misunderstanding he may have about the legalities of his actions. If not, Constance would drag him face down through his own mud. She chuckled quietly—she loved a good fight. Some things never changed.

"BROCK, I'M TELLING you straight, you won't win this fight." Brock's good friend and business manager, Chris Chase, leaned over the desk.

"I never lose. You remember that. I NEVER LOSE!" Brock pounded his desk.

"Well, sorry, but you're going to lose everything if you don't focus on business and let go of your need to punish people."

"Can't you understand? This is business—serious business."

"Yes, it's serious and wrong. You don't have a leg to stand on."

"They don't know that. They're just a bunch of dumb kids."

"You didn't think they were so dumb when you took their money and paraded them around the country promoting Follow the Leader."

Brock didn't say anything more. Instead, he glared at Chris.

"Now let's get down to the serious business of saving your program." Chris presented Brock with a folder. "Here are my recommendations to cut expenses, scale down your operation, and save your ranch."

Brock reluctantly opened the folder and scanned the first page.

"I'm happy to see you're going to allow me to offer a few courses this summer."

"Yes, and you'll be teaching. When students find out Brock Rodgers is teaching courses this summer, the ranch will be swarming."

Brock grunted. "Fine, I'll enjoy teaching again." His words were appropriate, but his face was sour.

"Good. When you have a chance to look at my recommendations, give me a call."

"Sure."

After Chris left, Brock got up and kicked his chair, sending it rolling across the room and crashing into a bookcase full of printed materials featuring his smiling face. Well, he wasn't smiling now. No one questioned Brock Rodgers, and no one told Brock Rodgers how to run his business. He knew how to save a few dollars and he would save a few when he fired Chris Chase—that thought made him smile.

Chapter Twenty-One

aine's phone vibrated against her belt.

"You said your mom was handling everything!"

"Hello, Hank, it's nice to hear from you, too." Lainie felt her joy at watching the students warming up in the arena quickly turning into anxiety. "Mom said she was speaking to Brock this morning and not to worry."

"You better worry. We still have a few friends on the ranch and one called me today to say Brock hired a couple of guys to locate and pick up what he calls *his horses*. And Shadow is first on the list."

Lainie's stomach rolled. "How can he do that? He can't just come and take Shadow. When did they leave Iowa?"

"I'm not sure but I think today."

"This is crazy. I'm calling Mom."

"Ok. Lainie, will you let me know what happens?"

"I'll try." *Oh, Father, help me, please.*

"Lainie, are you ok?" Cassy rode Treasure up to the fence near Lainie.

"I'm not sure. I need a few minutes."

"Ok, we'll keep warming up."

Lainie nodded and punched her mom's number. No answer. She waited to leave a message.

"Mom, help! I just got a call from Hank. Brock is sending someone to come steal Shadow."

Lainie stepped into the arena, put on her best face, and asked the girls to gather around. "Let's get started." Her voice quivered.

"No."

"Cassy?"

"No, something's wrong. We're your students but we're also your friends and you need to be honest. Whatever is wrong, we want to help."

"I'm sorry. I don't think you can help." Lainie shook her head. "It's not your problem. Let's get started."

All six girls answered as one. "No." They didn't shout, they whispered.

"Ok, have it your way, our practice is cancelled for today. I'll let you know when I schedule a make-up session." Lainie started to turn away but was stopped by two of the mothers—one on each side.

No one moved. No one said anything for what seemed like forever.

Lainie looked up with tears in her eyes. "I'm sorry."

"What can we do?" One of the mothers placed her arm around Lainie and pulled her into a hug. "Lainie, you're more than just a teacher, you're someone we care about. The girls love you. Please, what's wrong?"

"Brock Rodgers is sending someone to take Shadow. He says he never gave her to me and she belongs to Follow the Leader."

"What? That's crazy! What about your mom? She won't lose the fight." Megan was always ready for a fight.

"I left her a message a few minutes ago."

All of the mothers gathered around Lainie and it was agreed the practice would be rescheduled. The horses were untacked and loaded into trailers. Only Cassy and Megan remained. They decided to stay for a while. Although Lainie probably wanted to be alone, they didn't think that was a good idea.

"We could take Shadow to Jennie's place." Megan was already scheming.

"No, I don't want to create a mess for Jennie." Lainie shook her head.

"When do you think they'll get here?" Cassy asked.

"I'm not sure. I don't know when they left Iowa, but they could get here late tonight."

"Dad won't let them on the property." Megan promised.

Cassy added, "Don't worry, Lainie, no one is taking Shadow."

Cassy led Lainie to a chair in the barn aisle as Megan jogged upstairs to get Lainie a bottle of water. Lainie sank into the chair. She didn't have the energy to resist.

While upstairs and away from Lainie, Megan left messages for her dad, Jennie, Sam, and Jeremy. It was time to rally the troops.

CONSTANCE PRESSED off on her phone, pleased with the results of her conversation with Brock. He seemed speechless at first, quickly became arrogant, and then subdued as she explained exactly what he faced if he continued to harass his former instructors. As for the matter of who owned the rescue horses, she didn't reveal details. She simply stated legal jargon insinuating it would be wise if he changed his mind about that issue, also. He was a bully, and when bullies were confronted—or slapped in the face with truth—they often backed down.

Constance couldn't wait to call Lainie and report how Brock tried to talk his way out of the corner. She decided to get a cup of coffee before making, what she thought would be, a relaxing call.

BROCK STUFFED the phone into his pocket. *How did those punks hire an attorney? Who did she think she was, anyway, with her smug veiled threats? Did she think he was stupid? How did he know if she really was an attorney? She could just be someone acting the part. No, he wasn't stupid. And I'm not calling my boys back. Let them pick up Shadow and the other horses as planned.* He needed money, and he already had buyers for well-trained horses.

"HE DID WHAT?" Constance sat up in her chair, spilling her coffee. "I just talked to him. It's all settled."

"I don't think so, Mom. Hank said Brock hired two guys to pick up all the horses. They're already on the road and Shadow is first. They could get here late tonight."

"I'm on it, Lainie. If Brock wants to play this game, I'm ready and willing."

"Thanks, Mom."

"Are you alone?"

"I'm not alone right now. Cassy and Megan are here."

"Ask them to stay or ask someone to stay with you."

"Ok, I'll ask Jeremy or Sam." Lainie hated the thought of asking her friends into this mess.

"I promise I will get this sorted out." *No one was taking her daughter's horse. Not again!*

"THANKS FOR CALLING, Megan. I'm leaving work now. I'll stop at home and check on the ponies and Julep, then drive to your place. Are Treasure and Starlight with you?"

"Yeah, so maybe you could bring their supper and breakfast? They may be having a sleepover."

Jennie laughed. "Don't forget, you have my truck and I have your mom's car. I don't think your mom would like hay in the back seat."

"Oh yeah, I forgot. I'll ask Lainie if we can have some of her hay and I'll pay her back."

"Don't worry, Megan. Jeremy and I are on our way."

"Thanks, Jennie."

"THANKS FOR LETTING me know, Jeremy. I have two more horses to shoe, then I'll head straight to the Peterson farm. No one is taking Sadie's pasture mate." Sam wished he could go to the farm immediately but didn't think it was good business to reschedule his clients at the last minute.

"CHARLIE, I JUST HEARD at the Bake & Shake that a mean man is coming to take Lainie's horse, Shadow."

"What mean man?" Jennie's grandpa put the footrest of his recliner down. "Lizzie, what mean man?"

"You know that guy on RFD TV. The one Lainie traveled with for a bit. He says Shadow is his horse and he's coming to take her."

"Why I don't believe that's true. I remember seeing Lainie in a few of those episodes."

"It may not be true but he's coming. We need to get out there."

"Ok, calm down. I'll call Ellen for a ride and we'll pick you up."

"WHAT ARE YOU TALKING about, Dad?" Ellen turned down the burner on her stove before sitting down on a kitchen stool.

"You know that cowboy guy Lainie traveled with for a bit? He's taking her horse."

"Ahh, but Jennie said Mrs. Anderson is an attorney and she won't let that happen."

"I think he plans on stealing her before the law gets involved. We need to get out there as back up."

"Ok, Dad, Ed's in the garage. We'll pick you up within the hour. I have vegetable soup on the stove. I'll bring it out, too."

Ellen rushed into the garage and quickly relayed the story to Jennie's dad, before rushing back into the house to gather paper bowls, plastic spoons, and other supplies. She packed everything in a large picnic basket. The pot of soup went into a box with old towels packed around the perimeter to keep it from sliding. Ellen was a pro at moving large amounts of food.

"SUSAN, TELL MEGAN I'm running a little late, but barring any emergencies I'll be home in about an hour."

"I will. I was just getting ready to walk down to the barn to see what I could do to help. A few cars and trucks are here. It looks like the word is getting out around town."

"Do you recognize any of the trucks?"

"I think so. Some are students and their parents. I'm packing some food. It looks like we may have a few people here this evening."

"I didn't expect something like this to happen. I'm sorry. Maybe I shouldn't have leased our barn to Lainie."

"Don't you be sorry. It'll be fine and it's certainly not her fault."

"I didn't mean it was her fault."

"You just get home when you can. We know most of the students and their parents. I'm not worried."

Adrian put his cell phone back in its holster before entering the examination room. Two more clients—a dog and a cat—and he would be on his way home to the farm.

CHARLIE GANTZLER was waiting on the curb in front of his apartment when Ed and Ellen pulled up.

"Hello, Dad. Are we picking up Mrs. Williams, too?"

"Yes. We need an army.'"

"I didn't think you liked fighting, Dad." Ellen turned slightly in the front seat to look at her father.

"I don't like fighting, I prefer to do all my fighting as a prayer warrior, but sometimes you need to fight for what is right and taking a young lady's horse just isn't right."

"I agree, Charlie. We're not going to let that happen tonight." Ed answered but kept his eyes on the road.

They pulled up at Mrs. Williams's house.

"She has Moose with her. I wasn't planning on a big dog in my new car."

Ellen laid her hand on her husband's arm. "I'll clean up any smell or mess, I promise."

Ed grunted but rolled down his window to welcome Mrs. Williams. Moose climbed into the car and plopped himself right in the middle of the back seat.

BY THE TIME Jeremy and Jennie arrived at the Peterson farm, two cars and four trucks filled the small parking area in front of the arena, with more driving down the road.

Jeremy sized up the situation. "Lainie, let's open the gate and let people park in the pasture."

"Ok, go ahead." Lainie was in a daze as she watched students, their parents, and all her friends arrive and unload their vehicles. She watched tables being unfolded and placed in the aisle as food magically appeared. Everyone moved with purpose. The atmosphere was full of energy but not exactly festive.

"Woof!" Moose made his entrance.

Lainie reached down to scratch under Moose's chin. "Hey, Buddy, did you come to help me?"

"Woof!"

Ellen McKenzie and Susan Peterson were old friends, and it didn't take them long to whip the impromptu gathering into shape. They soon had the tables lined up and food organized.

"Ok everyone. Susan has asked me to lead this group in prayer before we eat. Thank you all for coming out in support of Lainie and Shadow, and for not coming empty-handed. We don't know if Brock's crew will arrive tonight, but if they do, they'll be surprised." There were a few chuckles at Jeremy's words before the bowing of heads.

"Father, we thank you for everyone here tonight and for the food we share. Please be with us as we support Lainie and Shadow. Give us wisdom to do what we need to do to protect our friends. We trust you and love you. Amen."

Marcy arrived as the prayer finished. "I heard all about it at the hospital."

Sam was right behind Marcy. "My last client heard the news and offered to switch her appointment so I could get here."

"I'm here for you, Lainie and Shadow!" Trina called out as she entered the barn.

"WE'VE BEEN ALERTED to the situation, Adrian, and I'll have a car ready; however, I don't foresee a problem at this time. According to Mrs. Anderson, the attorney who called, Brock Rodgers has no legal grounds to take the horse."

Dr. Adrian Peterson knew the Appleridge police chief well. "Thanks, George. I just wanted to make sure we wouldn't be faced with any sort of notice of seizure or legal documents."

"No, nothing has been filed. We'll stop them from removing property, but I don't think it will go that far."

"But if we need you, you'll be ready?"

"That's correct. It's my understanding the man in question, Brock Rodgers, has not left the state of Iowa. It's my guess he hired a few guys to go on this wild goose chase."

BY THE TIME Adrian arrived home, the group was fed and fairly quiet except for a few scattered conversations. Susan motioned for him to get a plate and indicated an empty chair near the door.

"Do you have any news?" She asked. She knew her husband well. He would have checked in with the Appleridge police chief before driving home.

"Yes." He smiled. "Nothing official was filed. They have no legal recourse to take Shadow or come onto this property. But let's not say anything yet. This is a nice gathering for Lainie."

Susan nodded. "Appleridge considers her family."

JUST BEFORE ELEVEN they heard a diesel truck driving slowly up the road. It slowed almost to a stop before pulling into the drive. The waiting group was smaller now as some of the parents needed to take children home. It was a school night, after all. Although it was also a work night, fourteen friends remained—Jennie, Jeremy, Cassy, Megan, Marcy, Trina, Sam, Ed and Ellen McKenzie, Dr. and Susan Peterson, and surprisingly, Mrs. Williams, Grandpa, and Moose. And they all stood as a group to block the drive leading to the barn.

"Holy crap, what's going on?" The driver pulled to a stop.

"I don't know, but we're not getting paid enough for this crap."

The driver and his sidekick climbed out of the truck to face the crowd.

"We're here to pick up a horse." The driver spoke with as much authority as he could muster.

"I'm afraid you wasted a trip, boys." Dr. Peterson stepped forward. "This is my property, and unless you have a legal document giving you the right to be on my property, I suggest you get back in your truck and hightail it back to Iowa or wherever you're from. And don't worry about collecting any more horses. I suspect old Brock will be too concerned about the mess he's in to worry about you."

"Says who?" The sidekick wanted to make sure he got in his two cents.

Lainie stepped forward. "Says my attorney! She's on the phone and has the Appleridge PD on the other line. She has also been in contact with the authorities in Iowa. Brock Rodgers is in a bit of trouble. I wouldn't expect to get paid for this job, if I were you."

As the trailer backed slowly out of the drive, Lainie started to breathe again. It felt like she hadn't taken a breath in hours. She turned to face her friends, all standing with huge smiles on their faces. "I don't know what to say. Thank you all so much."

"It's your mom who fought the battle. We just stuck around as support." Jeremy motioned for everyone to gather around Lainie. "It's what friends do."

"Mom! My mom!" Lainie looked at her phone. "Mom, are you still there?"

"Yes, honey, I'm here. I've heard it all. You hang up now and celebrate with your friends. I'll send a text to Hank and I'll talk to you both tomorrow. Bye, sweetie." *Yes, Lainie, I'm here for you this time. It's what a mom should do.*

Chapter Twenty-Two

The B & S club met at the Bake & Shake early the next morning. Today the conversation would be more truth than speculation. After all, Charlie Gantzler was an eye witness.

"I heard there was quite a commotion at the Peterson farm last night and it involved another Moose." Joe Moore, the retired Appleridge police chief, laughed.

Charlie spoke up with a grin, "Now Joe, you know that's how rumors get started."

"So, Charlie, were you at the party?" Joe knew the answer, but he wanted to keep the conversation moving.

"Yes, me and a few friends showed up to support Lainie Anderson. And, yes, Moose was there, too."

"I heard two horse thieves were caught on the property."

Charlie turned to look at one of his cohorts. "Well, I guess if they tried to take the horse, they would have been horse thieves, but they didn't get that far. Once they spoke to the attorney—who happens to be Lainie's mother—they weren't so eager to risk their necks for the job. Apparently, Brock Rodgers hired them to gather up a few horses he claimed as his own."

Joe knew his law and added, "I bet they'll be a bit more careful about the jobs they take from now on."

"They couldn't leave fast enough. I think one said he didn't agree to steal any horses. Brock has a lot of explaining to do."

The B & S club found the story very entertaining.

SEVERAL OLDER LADIES arrived at the Bake & Shake for a noon lunch.

"Did you hear? Two horse thieves were caught out near the Peterson farm?"

"I heard they also caught a moose."

"Now you know we don't have moose in Appleridge."

"That's what I hear—I'm sure I heard someone mention a moose."

It could have been Lizzie Williams's dog named Moose. Why that dog sure does get around and causes all sorts of trouble."

"Why he does. Do you suppose we should say something to Lizzie about watching her dog a little closer?"

"I heard she's watching Charlie Gantzler pretty close. Didn't they look like sweethearts in the Appleridge parade?"

Those nearby looked over and smiled at the giggles coming from the ladies' table.

THE MILKSHAKE CROWD arrived at the Bake & Shake counter after school.

"Did you hear about the moose thieves in Appleridge last night? Someone tried to steal Dr. Peterson's moose."

"I don't think Dr. Peterson has a moose."

"Yeah, he does."

"I heard they tried to steal a horse, not a moose."

"Anyway, if it was a moose, they'd be called moose thieves, right?"

"Yeah, you're right."

"I think they hang horse thieves. That's what they said in a movie I saw one time."

"Yuck!" The girls shook their heads and walked to another table.

"They didn't hang anybody, but we sure did stop those thieves."

"How do you know?"

"I was there. My sister takes lessons with Miss Lainie at the farm and we went out to help her last night. Lots of people were there."

"Did you see a moose?"

"Yeah, a dog named Moose and he was huge!"

"See, there was a moose." The boys laughed at the joke.

JENNIE STARED at her computer screen. It was time to write her story about Lainie. It was also a story about Appleridge—about friends helping friends. Lainie was already part of the Appleridge family. She was honest, hard-working, and wanted the best for her students and their horses. Jennie pondered those thoughts. She would love to be described as honest, hard-working, and someone who cared about other people. Wouldn't anyone? No, probably not. Some people preferred to be called wealthy and powerful. Mrs. Anderson was wealthy and powerful, but she wasn't happy—maybe she was happier now since she mended her relationship with Lainie. Jennie thought maybe Mrs. Anderson would choose a different description now. Yes, she was sure that was true. Happiness didn't come from wealth and power; it came from having people genuinely love you. She needed time to think before she started to write. She would work at home. It was time to shut down her computer, leave the office, and meet Sam at the farm. He was bringing Sadie this evening.

AFTER THE EXCITEMENT several nights ago, Cassy and Megan nervously spoke to Jennie about keeping their mares with Lainie instead of bringing them back to Fawn Song Farm. Jennie gave them both a hug and assured them she understood. She hated to see them leave her farm, but she understood. Lainie's place was the best place for two adventure-loving young ladies. She also assured them both Sam and Sadie were welcome to move and pretended she didn't know it was already discussed.

Jennie smiled to herself. Sometimes it's fine to keep a few secrets.

Excerpts from the
Farm & Family Country Chronicle

Lessons with Lainie

By Jennie Hope McKenzie

The young instructor spoke to the group of students with both authority and kindness. It's a learned skill—to be a great leader with kindness, and Lainie Anderson has learned it well. As I sat arena side in my folding chair, I was intrigued. I didn't know much about the horsemanship program being taught, and I certainly didn't know Lainie, but I saw something special happening between horses and their owners.

The students in the arena were all ages and appeared to be at various levels in their horsemanship. I noticed that some of the horses were very alert and interested in the exercises, a few others appeared bored, and one looked very unconfident. Lainie worked with each human and equine, helping them connect as a team. For the most part, she was successful. I was impressed with Lainie's ability to stay focused, patient, kind, but yet firm, as she faced several challenges.

Before Lainie Anderson started teaching horsemanship clinics, she successfully competed and trained as Elaine Anderson, and was short-listed for the United States Olympic Team. Competition has a way of bringing out the best and the worst in people, and unfortunately, Elaine, aka Lainie, experienced some of the worst. She was ready for a change, and a horsemanship program sharing the message of partnering with your horse instead of using force, drew Lainie like a moth to light.

Lainie went about the business of teaching as her passion. She taught what she felt in her heart—sharing her best in Appleridge. And then she found something she didn't expect—she found friends. Lainie thought she was in Appleridge to simply share her horsemanship knowledge, but she soon discovered her new friends were also willing to share.

When the clinic finished, it was time to leave Appleridge. Lainie was scheduled to teach other clinics in other places. She didn't want to leave, and vowed to return some day, if possible.

Soon after she drove away from the community of people who held a piece of her heart, a tragic accident destroyed her truck and trailer. The Appleridge community rallied, and she found a new future. When a bully threatened to take her horse, Appleridge rallied, and she found strength.

This is a story about an amazing person—someone who clung tight to her passion of helping horses and humans, while at the same time, staying true to her beliefs. But it quickly became apparent that it wasn't only a story about Lainie. The real story is about our community surrounding a new friend in her time of trouble—welcoming her home. It is also a story of faith. In Lainie's own words, "I didn't understand what I did to deserve such kindness." Lainie soon learned that amazing kindness is found in those who have amazing faith.

Lainie Anderson has found a new home in Appleridge, and Appleridge has found a wonderful and caring teacher for both horses and their humans.

Contact Lainie for lessons, training, and an exciting performance team opportunity for both youth and adults.

Fall Fun in Appleridge

By Jennie Hope McKenzie

The Appleridge Festival Queen pageant, held Friday evening, served as the perfect festival opening event. Appleridge High School Senior, Cyndi Jones, mesmerized the judges with her violin solo and grace, winning the crown. Jane Woods, a Richburg College Junior, wears the Runner-Up sash. Pageant contestants elected Sharon Blass, Miss Congeniality.

Saturday, crisp as a fresh red apple, began early as street venders prepared tents and tables for the festival crowd. The parade kicked off at 11:00 AM with participants embracing the theme, Apple of Your Eye. A patriotic crowd stood at attention as the fire and police department flag squad marched in uniform, followed by Mr. Robert Ross's team of matched Morgan geldings pulling a restored antique steam pumper—the pride and joy of Appleridge. This was the first time the restored and polished engine was hitched to a team since its early twentieth century retirement.

The crowd cheered for the Appleridge High School marching band and waved at the parade honorees, Queen Cyndi, and visiting festival queens. Children scrambled for candy thrown from floats and jumped up and down with excitement when they spied Marcy Streeter's pair of Welsh ponies pulling a carriage decorated like a treasure chest. The prancing ponies caught the attention of all horse lovers, young and old.

Following the parade, a large crowd enjoyed a tasty selection of festival food on The Green, while listening to music at the gazebo. The festival ended with a dance and concert under white lights and a full October moon.

The Appleridge Apple Festival Committee would like to thank all the festival sponsors: Karol's Music Store, stage and sound equipment; Apple Tree Market, apples and prizes; Our Savior Lutheran Church, water station before and after the parade for all parade participants; Trinity Methodist Church, folding tables and chairs; Wagging Tails 4-H Club, organizing youth contests; Appleridge Soccer Association, games and demonstrations; Appleridge High School, vendor and street signs; The *Farm & Family Country Chronicle*, festival flyers; Appleridge Rotary Club, parade line up; and the entire town for their support and participation.

The Committee would also like to recognize their advertising sponsors: Ann's Dress Shoppe, Apple Core News Stand, Apple Tree Market, Appleridge Senior Apartments, The Bake & Shake, The Café, Casey Law Office, The *Farm & Family Country Chronicle*, Karol's Music Store, Lessons with Lainie, Orchard Pharmacy, Peterson Animal Clinic, Richburg Country Inn, Richburg Deli Depot, Seamstress Ellen McKenzie, and Town Trash Service.

Congratulations to all the parade and contest winners. A complete list will appear in next month's edition.

Enjoy a Sneak Peek!

Finding Fare
Faith, Family, Friends & Horses, Book 3

"I don't see anything that looks like a Morgan horse going through the sale. Let's take a peek at the horses behind the barn." Kerry thought this was the worst job ever. She hated looking at the horses behind the big barn—horses sold in backdoor deals to meat buyers. How many times would her heart break, seeing the horses squeezed into pens, waiting for their nasty trip to slaughter?

Deb nodded. "At least the horses actually going through the sale have a chance to end up in good homes. These guys back here never have a chance." She shook her head. "It never gets any easier."

As volunteers for Save a Lost Morgan Rescue, Kerry Casin and Deb Thomkins visited the sale, looking for horses in danger. Then they would do whatever they could to get the horses to safety quickly—and with very limited funds they weren't always successful. They couldn't save them all, but they tried to save a few.

The various rescues worked together; some, like the Morgan rescue, focused on a particular breed of horse. The kill buyers liked working with the rescue groups—not out of compassion, but out of greed. It was easy money selling to a rescue, knowing those *horse lovers* would move heaven and earth to raise the funds. If they couldn't raise the money, too bad. The kill buyers could still turn a profit by throwing the horse on the next load leaving for the slaughter plant. It didn't make any difference to them. Money was money.

"Kerry, look." Deb stopped and grabbed Kerry's arm. "That's got to be a Morgan. The skinny chestnut with the really light mane and tail."

"Let's talk to the dealer. We've gotten horses from him before. His name is Mack. He'll talk."

"Hello, ladies. Which one can I send home with you today? I bet it's that little chestnut, and I think I have some papers on him, too. Well, at least I did. I may have thrown them in the trash. It's not like he'll need them where he's going." He snorted and held out his hand. Neither Kerry nor Deb offered a hand in return. They didn't respond to Mack's sick humor. Instead, they turned to focus on the gelding. This was business—a business they hated.

"He's a Morgan?" Kerry was pretty sure he was.

"Yup, pure blooded. I can let you have him for a little over my cost. Let's say $550 and he's yours. He's a *little worse for the wear*, as my grandma liked to say. If he had a few more pounds on him, I'd get more money."

She wondered if Mack's grandma would think he was *worse for the wear* for doing what he was doing. Kerry reached for the papers he offered. Maybe they could contact a name listed on the papers. Sometimes a former owner would donate funds.

"How much time do we have?" Deb knew they didn't have much in the bank. She would need to make calls and get a campaign running on social media as soon as possible.

"Well, I can give you until 9:00 tonight." The dealer grinned, revealing tobacco-stained teeth.

"That's not much time. Can you give us a few days?" Kerry hated pleading but she'd do it for the horse.

"Naw, sorry. There's a truck leaving tonight." Mack didn't look very sorry.

"Could you at least get him out of this pen?" The pen was crowded with scared horses. Deb didn't want the little guy to get kicked or injured.

The horse turned his head and gazed with soft brown eyes at the girls. It was if he were saying, "I know you're trying to help me."

"Are you interested? If not, he'll be just fine where he is."

"We're interested. We just need to get the money together." Kerry somehow kept her tone friendly. She should get an academy award for hiding her true feelings. What a sleaze! She wanted to give old Mack a piece of her mind, but first they had a horse to save.

"Show me the money and we'll talk. And, ladies, you only have seven hours so I would hurry if I was you." Mack turned and chuckled as he walked back to the barn.

Kerry turned to look at Deb who was already on her phone.

ABOUT THE AUTHOR

Linda Amick Algire loves to write inspirational stories with entertaining characters—including horses. Linda's stories of faith, family, friends & horses turn a messy world into a place of love and acceptance. When Linda isn't writing, she enjoys playing her fiddle at jam sessions, and spoiling her grandsons whenever they visit. She also enjoys learning new things with a little horse named, Wren, and his buddy, Clyde.

Linda loves connecting with readers!
Send Linda a note a linda@fawnsongfarm.com

Follow Jennie and her Appleridge friends at
www.fawnsongbooks.com

CPSIA information can be obtained
at www.ICGtesting.com
Printed in the USA
LVHW031115141019
634125LV00001B/201/P